T0011043

But why had Grayson boug[...] **Surely they weren't moving back. Or were they?**

"Does this mean—"

A door banged in the back corner, and a young girl walked out of the office space. "I hope the house is better than this junky old place."

Sage's whole body went numb, and her vision wavered. She'd thought seeing Grayson was the biggest emotional shock of the day, but there was no mistaking the teenager walking their way. A child she'd never expected to see again but had thought about often over the years. Her light brown hair was long and falling loose around her face as if she was trying to hide.

"Loren," Sage said with a hand pressed tight against her stomach as if that would hold in the rush of emotions.

The young girl's head snapped up, and her curious gaze flicked over Sage's unfortunate state of dress. Her face was definitely more expressive than her father's and was somewhere between horror and humor. "How do you know my name?"

Sage worked her mouth, but words refused to come.

Dear Reader,

Welcome back to Channing, Texas! *Her Secret to Keep* is the second book in my new series, The Women of Dalton Ranch. It's set in a fictional small town near Dallas.

Sage Dalton owns a successful horse ranch with her twin sister, but what she wants most is a child of her own. The question is how to make that happen. When widowed single father Grayson DeLuca returns to Channing with his thirteen-year-old daughter, Sage is more surprised than anyone. Sage and Grayson have a second chance, but there's a secret that must be kept. Or does it?

I hope you enjoy *Her Secret to Keep* and will visit Dalton Ranch again when the third book in the series is released. I can't wait to share the story of Sage's twin sister, Daisy Dalton. As always, thank you for reading!

Best wishes,

Makenna Lee

HER SECRET TO KEEP

MAKENNA LEE

HARLEQUIN
SPECIAL
EDITION

If you purchased this book without a cover you should be aware
that this book is stolen property. It was reported as "unsold and
destroyed" to the publisher, and neither the author nor the
publisher has received any payment for this "stripped book."

HARLEQUIN®
SPECIAL
EDITION™

Recycling programs
for this product may
not exist in your area.

ISBN-13: 978-1-335-59468-6

Her Secret to Keep

Copyright © 2024 by Margaret Culver

All rights reserved. No part of this book may be used or reproduced in
any manner whatsoever without written permission except in the case of
brief quotations embodied in critical articles and reviews.

This is a work of fiction. Names, characters, places and incidents
are either the product of the author's imagination or are used fictitiously.
Any resemblance to actual persons, living or dead, businesses,
companies, events or locales is entirely coincidental.

For questions and comments about the quality of this book,
please contact us at CustomerService@Harlequin.com.

TM and ® are trademarks of Harlequin Enterprises ULC.

Harlequin Enterprises ULC
22 Adelaide St. West, 41st Floor
Toronto, Ontario M5H 4E3, Canada
www.Harlequin.com

Printed in Lithuania

MIX
Paper | Supporting
responsible forestry
FSC® C021394

Makenna Lee is an award-winning romance author living in the Texas Hill Country with her real-life hero and their two children, one of whom has Down syndrome and inspired her first Harlequin book, *A Sheriff's Star*. She writes heartwarming contemporary romance that celebrates real-life challenges and the power of love and acceptance. She has been known to make people laugh and cry in the same book. Makenna is often drinking coffee with a cat on her lap while writing, reading or plotting a new story. Her wish is to write stories that touch your heart, making you feel, think and dream.

Books by Makenna Lee

Harlequin Special Edition

The Women of Dalton Ranch

The Rancher's Love Song
Her Secret to Keep

Home to Oak Hollow

A Sheriff's Star
In the Key of Family
A Child's Christmas Wish
A Marriage of Benefits
Lessons in Fatherhood
The Bookstore's Secret

The Fortunes of Texas: Hitting the Jackpot

Fortune's Fatherhood Dare

Visit the Author Profile page
at Harlequin.com for more titles.

To my sisters-in-law, Raye and Kelly.
Thanks for being the sisters I always wanted.

Chapter One

Why is Grayson DeLuca here?

Sage Dalton had tried for over a decade to forget what she'd done to save her horse ranch, and now a living reminder was standing right in front of her with a broad shoulder braced against one of four massive posts that ran up to the peaked timber roof two stories above them. A businessman out of place in this hundred-year-old abandoned building.

She wrapped her arms around her body as a team of arial flyers swooped around her stomach, but her vocal cords were stuck in freeze-frame mode.

Grayson's jade-green eyes had a few fine lines at the corners, but he had the same thick, dark hair, always on the verge of needing a haircut while still managing to look perfectly put together in a roguish sort of way. He had the same good looks, more rugged than refined. The same self-assured posture. And the same achingly exquisite heart tug that had made her fall for him years ago.

As for having the same smile…she had no idea. The only hint that he'd even seen her was a flicker of awareness in his wide eyes.

"Hi, Sage." His familiar deep voice was kind and steady but also gave nothing away.

"Hello, Grayson. It's been a while," she said needlessly and mentally rolled her eyes. They both knew exactly how long it had been—to the day. She needed to pull herself together because it wasn't the late summer heat causing her sudden flush. She was barely holding herself together while he was Mr. Chill-as-a-Popsicle.

"Thirteen years," he said. His pearl-gray tie hung loose, and the top two buttons of his tailored white shirt were undone. With his sleeves rolled up, the simple movement of hooking his thumbs in the front pockets of his charcoal slacks showed off the corded muscles of his forearms. He looked ready for a photo shoot.

She, on the other hand? Sage inwardly cringed. Not good. Not good at all. Was it too late to backtrack and pass herself off as her tomboy twin sister, Daisy?

A sparrow flew across the wide-open interior of the red brick building, and they both followed the bird's path to where it landed on a crossbeam. Bits of straw and twigs poked out of its nest, probably like the mess on her head.

Sage brushed both hands through her shoulder-length blond hair, frizzy from bathing the mischievous new foal who'd rolled in the dirt. Her butter-yellow T-shirt and worn jeans were mud splattered, and one sleeve was partially torn off from where the horse had grabbed it with his teeth. She wasn't even wearing lip balm, much less a carefully applied full face of makeup, and the only cute item she had with her was her black-and-white Kate Spade handbag.

She was the sister who was always well put together before leaving the ranch, but when she'd received a call about the anonymous buyer showing up, she hadn't wasted a second before hopping into her truck and heading to town. Big mistake.

"How did you know it was me and not my sister, Daisy?"

"You might be identical twins, but I can tell you apart."

One corner of his mouth twitched as if he would smile, but the moment passed.

Her stomach clenched. Managing things around her made her feel in charge of her own life, and she hated this sudden lack of control over her emotions. The deep ache being dredged up would take time to unpack, sort through and be delt with in a way she hadn't done properly in her early twenties.

She tried to adjust her torn sleeve, but it was no use. "I seem to be in the right clothes to start cleaning up this place, but you're a bit overdressed for poking around an abandoned building."

He glanced down as if he had no idea what he was wearing. "I had a meeting this morning before leaving Houston."

"What are you doing here?" She circled her hand to encompass the whole of the space she hoped to turn into a community center. It was the perfect place to reinstate the Old Town Christmas celebration that her mother had chaired for so many years.

"I just bought it."

"You bought the grist mill?" It seemed so unlikely that she was having trouble making sense of it.

"That's right. I'm the new owner."

"Really?" She'd been so distracted by the sight of him, she hadn't connected the obvious dots.

"You find it hard to believe?"

"It's unexpected. I didn't think you would ever come back to Channing."

"Me either," he said under his breath and then turned in a slow circle while looking up at the crossbeams. "It looks pretty sturdy."

"You're the architect, and if you say it is, I'm sure it's true." The anger she'd carried into this meeting vanished. She had been prepared to hate the out-of-town buyer, especially if they had plans to tear it down. His owning it was great news, and a worry lifted from her mind. Grayson's great-great-grandfather had helped build this grist mill beside Channing Creek, and there was no way he would tear it down.

But why had he bought this building? Surely they weren't moving back. Or were they? "Does this mean…?"

A door banged in the back corner, and a young girl walked out of the office space. "I hope the house is better than this junky old place," she said.

Sage's whole body went numb, and her vision wavered. She'd only thought seeing Grayson was the biggest emotional shock of the day, but there was no mistaking the teenager walking their way. A child she'd never expected to see again but had thought about so very often over the years. Her light brown hair was long and falling loose around her face almost as if she was trying to hide.

"Loren," Sage said with a hand pressed tight against her stomach as if that would hold in the rush of emotions.

The young girl's head snapped up, and her curious gaze flicked over Sage's unfortunate state of dress. Her face was definitely more expressive than her father's and was somewhere between horror and humor. "How do you know my name?"

Sage worked her mouth, but words refused to come.

"This is Sage Dalton. An old friend." When Grayson said the word friend, his throat bobbed.

"It's very nice to see you again, Loren."

"Nice to meet you." She tugged on the hem of an over-sized black T-shirt that went along with her black leggings and sleek motorcycle boots adorned with shiny silver Prada buckles. "What happened to your clothes? Were you in a fight or an accident?" Loren asked Sage.

Grayson spun away from them, and she had the feeling he was fighting a smile he didn't want her to see.

"Not exactly." Sage hadn't missed the young girl's amused reaction to her disheveled appearance. She dusted off more flecks of dried mud while her cheeks flamed. "I was trying to bathe a very feisty foal."

"A foal?" The tilt of the teenager's head was so much like her father's.

"A baby horse. I own a ranch." Why had she thought it would be okay to come into town looking like this, and what were the chances of them showing up on the first major fashion-don't-day she'd had in the past ten years?

Loren scuffed the sole of one designer boot against the dusty concrete floor. "Dad, we have to be at the house before the moving truck gets there."

Moving truck? So they are moving back to Channing.

The metal band of his TAG Heuer watch shifted with a soft clink as he raised his wrist to check the time. "The truck won't be here for a couple more hours."

"But I haven't even seen this old house you're moving us into. Don't we have to move stuff out before we can move in?" Her arms spread wide and then dropped in a theatrical move that could only come from a dramatic teenage girl.

"We might have to pile some of the existing furniture into one room for a while."

"But Dad... I haven't even picked a bedroom, and who knows how much crap—" She cut off her words when he cleared his throat. "How much stuff will be in the room I want. And what will I do if my furniture doesn't fit?"

Grayson sighed and wiped sweat from his brow with the back of one hand. "We'll figure it out."

Was this obviously unwanted move from big city to small town the source of the teen's angst, or was it something deeper? There was a sadness in Loren's eyes that made Sage's heart ache, and she forgot about her own unfortunate appearance. She wanted to pull Loren into her arms and tell her everything would be okay, but Loren didn't know her. It would only make things more awkward than they already were.

Sage adjusted the thin purse strap on her shoulder. She needed to get out of here before she did or said something to embarrass herself like she'd done the last time she'd been in a room with Grayson and Loren—and before the third member of their family showed up. She'd had enough emotional upheaval for one day.

"I need to get going." Sage took a few steps back. "I'm sure I'll see you two around town."

"I'm sure you will." His brow creased, but he held up a hand in a quick wave and finally gave her a small smile. "Bye, Sage."

As father and daughter refocused on one another, she allowed herself one more quick glance at them before turning to go. How was she going to handle randomly seeing them around town?

Back out in the midday sunshine, she took a long, deep steadying breath. A pivotal part of her past had hurtled back into her life without warning, plunging her into painful memories. She was too rattled to be around a bunch of people who might want to stop and chat. Since so many of the businesses had opened over the last month, this original part of Channing, known as Old Town, was bustling with people—both local and tourist. She needed time alone to sort through the roar in her head and heart.

Instead of taking the shortest route along the sidewalk to where her truck was parked in front of her friend Emma's new boutique, Glitz & Glam, Sage walked behind the row of shops on the oldest part of Main Street. Too bad she hadn't made a stop in the boutique for a speedy wardrobe change.

On her way to the gently sloping incline that stretched all the way down to Channing Creek, she had to walk through a wooded area of oaks, elms and Texas redbuds that changed with the seasons. Redbuds were her favorite, and it's why they'd planted them along each side of the long driveway at Dalton Ranch. She stopped under one and plucked off a shiny green heart-shaped leaf. It was smooth between her fingers, but she crumpled it in her fist—because that's how her heart was feeling.

Wounded and put away years ago without fully healing. Forever bruised.

As she came out of the trees, she walked closer to the water's edge where bald cypress dipped their roots into the briskly moving creek. A string of ducks floated by on a current that forced them to drift in a wavy pattern. She could sympathize because it felt as if she'd been caught up in a strong riptide.

It was unnerving to have Grayson turning up at the precise time she was soul searching about the next phase of her life. At age thirty-six, her biological clock wasn't just ticking, it was gearing up for the final sprint of life's timed race. She needed to make a decision about whether or not to become a single mom. Soon. Was it time to get serious about seeking medical assistance?

Her phone chimed and startled her. She pulled it from her purse and read a text from her sister, asking her to bring home a gallon of milk. She sent an affirmative text message, and with a reluctant sigh, she started up the creek bank, keeping her head down and hoping no one would approach her.

Talking all this over with Daisy would help. Her sister would be as surprised as she was about the town's newest residents. It was already apparent that her feelings for Grayson had not died as she'd tried to convince herself of over the years, but this time she would have to do a much better job of hiding them. He wasn't hers to love and never would be. Neither of them were. Brittany DeLuca had that honor.

When she got into her silver BMW, she instantly spotted her pink linen shirt draped across the passenger seat. "Ugh. Why didn't I put that on *before* going into the mill?"

She found a hair tie in the console, and as she was pulling her hair into a ponytail, she caught sight of Grayson in front of the coffee shop, Crafty Coffee. He was turning one way and then the next, looking around with obvious concern. Loren wasn't in sight, and she had a feeling that's who he was looking for. His parental concern was something she couldn't ignore. She grabbed the pink linen shirt, put it on over her T-shirt, buttoned it and tied the shirttails in a knot at her waist and then got out of her car.

In a town the size of Channing, she couldn't avoid seeing him, but if she wanted to get Grayson on board with turning the one-hundred-year-old mill into a community center, she would have to see him fairly frequently. That thought made her heart race, and she wasn't sure if it was from excitement or anxiety.

He saw her coming and held up both hands in a *what are you going to do?* gesture. "Have you seen Loren?"

"No, I haven't." Where was Loren's mother while all of this was going on? "Want me to help you look for her?"

He hesitated. "You don't have to."

"It's no trouble." But just being around him could get her into more trouble than she needed right now…or ever.

"Then yes, please. Let's head this way." He pointed up the street toward the Rodeo Café.

She fell into step beside him. "What happened?"

"We got a call that the moving truck full of our furniture was in an accident."

"Oh, no."

"Everyone is okay, but Loren got upset and took off." His hand shot forward in a speeding motion. "Running away is her newest rebellion tactic. At least here I'm not nearly as worried as I was when she did this in Houston. It's a big part of why we left."

So many questions tumbled through Sage's head, most of which were too intrusive to ask this soon. "There's not too much trouble to get into here, especially in the middle of the day. Want to tell me what's going on?"

"She was hungry, and I'm hoping she only ran as far as the café."

Not exactly what she was asking, but her curiosity would have to chill along with the rest of her. "Have you called Britt? Maybe she's heard from Loren."

His steps faltered and he came to a complete stop, his face showing all the emotion it hadn't before. "You don't know?"

Chapter Two

Standing in the middle of a busy sidewalk with Sage, Grayson DeLuca was tragically close to losing his faltering hold on his emotions. Seeing her after so many years came with feelings more intense than he'd anticipated, and to keep from doing anything he'd regret, he was hardly showing any emotions at all—his standard fallback while he made a plan and stuck with it.

Several passersby went around them, but he remained rooted in place in front of an ice cream shop. He had assumed everyone knew about Britt's death, but now that he thought about it, he'd never actually called anyone in Channing or anyone who had any ties to the place. Now the news of his wife's sudden death would be new to everyone here, and they would have to go through all the condolences all over again.

"Grayson, please, tell me what's happened?"

Her hand was warm against his forearm, and it would be so easy to draw Sage against his chest and find comfort in her arms. The contact would feel so good.

Guilt hit him hard and fast. A knife to the chest. The embrace feeling good was the problem. He shifted away from her touch and started walking. "We lost Britt almost two years ago."

Sage rushed to catch up to him, with her hands clasped against her chest. "Oh, Grayson, I didn't know. I'm so sorry."

"I appreciate it." He'd never get comfortable responding to sympathy, and he was not looking forward to a whole new batch of it. Reliving this was something he had not anticipated when making this move to Channing.

"I'm sure that has a lot to do with why Loren is acting out," Sage said.

"It's been coming on since then." He couldn't admit that he didn't know what the hell he was doing. When Loren was little, he'd worked so much that she'd been much closer to her mom, and now that it was just the two of them, he was fumbling everything.

He opened the café's door, and he made a quick pass through the restaurant while Sage checked the women's restroom, but there was no sign of his daughter.

They stood out in front of the restaurant, both scanning the area. Was Loren somewhere watching him search for her? He should have anticipated a move like this. Payback for making her leave her life and friends in Houston, but he'd had no choice. Paying a lot of money for a private school hadn't meant there weren't bad influences, peer pressure and trouble to get into.

"You didn't say how bad the accident was. Are your belongings okay?"

"The truck landed on its side and the back doors popped open. Some of our things are ruined, but I'm not sure how much of it."

"Oh, no. Poor sweetie. This accident has probably made Loren feel like she's lost something else."

He internally winced at Sage's assessment. "Probably so." He hated this upheaval for his daughter and wanted more than anything to give her a happy childhood. "At least our clothes, photos and the really important things are in a U-Haul trailer behind my Escalade." Thank goodness he'd done that and not risked the items and memories that were most important.

"Maybe we should split up to cover more ground," Sage said. "Want to give me your phone number so I can call you if I see her?"

"Good idea."

With numbers exchanged, they set off in two directions. Now all he had to do was find his daughter, start over in a town that he'd thought was part of his past and figure out how Sage Dalton fit into their lives.

Sage spotted Loren sitting on the polished limestone rim of the courtyard fountain where water splashed over the sculpted body of a rearing stallion. She slowly approached and took a seat near the teenager.

"I'm glad you're getting a chance to explore our town," Sage said.

"Doesn't seem like much to see." It wasn't said in a bratty way but more weary and sad. Understandably so. She'd just had her whole world upended.

"It definitely isn't Houston, but I promise there will be things you'll like about it. And we aren't too far from Dallas. Fort Worth has some fun things, too. My niece, Lizzy, is an opera singer and performs there." She slipped her phone from the side pocket of her purse and typed a quick message letting Grayson know where they were. "What kind of music do you like?"

"Rock." Loren ducked her head and let her long hair swing forward and cover her face.

Sage kept talking, even though Loren mostly responded with nods and one-word answers. She was considering it a win that the teen hadn't gotten up and walked away.

Grayson was slowly approaching from the side, weariness on his face.

Loren stiffened when she saw him and then shot Sage a suspicious side-eyed glance.

"Ready to eat?" he asked his daughter, completely ignoring the part about her running off alone in a new town.

Was he just not willing to reprimand his child in front of her, or was he going to ignore the behavior completely? Sage had a feeling the teen was doing it to get his attention, and ignoring it wasn't going to help. But it wasn't her place to say any of this.

Loren stood and tugged on the front of her oversized T-shirt. "Can we just go see the house and order a pizza?"

"I'm afraid the new pizzeria just opened and won't start its delivery until next week," Sage said.

"That figures," Loren mumbled with an impressive eyeroll.

"Is it your aunt Tilly's house that you're moving into?"

Grayson nodded. "Yes. I haven't been inside of it…since we moved away."

Sage could see this situation going badly. There was no telling what they'd walk in to find. "Has anyone been inside of the house to check on the condition?"

"I've been paying someone to stop in a few times a month to run the water and keep the air and heat at a reasonable level and do light cleaning."

"And you're planning to sleep there tonight?"

"See, Dad. Even she thinks it's an epically bad idea." Loren crossed her arms in a huff.

Sage felt bad for adding to the drama and angst. "Tell you what. Why don't you two go to the house, and I'll bring over a pizza as a housewarming meal."

While Grayson appeared to be searching for a way to say no, Loren had a different idea and didn't hold back.

"Yes, please," the teen said. "I like pepperoni and cheese."

"I guess we'll see you in a little while," he said. "Thanks, Sage."

"I need a miracle—stat," Sage said as she rushed into Glitz & Glam, sidestepping to avoid two women leaving with armloads of bags.

Emma Hart, a high school friend who'd recently opened the boutique, put her hands on her hips. "Girl, what on earth are you doing in town dressed like that?"

"It's a long story. And to change this—" she waved a hand along her mud-spattered clothes "—I have the amount of time it takes to make and bake a pizza to transform myself."

"Got it." Emma shooed her toward the back staircase that led up to her small apartment above the shop. "Go use my bathroom and wash up a bit while I gather some options in the dressing room."

Since her friend knew her style and size, Sage went all in for a full shower. The quickest one of her life. She towel dried her hair, smoothed in some of her friend's lavender-scented hair balm and scrunched it. It wouldn't give her the soft curls she got with her curling iron, but when desperate, you did what you could. She dug out her emergency tube of mascara and swiped on soft pink lipstick. She wrapped herself in one of Emma's robes before going down to the dressing rooms at the back of the boutique.

Her name was printed on a miniature chalkboard that hung from the door of the last room. Inside, she found a small stack of undergarment options on the hot-pink tufted velvet chair. The red wrap-style dress was just her style, but it was too fancy for a casual pizza delivery. She was *not* getting ready for a date. She just wanted to make a better impression than the farmhand fashion she'd been sporting. The floral maxi dress was a possibility. She'd have to see it on.

"I have one more option," Emma said from outside the dressing room.

Sage opened the door a crack, and Emma handed her a blue dress made of soft chambray cotton denim. "I like this one. I'll try it on first."

"I'll grab another just in case and be right back."

The dress had a knee-length skirt and a halter-style top that tied around her neck. She slipped it on and liked the silhouette it gave her. It was a casual everyday dress but with a touch of sexy flare.

"How does it fit?" Emma asked.

"Perfect. This is the one. Do you have any cute sandals?"

"Of course I do. I'll grab some, and then it's time to spill it," Emma said through the door. "I'd love an answer to why we're doing this rushed fairy-godmother thing."

That was a damn good question. What exactly did she think she was doing? She groaned. The problem was the fact that she wasn't thinking ahead. Being this impulsive and reckless wasn't like her at all.

Sage smoothed the skirt of her new dress and looked at herself in the mirror. Her cheeks were rosy from all her running around and the hot shower, and her hair was forming lose waves. It wasn't her usual level of dress, but it was a definite improvement.

What am I doing? I'm not a twenty-three-year-old. I'm a thirty-six-year-old business owner who has responsibilities and should have more sense than this.

"I've got two shoe options." Emma's voice interrupted her thoughts and reminded her that she was in a hurry.

Sage opened the door and studied the sandals. A gold,

bejeweled pair that might go well with the red dress, or a braided-leather pair the color of hot chocolate. "I think I'll go with the simple ones. Thanks, Em. I owe you one big time."

"Remind me again why I'm helping you?"

Sage slipped on the shoes. "I ran into someone I haven't seen in years."

"Anyone I might know?"

"Do you remember Grayson DeLuca?"

Emma's grin grew into a wide smile that showed off her dimples. "Of course. Who could forget that handsome man? He hasn't been around in ages."

"And as you saw, I made a wonderful impression. And since I'm taking them a pizza, I didn't think it would hurt to improve things a bit."

"Well, I'm glad you came in. It's a total transformation. I put your dirty clothes in this bag." Her friend held out one of the pink shopping bags with their logo.

"Thanks a million for the save. Will you put the red dress aside for me? I want to come back and try it on when I have time. And put everything I'm taking with me on my tab."

"You got it. Good luck. Later I want to hear the details," Emma called after her.

She rushed to her car, put her things in and then dashed across the street to get the pizzas she'd ordered.

Was she being totally foolish?

Grayson had barely smiled, and neither had Loren. He'd barely even talked to her, for goodness' sake.

To answer her own question, yes, she was being completely foolish. And yet that didn't seem to be stopping her.

Chapter Three

Sage parked in front of his great-aunt Tilly's old house. The street was shaded with huge mature oaks, and the houses ranged in age from the 1920s to a couple of brand-new ones. A black Cadillac Escalade towing a U-Haul trailer was parked in the long driveway that led to the detached garage. The front yard wasn't completely overgrown but was overdue for a trim, and the mossy-green paint was peeling around the red bricks. She could only imagine Loren's reaction to her new home.

Loren was a big part of the reason she wanted to spend time with the two of them. She'd thought she'd never see her again, and this unexpected chance had been too much to pass up.

With two pizza boxes, she made her way to the front door. Weeds grew through cracks in the sidewalk, and she stepped around a suspicious crumbling spot on the front steps. The doorbell didn't seem to work, so she knocked.

The heavy wooden door stuck slightly as Loren pulled it open and then looked at her curiously.

"Pizza delivery," Sage said.

"Oh, it's you. You look different."

"Better, I hope?"

Loren looked slightly embarrassed. "Yes. Every time I see you, you're a little more…"

"Presentable?" Sage suggested with a small laugh. "I had a rough morning. This is a little closer to the norm."

Loren held the door open wider. "Come in, but I can't promise that this creepy old place isn't haunted."

Sage stepped forward just as Grayson came down the stairs.

"Loren, who's at the door?" He walked up behind his daughter and then stopped short as his deep green eyes skimmed over Sage from head to toe. "I…um…"

If his sudden speech problem was any indication, he'd noticed her wardrobe change as well, but he didn't look any happier to see her than he had at the mill. No broad smile that made his eyes crinkle slightly at the corners. No joking around. Just treating her like a long-ago casual acquaintance, like he hadn't given her a second thought over the years. Had he changed that much? Where was the man who smiled even when a joke was terrible?

Sage's insides crumpled. She dressed up to make people think her inner self matched her put-together and poised outer appearance. But at the moment it did not. Coming here had been a huge mistake. Getting all dressed up before coming had been an even bigger mistake, and she was making a fool of herself.

"Enjoy your pizza." She handed the boxes over to Loren and spun to go. "I have your drinks in the car. I'll get them and then be on my way," she called back to them without turning around.

But Grayson followed. "Sage, wait."

She stopped and turned to face him with a pleasant smile in place. One that she hoped masked her true emotions.

"Stay and eat with us. You might as well see the mess I've gotten myself into." He waved a hand toward the house that was built in the craftsman-style with four tapered columns on brick piers supporting the roof of the front porch. Decorative brackets were mounted under the overhanging eaves and needed a new coat of white paint.

"More than you bargained for?"

He scratched the side of his head and sucked air in between clenched teeth. "You could say that. I don't know what I expected. Loren might be right to be mad about moving her here."

She caught a flash of vulnerability she didn't expect from Grayson DeLuca. It only lasted a split second and was gone as fast as they had disappeared from her life years ago. She felt petty for being so concerned with her appearance and insecurities when he was going through such a hard time. "I'm sure it's nothing that can't be cleaned up and repaired."

He scoffed. "You should probably see it before you say that."

"All right, let's see what you're working with." She opened her car door, got out the cardboard carrier with two of the drinks and handed it to him, hoping it would look like her drink wasn't with theirs because of course she hadn't assumed that she would stay. She reached back in and got her iced tea from the center cup holder, then fell into step beside him. She should've gotten in and driven away, but she was apparently adding a little more torture to her day.

He'd ditched his suit and was in dark jeans, a designer T-shirt and expensive ostrich-skin boots. He had apparently done well for himself, but so had she. Dalton Ranch had become well known for prized horses and was extremely profitable.

They stepped into the front room where Loren was kneeling beside the coffee table eating a slice of pepperoni straight from the box. "I'm not sure it's sanitary enough to eat in here, but I'm too hungry to care."

A pile of dusty drop cloths had been removed from the

antique furnishings. Covering everything had helped, but the room as a whole had been neglected. The woodwork around the fireplace and built-in bookcases was dull with layers of caked on dust, years of spiderwebs and forgotten memories.

He sat on the floor at one end of the coffee table and grabbed a slice, and Sage did the same across from him.

"Since Aunt Tilly passed away, I've been paying Mrs. White across the street to check in on this place every month."

"You wasted your money," Loren said and took another bite.

"Oh, Grayson. Mrs. White died a year ago. And she was in poor health for a year or so before that."

He stopped with a slice halfway to his mouth and then put it down. "Oh, no. She was a sweet woman. I always mailed a check for a whole year at a time. I wonder who's been getting the money."

"And *not* doing the job," Loren mumbled around a mouthful.

"Were the checks cashed?" Sage asked.

He took a moment to think. "I'm not sure. I've had a lot going on the last couple of years."

"Mrs. White's grandson, Nathan, lives in her house now. I'd start by asking him."

"I'll do that."

"Are you keeping all of this antique furniture?"

"No!" Loren said with an animated face that made Sage hide a grin.

"Maybe some of it," Grayson said. "The replacement moving truck will be here tomorrow afternoon, and then we'll assess what we need to keep."

"We one million, billion percent can't sleep here tonight," Loren said in her best horrified voice. "There's only one bed with a mattress, and I am *not* sleeping on it. It's so filthy it would be like sleeping in a dustpan."

"We'll go to a hotel for the night," he said.

Loren continued her assessment. "I tried to wipe some of the dust off the fireplace mantle, and it wouldn't come off because it's sticky. It's going to take a miracle or a fire hose to clean this place."

Her nose scrunched up, and the expression reminded Sage so much of Britt. Cold fingers of sorrow grasped her heart. She and Loren's mom had been good friends once upon a time, and she'd thought about her often and missed her over the years. One of her biggest regrets in life was the way things had ended between them.

"I have something that will clean the woodwork," Sage said. "It's a mixture my mom used to make. We call it witch's brew because it works like magic. It will take off that sticky layer and oil the wood. I'll bring some over tomorrow."

"You're going to help us clean up this mess?" Loren asked.

"No." Grayson put his paper cup down hard enough that the plastic lid popped up on one side.

The pizza was suddenly like rocks in Sage's stomach.

"We can't ask you to help us with something this big. You've already done enough."

"Dad, I don't see how just you and me are going to be able to handle this mess. Can't we just hire people?"

"I'd be happy to help," Sage said. "I find it calming to watch things go from messy to clean. And I know someone who owns an antique store in town. I'm sure they'd be happy to buy some of this or sell items on consignment."

Loren raised up onto her knees. "Can you ask them to come now to get the junk we don't want? Then we'll have room for our stuff."

"I don't know about today, but I'll contact them and see if they can come take a look tomorrow." Sage pulled out her phone and messaged back and forth for a few minutes. The couple who owned the shop were eager to come because they had always wondered what treasures were sitting in Tilly DeLuca's old house.

"Alex and Susie Rios will be here tomorrow before lunchtime," she told them.

"Oh, thank God. Dad, did you call the moving company again and ask how much of our stuff got broken?" Loren asked.

"I don't have a full list, but..." He hesitated. "Some of our furniture fell out of the back end of the truck when it tipped over."

Loren made a pained sound in her throat and knocked a piece of pizza crust onto the old rug as she jumped to her feet. "My bedroom furniture was in the very back." She ran up the stairs and slammed a door so hard that miniature dust clouds poofed up around the room.

Grayson sighed. "It's her own fault. When the movers came to load the truck, Loren locked herself in her room. So her things ended up in the very back of the truck."

"Oh, no."

"I asked them to pick up all the pieces they could, even if they were broken. I do know that our dining table is in too many pieces to save."

Sage's heart ached for the young girl. She ached for both of them. "I should probably go and let y'all get to what you need to do."

"You know about antiques, right?" he asked.

"A bit."

"Since your friends are coming in the morning, do you have time to stay a few more minutes and look through the house with me and help decide what to keep and what to sell?"

"Sure." The giddiness that hit her was a childish kind of emotion, and as her mama used to say, it was going to land her in hot water in a hurry. But at the moment, she wasn't afraid of the possible burn.

Tilly's dining room table and chairs were a fitting style for the era of the house, and since his was broken, he decided to keep it. In the living room, the only things they were keeping were the square coffee table they'd used for their indoor pizza picnic, a long, low bookcase and a sturdy wooden rocking chair built in the craftsman style with wide slats up the back.

Loren had come back down and been quietly trailing a few paces behind them as they headed into the hallway by the staircase and toward the one downstairs bedroom. She paused and went into the bathroom.

"Hey, Dad." Her voice was drawn out in a dramatic way. "You should see this."

He turned back. "What's wrong?"

"When I used this bathroom earlier, I assumed there was a shower behind that curtain, but it's just a closet with no door. There's no bathtub or shower in here."

"I know. The only full bathroom is upstairs."

"Seriously? I sure am glad *my* room is upstairs."

Sage had to agree with the teen on that one.

In the bedroom that would be Grayson's there was a full set of ornate French provincial furniture that was not at all his style, and it was all marked to go.

Upstairs, one bedroom was empty except for an old-fashioned sewing machine you had to pedal with your foot and an impressive collection of antique manual typewriters. Another had mismatched pieces from several eras, and it was all marked to go. The largest upstairs bedroom that Loren had picked had a window seat and held a full set of dusty Art Deco furniture.

"You should definitely keep this set," Sage said. "I would've loved to have a dressing table like that when I was your age." She brushed her fingers over the top of the large round mirror. "It's hard to tell now, but it's going to be gorgeous once it's cleaned up."

The teen looked skeptical and caught her lip between her teeth like she might cry but only shrugged and went back downstairs ahead of them.

When Sage walked into her house through the kitchen door, her twin, Daisy, turned from the refrigerator and cocked her head. "No milk?"

"Oh, shoot—I'm sorry. I got busy and completely forgot."

"That's not what you were wearing when you tore out of here to get to the mill. You were a hot mess, and now..." She grabbed an apple from their mom's chipped pottery mixing bowl and looked her sister up and down. "Did you come home and change without me knowing?"

Sage dropped her purse onto the center island and propped her arms on the marble top. "Funny story. I had to make an emergency stop at Glitz & Glam to let Emma work her magic."

"Why?" Daisy drew out the word in a suspicious tone and then leaned on the opposite side of the island.

"Grayson has moved back to town."

Daisy froze with her teeth pressed against the flesh of her apple and then put it down. "You're not kidding?"

"Nope. They're moving into his aunt Tilly's house."

"Are you telling me you've been with them this whole time?"

"Yep." She let out a long dramatic sigh that could rival Loren's attempts to be acknowledged.

"Does Loren know—"

"No," Sage said, cutting off her sister before she could even finish her question.

"After what she said back then, I can't believe Britt is suddenly okay with you being there."

Sage's skin chilled as her mind flashed back to the memory of that day in the hospital thirteen years ago. The last time she'd seen them. Shaking off the past, she looked into a face identical to hers. "Britt died two years ago."

"Oh, no. How? What happened to her?" Daisy once again put down her apple without taking a bite.

"I don't know how she died. It didn't seem like the right time to ask for details because he wasn't really in a sharing mood."

"Now I understand why you were there. How was it seeing them again?"

Before she could give her any details, the sound of their niece Lizzy's singing came closer and in chorus with her son's crying.

Happy to think of something else, Sage reached for the toddler. "What's the matter, sweet Davy?"

Lizzy handed him over with a kiss on the top of his head before letting go. "He's mad that the cat wouldn't get into the bathtub with him."

They all chuckled, remembering the time Davy had pulled their white cat, Lady, into the tub. She'd sprung into the air like a cartoon animal and hidden under the bed for hours.

Sage cuddled the baby boy, and he quieted to play with one of her curls. She smoothed his hair, still damp from his bath and scented with baby shampoo. This sweet child had come to them as a foster baby when he'd been an orphaned newborn and some people had been reluctant to take him because of his Down syndrome. But Lizzy had fallen in love with him immediately and fought to adopt him. Shortly after her wedding, Lizzy and her husband, Travis, had done just that.

Lizzy handed a bottle of milk to Sage. When her niece and Daisy began discussing a book, she took the bottle and walked out of the kitchen. Davy stuck a thumb into his mouth and rested his head on her shoulder as she made her way through the house to the living room. She sat in her pink velvet chair beside her sister's powder-blue one, and he settled back in her arms and took his bottle.

His cuddles always made her tension ease. Having Davy living in the house with them was wonderful and fulfilled some of her maternal longings, but he was also a reminder of the child she didn't have. She yearned for the chance to do this with a baby of her own, but it never seemed to work out for her.

Davy, who was super limber, lifted his little foot to put his toes on her chin.

"What are you doing, silly boy? Am I not paying enough attention to you? I'm sorry, angel." She tickled the bottom of his foot, and he giggled around the nipple on his bottle. "I'll tell you a story about the time your mama painted herself with mud."

The two of them snuggled, and as she talked, he drifted off to sleep in her arms.

Was it time to seriously do more than only consider using a sperm donor and becoming a single mom? She could make an appointment with her doctor and get things officially moving forward. Even without a husband, she had plenty of support. But her baby wouldn't have a dad. Was Grayson's return to Channing a sign that she needed to make a decision? Or was this a sign she should wait a little longer and see if there was any chance that he—

"I can't let my mind go there."

She gritted her teeth and scolded herself for even letting in a sliver of hope that Grayson would want to have a baby with her.

Chapter Four

By the time Grayson got to the small hotel that was fifteen miles away from Channing, there were no suites or even adjoining rooms. There was only one room with two double beds.

"I'm taking a shower to wash off the filth," Loren said the second they got to their room. She grabbed her bag and went straight into the bathroom and started the water.

He had to agree with needing a shower and hoped she wouldn't take too long. He went to the window and looked out at the car headlights zipping by on the highway.

Mixed in with the sound of the shower, he could hear his thirteen-year-old talking to a friend on the phone. Bits and pieces of the conversation made it clear that she was unhappy about her new home. Loren's behavior was partially his own fault for letting her get away with so much for so long, but since becoming a single parent, he was more unsure than he'd ever been in his entire life. It was time to have a talk about how things would go from here on out.

He hadn't missed the way Sage's forehead had furrowed when he'd let Loren get away with running off and then storming upstairs and slamming a door with no consequences. But she didn't know their full history or the things they'd been through.

Or my unfortunate lack of preparedness for parenting a teenage girl.

Sage hadn't mentioned a husband or kids, and knowing her, if she had either she would've told him all about them. It surprised him that she didn't have a family.

Being with her only hours after arriving in town was breaking the promise he'd made to Britt right after Loren's birth. His promise to never see or speak to Sage again. It felt like she was the one woman who was off-limits.

"I'll set boundaries with Sage," he said to himself, as if saying it aloud would make it so. He could do it. It would be fine. He'd never been unfaithful in his marriage—except in his mind. He'd made a promise to his wife and stuck to it for all these years.

Until now.

But Britt is gone.

Loren came out of the steamy bathroom, and he grabbed what he needed for his turn. "I wish you would try to give our new home a chance."

"I didn't get a vote about moving here," Loren said and crossed her arms.

"Oh, yes, you did get a vote. Every time you got yourself into a potentially dangerous situation in Houston. They all added up to this being our new home."

"This isn't fair because you didn't even talk to me about it. You just announced that you were selling our house and blowing up my world."

He plowed a hand through his hair. "Huh."

"You *want* to live here in this tiny town in that crummy old house, but I don't."

"Loren Grace DeLuca, do you think I want to be living in an old fixer-upper with no maid, gardener or chef?" Until he started a new business, they were living on savings and he had to be cautious. "Doing all the work ourselves isn't my top pick either, but for now, it's what we've got."

"For now?" she asked, her expression perking up with hope. "Does that mean living here might be temporary and we can go home?"

"I did not say that, but I'll tell you what… Let's just focus on now and see how it goes. Do not leave this room while I'm in the shower."

"You think I'm going to run away?"

He gave her a serious look. "It's crossed my mind."

She threw out her arms and fell backward onto the bed. "Thanks to you, I don't have any friends here to run to."

Which was the reason he'd moved them here to a small town that wasn't as dangerous. But how long would it take to settle in? "I promise you'll make new friends." He pointed to the hotel room door. "Do not even open it."

"But Dad—"

"I mean it, Loren." He took a breath and calmed his voice. "I'm too tired to worry and go chasing after you tonight."

"Then don't chase after me!" she yelled. "You didn't worry about what I was doing for all the years when Mama was alive."

He felt instantly gutted. He dropped the things he'd gathered for his shower onto the corner of the bed. "That's not true. Your mama and I just took on different parenting roles, but I always kept track of what you were doing and made sure that you were okay. Since the first moment that you cried in the delivery room, I've loved you with all of my heart and wanted to protect you."

Loren continued to stare at the ceiling, ignoring him. But she ran her top teeth over her bottom lip like she always did when she was thinking hard about something.

"You and I are both still adjusting to our new way of life.

But you're right that I wasn't around enough when you were little, and I'm more sorry than you can know about that. I'd like to change that and also set a few ground rules."

She sat up. "What kind of ground rules?"

"Why don't we start with something easy to do. No running away."

Her sigh was long and drawn out.

"Believe it or not, I didn't move us here to torture you." *Or myself.* "You need to understand where I'm coming from. I've already lost the woman I loved. Having your mama taken so unexpectedly has been hell on both of us, and it's past time for us to get a few things worked out. I can't bear the thought of anything happening to you. Do you have any idea how scared I was every time you ran away?"

"No. Not really." She chewed on her thumbnail.

"The thought of something horrible happening to you and never seeing you again—or, God forbid, never knowing— is…" He choked up as sweat broke out on his forehead. "Unthinkable."

Some of the fight left Loren. "I didn't mean for you to feel that way. I promise I'll stay in the room while you shower."

"Thank you." He picked up his pajamas, turned for the bathroom and took a few steps.

"Dad? What did Mama do when I cried for the first time in the delivery room?"

The breath hung in his lungs and formed ice crystals. He chose his wording carefully so he wouldn't be lying. "From the first moment she saw you and heard you cry, your mama was head over heels for you. She loved you more than anything else in the whole world. Never doubt that."

He could not let Loren know that her mother, Britt, hadn't even been in the delivery room for the birth. He'd sworn to his wife to keep that secret.

* * *

The next morning, Grayson ducked to avoid a spiderweb that was dangling from the ceiling and swaying in the breeze coming in through the open living room windows. He'd been so focused on other things, he'd forgotten that all their cleaning supplies were in the moving truck, and this old broom from the pantry wasn't doing much good. He would have to make a trip to the store.

He'd been surprised to inherit his great aunt Tilly's house where he'd lived with his straitlaced aunt and his mom for his last three years of high school—not by his choice but due to his parents' divorce and his dad moving away with a new wife. He should've sold this place years ago, but for some reason, every time he'd considered it, something had stopped him. Once he'd gone so far as to hire a Realtor, yet he'd held on to it.

Too bad I didn't take better care of it.

Had it been his subconscious or some intuition telling him there was a reason to keep it? Was this where they were supposed to be, or had he made a huge mistake trading their lives in Houston for the same location he hadn't wanted to live in when he hadn't been much older than Loren?

What choice did I have?

He could sympathize more than she realized, and once they settled in, he'd tell her about when he'd started high school here in Channing. He'd made friends quickly and hoped she would too once classes started, but he'd been outgoing and into sports, and he hadn't been as angry, withdrawn and rebellious as Loren.

"Good morning." Sage came through the wide opening between the entryway and living room where the pocket doors were stuck in the wall and refused to slide closed. She was rolling a vacuum with one hand, carrying a bucket of rags in the other and held a mop under one arm like she was ready to do battle.

"Morning." He reached out to take the bucket and mop. "I didn't know you'd arrived. Why didn't you ask me for help?"

"Loren is helping me unload."

"There's more?"

She smiled. "I brought extra supplies just in case. I figured your vacuum and stuff were probably on the moving truck."

"And you'd be correct. Thanks. This saves me a trip to the store." Sage had come to his rescue. Again.

Was it his imagination or did she look prettier every time he saw her?

Yesterday, when he'd first seen her at the mill, she'd been disheveled and mud splattered, but the dirt and torn shirt hadn't been able to hide her natural beauty. When they'd searched for Loren only a short while later, she'd tidied herself up a bit. And then less than an hour after that, she'd shown up at his house with damp hair and a pretty dress that had shown off her smooth bare shoulders. He couldn't remember her to be one to change her clothes several times a day, but it had been years since he'd seen her. The many looks of Sage Dalton.

This morning, she'd come dressed to work in jeans, tennis shoes and a maroon T-shirt that was fitted just enough to show off curves, all free of mud splatters. But she had on more makeup and her hair was smoothed into big shiny curls.

"What? Do I have something on my face?" She touched her cheek.

Great. Now I'm staring at her. "More makeup than I've seen on you before."

She shrugged. "It's been a long time, and I'm older and need the camouflage."

"You don't look older."

"I see you're still a charmer."

Before either of them could say more, Loren trailed in with a big plastic tub filled with cleaning supplies and a dust mop balanced across the top. She put it on the coffee table. "That's everything from your car."

"Thanks, Loren."

The teenager twisted her mouth into a thoughtful expression. "Can you call me Ren, please?"

"Of course," Sage said. "I didn't realize you went by a nickname."

"I didn't, either," Grayson said. Where was this coming from?

"If I have to start a whole new life I might as well have a new name."

"Any chance Ren will give small-town life a chance and want to wear something other than black?" His daughter got a gleam in her eyes, and he had no idea what his comment had sparked, but he hoped it wasn't more rebellion.

"To be determined. Another reason to go by the name Ren is because a lot of people pronounce Loren like the name Lauren, and it makes me nuts. It's supposed to be said like Sophia Loren. My mama was a big fan of hers and watched all her movies."

"Yes, I remember that about her." Sage glanced at her feet as if hiding her expression.

"Now that we've got that settled," Grayson said. "I have a plan of action for the day."

Loren rolled her eyes. "Of course you do."

He shot her a *watch it, kid* look.

"Dad always has to make a plan," she said to Sage.

"I know. He was like that even in high school. And I'll admit, I also like to make plans and be in control of things."

"Sometimes it drove Mama crazy. She liked to be more spontaneous."

He swallowed hard. That had been one of their conflicts, but he hadn't realized Loren had picked up on it.

Sage looked at her pink watch. "My friends, Alex and Susie Rios, will be here any minute to pick up furniture for their store. You'll have to work out with them what they buy and what you want to sell on consignment."

"Awesome." Loren went over to the faded old sofa and started trying to push it toward the door.

"I don't think you need to move that yet, kiddo," he said, but he liked her eagerness to help. "Part of my plan is to clear out the odds and ends left in some of the furniture pieces that are going away."

"Good idea," Sage said. "It will save a lot of time and help Alex and Susie get furniture out of the house and into their truck. Let's make a box for items to keep, one for donate and one for trash."

Loren put her hands on her hips and looked around. "So, a shoebox for keep, moving box for donations and refrigerator-size box for trash."

Sage chuckled, and Grayson had to admit it was funny. With the way things had been lately, any time his daughter joked around he was going to take it as a win.

In the time it took them to put books, photographs and random knickknacks into plastic tubs and boxes, Sage's friends had arrived with a large truck and two helpers. It took less than an hour to haul things out of the house, and the antique dealers drove away with a full truckload.

He heard Loren talking to someone in the front yard and stepped out onto the porch.

A tall young man with curly black hair raised a hand in greeting. "Hi, I'm Nathan White from across the street."

"Grayson DeLuca. Nice to meet you."

"I'll see you around," his daughter said to Nathan and went back inside.

"I'm sorry I haven't gotten around to mowing your yard the last few weeks. I've been out of town."

"I didn't even realize you'd been mowing it," Grayson said.

Nathan cocked his head. "My grandma always had me take care of your front yard. I thought that's what the money was for."

At this point, there was no reason to go into the list of what hadn't been done inside of the house. "I appreciate you taking care of the yard."

"No problem." A car pulled up into his driveway across the street. "That's my girlfriend. I need to get going before we're late for a friend's party. Let me know if I can help you with anything."

"Thanks. Have fun," Grayson said and went up the front steps, noting the broken section that needed replacing—along with a growing list of other repairs. His bedroom was completely empty, along with two of the upstairs rooms and most of the living room. Loren had been right in her eagerness to clear things out. Now there was plenty of space for their belongings.

Sage pulled her shoulder-length hair into a ponytail and walked from the living room into the adjoining dining room that led through to the kitchen. The table and six chairs had been pushed to one side to create a wider pathway to walk through with boxes. She stopped beside the swinging door to the kitchen. It was propped open with a cast-iron doorstop made to look like a stack of books. "What's next in the plan? Do you want to start in the kitchen so that you'll be able to cook?"

"Dad isn't very good in the kitchen. We had a cook back home," Loren said. "If we're going to sleep here tonight, it has to be the bedrooms and the bathroom. Can we start upstairs and work our way down?"

"Bedrooms and bathrooms. That's a good place to start. Let's divide and conquer. Who's doing what?" he asked.

"Bedroom," Loren said.

"I call a bedroom," Sage said at the same time.

The girls looked at one another, and his daughter actually smiled before reverting back to her usual resting scowl. "That means you get the bathroom."

"Guess I stepped right into that one." He was so happy Loren had smiled, he didn't mind getting stuck with the dirtier job. If having Sage around came with the possibility of making Loren smile, then he'd suck it up and deal with the temptation she presented.

Upstairs, Sage went into the bathroom and turned in a circle. "It really isn't that bad. It could use some updating, but under the layers of grime, you can tell it's been well taken care of."

"Grime?" Loren grimaced. "That sounds gross."

"It's just layers of caked-on dust. There's no mold or funky stuff."

Grayson cracked his knuckles. "That's good news, since I'll be the one up to my elbows in here."

"Good luck and have fun with that." His daughter backed away from them with two thumbs up and a crooked grin.

He'd take that grin even though it was at his expense. He hadn't cleaned a bathroom in years and could already tell he was going to miss the housekeeper almost as much as he'd miss the cook they'd had in Houston. Once he got a new architectural firm up and running, they could go back to something closer to their old lifestyle.

"I'll get out of your way so you can make this room sparkle." Sage fluttered her lashes and shot him the teasing expression he remembered from when they'd seen one another every day.

He was rapidly recalling why he'd been unable to resist falling for Sage all those years ago. At least they had never crossed a line they couldn't come back from. But if she kept teasing him with her full pouty mouth and looking at him with those flirty green eyes, he was going to have a hell of a time keeping his distance.

How had he kept his attraction a secret from everyone all those years ago? He needed to find that strength again because he could not have Loren picking up on his attraction to Sage Dalton.

Chapter Five

Loren dragged her feet down the hallway. She stopped in the doorway of the bedroom that would be hers, fighting another round of tears that stung her eyes and burned the back of her throat. She hated crying in front of people. It was something she had to do alone.

With a resigned sigh, she went into the dusty museum of a room. Her old life was gone. This wasn't a bad dream she could wake up from.

My new life sucks.

Everything she knew and loved was gone. The house where she'd grown up. Her school and friends and clubs.

Her mama.

A few tears escaped the corner of one eye, and she let them fall because the barely there whispers on her cheeks were like the echo of her mama's touch.

She pulled out the round wooden stool from the dressing table that Sage thought was so cool, but she wasn't sure what was so special about it. Sitting with her elbows on her knees and her chin on her folded hands, she surveyed the old-as-hell room with dark woodwork and faded floral wallpaper. It was half the size of her bedroom in Houston and there was no attached bathroom, but she'd chosen it because of the window seat that looked out over the front of the house.

She didn't know which direction the house faced but was

hoping it would let in light that would be good for painting. It might be a place to set up her easel. She shifted on the stool to look at the other side of the room. The closet was laughably small and lit by a bare bulb with a pull string. It was the kind of closet where small children saw monsters in the dark. She shivered.

That's a door that will remain tightly closed.

Nailing it shut wasn't out of the question. It's not like she needed that much space. Since she'd outgrown all the pretty clothes she'd bought with her mama and only wore black, she didn't need that many. How many different black tops did one person need? But she was getting tired of black. She missed pastel colors and patterns but couldn't bear to pick things out without her mama.

Loren turned on the stool and picked up the large spiky seashell from one corner of the dressing table. It had been in one spot for so long that the outline of it had been left in the dust. After looking into the opening of the shell to make sure there were no spiders or creepy crawlies making it their home, she held it to her ear and closed her eyes.

The sound of the ocean was soothing and made her think of a family vacation they'd taken to the beach when she'd been little. Not to Galveston, near their home in Houston, but somewhere with white sand and palm trees and huge waves that crashed and foamed on the shore.

Who had taught her that you could hear the sound of the ocean in a seashell? A long-ago memory flashed. Hearing this same sound while sitting on her dad's lap and being so small that her feet had stuck out straight in front of her. Had he been the one who'd taught her this?

She hadn't put the shell into the boxes of giveaway stuff they'd packed up earlier because she kind of liked it. It was something that could've been in the yoga-and-meditation room her mama had decorated with a seaside theme.

She returned the shell to its place and was startled by her own reflection in the large mirror. Dark circles shadowed her eyes, and her mouth curved down at the corners. Her hair was the longest it had ever been, falling to the middle of her chest, but she'd forgotten to brush it and split ends made it scraggly. It wasn't the way she saw herself in her mind. Nothing was familiar right now.

Sage had said this furniture would be great once it was clean, and Loren had her doubts, but she hadn't cared enough to argue. Especially since the shiny white lacquer furniture that she'd had in her bedroom for as long as she could remember had probably been destroyed in the car crash.

Her throat tightened. Would nothing ever be the same again?

With her finger, she drew a spiral into the dust on the surface of the dressing table. It had a big round mirror and was the kind of furniture she'd seen in old movies where a woman sat to brush her hair with a fancy silver brush. She'd watched those movies with her mama and hadn't been able to watch them since.

Loren got up and crossed the room. There was a matching chest of drawers, a nightstand and a double bedframe minus the mattress. Since they were keeping this furniture, she hadn't checked the drawers when they'd boxed things up earlier.

"Please don't let there be someone's old underwear in there." She opened the top one and sighed with relief and then checked them one after another. Other than a few coins and a paperclip, they were all empty.

She could hear her dad clunking a broom or mop around in the bathroom, bumping into the toilet and tub as he worked.

Sage came into the room with the vacuum and tub of cleaning supplies. "I've swept and mopped the two empty rooms, and if you like, I can help you get your room done." She held out a microfiber duster. "Want to run this over the furniture and I'll come behind you with my witch's brew cleansing oil?"

"Sure." She was too depressed to argue, and she did want help. It was all kind of overwhelming. A lot of the dirt stuck to the microfiber of the duster, and she could see that the wood wasn't all the same color.

A horrible groaning, screeching and then thumping sound made Loren jump and fling the duster into the air as if something was coming for her.

Sage had let out a yelp and now had a hand to her heart. "It's just the water pipes," she said.

Her dad's loud cursing came from down the hallway, saying several words she definitely wasn't allowed to say.

"Everything okay in there?" Sage yelled down the hallway and tried not to laugh.

"Define okay," he yelled back.

Neither of them could resist rushing to see what happened. Loren was hoping for a reason to live somewhere else, and she wouldn't mind being able to say that she'd told him so. This place was a dump.

They found him on his knees beside the clawfoot tub and looked over his shoulder. A pool of brick-red water swirled around the drain, and Loren's stomach twisted. "Oh my God. What the hell is that? Blood?"

Her dad reached back and squeezed her hand. "No, kiddo. It's just rust in the old pipes."

They all three stood there silently watching as the water continued to run. It turned the color of tea and then finally ran clear.

"See?" he said. "Nothing to worry about."

Loren groaned. She really missed her sleek white bathroom with its walk-in shower and large countertop. This was archaic.

"I'm done talking to you. My life is over."

She went back to her room and continued dusting. She knew she shouldn't talk back to her dad, but sometimes she just couldn't help herself. Who else could she share her misery with?

Sage rejoined her a few minutes later. When she swiped the front of a drawer with an oiled rag, the wood grain that was revealed caught Loren's eye. "Wow. Your mom's witch's brew really works. That's what's underneath all this? Will all the pieces look like that?"

"I think so. Want to trade jobs so you can see the magic happen? It's kind of fun."

"Yes, please." Loren took the oily rag and bottle of homemade mixture that had separated into layers and needed to be shaken up every now and then.

"Make sure the lid is on tight before shaking it. I've made that mistake in the past, and it didn't turn out well."

"Got it." This old high school friend of her parents was hard to figure out. Was she just a nice person, or was she after something? Loren stiffened. Something like her dad.

Was Sage like all those awful women in Houston who'd started flirting with him right after the funeral? It had been horrible to watch.

She would have to keep a close eye on Sage and see if she had a hidden motive for helping them like this. Loren continued to rub the surface of the furniture with oil. Geometric patterns bordered each drawer and were made from three different kinds of wood. The interconnecting lines were like artwork.

"This furniture is even more beautiful than I thought it would be," Sage said.

Loren wasn't going to admit aloud that she agreed. "How old do you think it is?"

"It's Art Deco style, so it's probably from around the nineteen twenties."

"Wow. That's really old." Loren ran her hand along the curving corner of the footboard. "It's kind of like art."

"I think so, too. Are you into art?"

"I've been taking classes for years. Drawing, painting and some pottery."

"That's wonderful." Sage tucked a loose curl back into her ponytail. "I'm not very talented in that way. I hope you'll show me some of your work sometime."

"Sure." She was probably just saying that to be nice.

"What do you say we roll up this musty old carpet and get it out so we can clean the wood floor?"

"And definitely not bring it back in. I have a pink-and-turquoise rug to put in here. At least a rug is something that couldn't have broken in the crash."

"That's true."

They rolled up the musty threadbare area rug and slid it out into the hallway. Once they'd vacuumed and mopped the bare floor, her room was clean and ready for her things to arrive. When they saw the condition of her white furniture, then she'd decide which of these antique pieces she had to keep or move into one of the empty bedrooms.

Before going downstairs, they stopped to check out the bathroom at the end of the hallway. It looked surprisingly good. Although the clawfoot tub was really old, it was clean enough to stand in for a shower. But that was only if no more horror show water came out of the faucet.

"Let's go help your dad," Sage said on her way out of the bedroom.

Loren stared after her and once again wondered what she wanted from them—or, more particularly, from her dad.

I'll be keeping an eye on you.

There were currently two females in his house, and only one of them was speaking to him. And it was the wrong one. His daughter had announced that her life was over and she was done talking to him. Sage Dalton *was* talking to him, and that was a problem. She was tempting him more than he'd expected. He'd thought his feelings for her had been put to rest years ago, but he'd been fooling himself.

Grayson ordered food from one of only two places that delivered. He'd chosen the Golden Dragon because he knew Loren and Sage both liked Chinese food. At least he assumed Sage still did. He remembered a time when she had craved it.

He couldn't bring himself to tackle the downstairs half bath yet, so he moved into the kitchen and groaned at the amount of work it would take to bring it up to modern standards and make it livable. It needed all new appliances, countertops, backsplash, sink, flooring and who knew what else.

He couldn't blame his daughter for being upset about this house, and that was one of the reasons he hadn't been too hard on her for her bratty behavior. He would go through with his plan to set some ground rules, but there would be time for that once they were more settled in and he could think straight.

That and the fact he didn't know what the hell he was doing. He knew very little about the mind of a teenage girl. The ache of missing his wife had dulled over the years, but it sometimes still crept in without warning and gave him a prizefighter slug in the gut.

Loren came into the kitchen, followed by Sage. "Dad, I'm starving."

"I already ordered food. Sweet-and-sour chicken, broccoli beef and a couple of others. It should be here in a few minutes."

"Excellent choices," Sage said. "You did a great job cleaning the bathroom."

"Dad, you should see the furniture in my room after using Sage's magic oil."

"It looks better?"

"Waaay better."

"That's great. I'm glad you're speaking to me again." He liked seeing this level of excitement from his daughter, and when Sage caught his eye, he whispered a thank-you. Her answering smile made his stomach fill with something way to close to butterflies for a man who'd just turned forty years old.

A knock sounded on the front door, and he went to collect the food from the delivery driver and gave him a tip that made his eyes widen and thank him profusely. Apparently the young man wasn't used to the amount the delivery drivers expected in the big city.

The three of them sat at the dining room table and distributed the Chinese food onto paper plates. At first the meal was awkward, and they ate without talking.

"Tell me more about your pottery class. I've always wanted to try it but haven't had the opportunity."

"It's one of my favorite classes."

"She's really very talented," Grayson said, wondering why she'd never told him it was her favorite. "Thankfully I put all of her pottery projects in the trailer that I drove here."

"I'd love to see them once you're unpacked."

Loren added a scoop of rice to her plate. "Is Channing High School going to have a pottery class?"

"They didn't when I went to school there, but it's possible they've added that to the art curriculum." Sage speared a piece of broccoli with her plastic fork. "How are you already going into high school at your age?"

"I skipped a grade in elementary school. Dad did the opposite. He went to first grade twice. He was older than everyone in his class when he graduated."

"Thanks for sharing that bit of embarrassing history," he said with one eyebrow comically arched.

"It's okay, Dad. You just got off to a slow start, but you made up for it."

Sage cleared her throat and covered her mouth with a napkin, but her eyes gave away her amusement.

It had been Britt's idea for Loren to skip ahead a grade. He'd been against it because he didn't want her to be too young when she graduated. He watched her sit with one foot tucked under her, just the way she'd done when she'd been so little her feet hadn't yet reached the floor. Time had flown by. He had only a few more years to prepare her for the world.

The moving truck arrived a short while later, and he followed his daughter out front, worried her improved mood was about to take a major nosedive. The metal door rattled as one of the movers rolled it up to reveal their belongings. A jumbled stack of damaged furniture sat at the very back.

Loren made a whimpering sound, and he put an arm around her shoulders. "I'm so sorry, kiddo. We'll salvage and repair all that we can."

"Our old life is broken." Her voice came out in a strangled whisper.

"We're strong, and with a little time, we'll make things good here. We'll be okay."

They stood there waiting silently as things were unloaded. Her white lacquered dresser was in too many pieces to save, and the headboard was damaged but fixable. Her desk was the only piece of her bedroom furniture that was still completely intact.

Grayson approached the two movers. "Please put anything that is broken or badly damaged in the garage behind the house."

"Yes, sir. We'll do that first and then start moving everything else into the house."

"Thank you."

He went back to his daughter, who was sitting on the front steps with her arms wrapped around her drawn-up knees. Sage was sitting beside her, not talking but there for support all the same. "Do you want your desk moved into your bedroom?"

Loren's sigh was long and drawn out. "No. It won't fit. Can I have one of the other empty bedrooms to turn into my art room, and it can go in there?"

"That's a great idea." He was relieved by her suggestion— and even more relieved that she wasn't running off to who knew where.

"What do you say we go upstairs and see which room has better light for painting?" Sage suggested.

His moody teenager nodded and went into the house, dragging her feet without any enthusiasm.

"Thank you, Sage."

"I'm happy to help."

There was no more denying that he was glad Sage was here. Surely Britt wouldn't mind someone helping her daughter, even if it was the woman who she'd mistakenly feared would take her husband. She had not taken him away. No one had. As long as Britt had lived, he'd been faithful to her.

He helped the movers even though they said it wasn't necessary, but he needed the physical movement to keep him from overthinking. His bedroom furniture hadn't fared much better, and what pieces were salvageable, he decided to put in the other extra bedroom upstairs. He'd be left with nothing more than a mattress on the floor, but now that the time had come, it felt wrong to use the furniture he'd shared with Britt here in this house in Channing.

Since he'd broken his promise not to move back here— even though it had been out of necessity—he needed a fresh start, which included new furniture.

When the moving truck finally pulled away, all of the undamaged furniture was in place and boxes were stacked in their appropriate rooms. The broken pieces of furniture had been put into the garage just in case there was some way to salvage any of it, which he doubted. He did it mostly because Loren wasn't ready to let it go yet, and he understood. He'd put both of them through a lot of sudden changes.

"Dad, I need help." Loren called out as she rushed down the stairs. "There are bees flying around in my haunted closet."

Chapter Six

Sage opened the cabinet under Grayson's kitchen sink to find warped boards and a puddle of water. "Oh, no. I'm afraid there's a leak down here. Do you have a wrench?"

"Yes. Mine's not unpacked yet, but there's a toolbox in the closet. I'll get it and then take a look."

Today he was dressed for manual labor. His worn jeans and threadbare concert T-shirt were surprisingly sexy, and she couldn't resist watching him walk away. While he was out of the room, she got down on the floor and stuck her head under the sink, and that was how he found her when he came back in.

"Sage, what are you doing under there? You don't have to do that."

"I'm just seeing if I can fix it. I've done it before at home. Hand me a wrench, please." She thought she heard him chuckle before he put the tool in her extended hand. Fitting it onto the pipe, she gave it a turn.

And water sprayed her in the face. She yelped and covered the leak with her hand, but it was no use. Water continued squirting between her fingers as he appeared beside her. "I'm so, so sorry, Gray. I didn't mean to make it worse."

"Let me see what I can do." He was trying not to laugh as he took the wrench…and made it even worse.

They scrambled out from under the sink, and she slipped.

He caught her, and they held on to one another, both laughing and slipping.

"I have to shut off the water." He let her go and almost ran into his daughter, who was scowling at them with her arms crossed and her foot tapping. Grayson rushed by her and outside to the water main at the front curb.

Sage brushed her wet hair from her face and grabbed a clean dish towel, hating how unhappy his daughter was to see them laughing together. "Be careful, Ren. You don't want to slip like I did."

Loren's scowl flickered briefly to surprise—maybe from hearing her new nickname—but then she looked at the wet mess on the floor and then at Sage. She shook her head disapprovingly but didn't speak.

It must be my turn to get the silent treatment.

In a strange way, Sage kind of liked getting the silent treatment like Grayson had received from his sulky child. It was silly but it made her feel connected to them. She grabbed a broom and started sweeping the water toward the open door that led out into the backyard. This was the one time to be thankful that the house wasn't quite level and sloped in a helpful direction.

"You know...this newest problem might mean you don't have to stay here tonight," she said to Loren.

That made the teen perk up. "I thought the bees flying around my closet would do it, but dad said they were wasps, and he got rid of them and their nest. But this newest disaster..."

She walked slowly around the room, inspecting the painted cabinets, chipped tile countertops and avocado-green appliances that had been put in sometime in the late 1970s.

The water leak had stopped before Grayson came back into the kitchen. His wet T-shirt was molded to his chest, and Sage forced herself not to stare at his sculpted muscles that were revealed by the wet fabric. Now she had proof that he still liked to work out.

"Dad, as if the rusty water wasn't enough, now we don't have any at all. This place is a freaking disaster, and y'all are playing in the water like a couple of kids."

Sage flinched and stopped sweeping in time to see Grayson do the same. Loren was hurting and struggling with this move, and they'd been laughing. To a moody teen, it probably seemed like no one cared at all about her feelings or what she had to say.

Grayson rubbed a dish towel over his wet hair. "I knew this house would need some work, but damn. You're right, kiddo. It's a bit of a disaster."

Sage flung more water out onto the small back porch that looked out over a yard that had been reclaimed by nature. "You were paying someone and thought they were taking care of the house."

"Never assume," he grumbled and picked up the mop to help.

Sage really wanted to take away some of their stress and tension and make things better for them. "We're all tired and hungry again, and I think we've done enough for the day."

"You don't even have to be here," Loren said and propped her hands on her hips. "Why are you here?"

"Loren Grace," he snapped. "Talking back to me is one thing, but you will not be rude to Sage."

Sage hated the crestfallen expression on the teen's face. They'd started to form the beginnings of a friendship, only to backtrack by laughing together and upsetting her.

"It's okay, Grayson. Ren doesn't know me and has a right to be curious. I'm here because I want to help out an old friend. And I'm hoping I'll gain a new friend in you, Ren."

Loren's shoulders relaxed a bit. "Are you doing this because you want to date my dad like all those other women?"

With his fingertips pressed to his forehead, Grayson mumbled something under his breath.

"No, honey. That's not why I'm here," she said.

"Okay. That's good." Loren grabbed a second mop and worked on the water under the sink.

So many things rushed through Sage's mind. She was here for several reasons. She wanted to know Loren, and the *helping a friend* part was certainly true, especially after learning he'd been struggling since becoming a widower. What concerned her the most was the flash of jealousy that had accompanied Loren's statement about the women he'd been dating.

This could go so wrong if I'm not careful.

Sage felt the need to shift the conversation. "I admit I didn't realize what I was getting myself into by offering to help clean this house, but now I really want to see it all cleaned up. I love to see historic homes and buildings—like the grist mill you bought—come back to life."

"Don't remind me how much work that mill is going to be while I'm dealing with this," he groaned comically and squeezed the mop out into the bucket.

Sage stepped around a small puddle of water. "I have the number for a good plumber."

The kitchen light flickered, and all three of them froze and stared at it, waiting for what would happen next.

"Haunted," Loren said in a spooky drawn-out voice.

Grayson sighed and turned to Sage. "Do you also know any good electricians? An inspection might not be a bad idea."

"I sure do."

"This whole kitchen, too," Loren said. "And while we're at it, the bathrooms should be totally redone. We should probably find another place to live." The teen's earnest expression was an attempt to be taken seriously, but her hopefulness was showing through.

Sage could tell Grayson wanted to smile as much as she did. Loren was quite the negotiator. She was working the situation to her benefit, but she wasn't wrong. This house was not ready to be occupied.

"I guess it's back to the hotel until I get some things figured out."

Sage propped her broom on the floor and leaned on the handle. "I have a better idea."

Chapter Seven

Grayson plowed his hands through his wet hair. Everything was spiraling down the drain like the red water in the bathtub. "I don't look forward to staying long term in a hotel, so I'm up for other suggestions. What's your idea?" he asked Sage.

"We have a one-bedroom log cabin on the ranch. It's empty, and you're welcome to use it."

"Only one bedroom?" Loren said.

"Would you rather stay here with no water?" His child was spoiled, and it was his own fault.

"I'm sorry, but I do not want to be bunkmates with my dad like we're at summer camp."

He rubbed his shoulder that had grown stiff from lifting so many boxes and pieces of furniture. Staying at Dalton Ranch would put him in an awkward position where he'd have to actively resist his attraction to Sage. Like he was doing right this very moment. How had he managed to keep his feelings for Sage in check and locked away all those years ago? Because he needed to do it again.

But he was running low on options and energy and needed something to go right. "We would appreciate using the cabin for a few nights."

"We also have a spare room in the farmhouse that Ren is welcome to use."

She glanced suspiciously between the adults and then looked at Sage in a way he'd seen when she was planning something. "I'd like to stay in the house, please."

He had a feeling it was not only his daughter's way of getting her own room but also to keep an eye on the woman who dared to laugh with her dad like her mama used to do. He didn't want his daughter to think of Sage as the enemy. Maybe spending time together would be a good thing.

Please let this be the right decision.

Sage pulled out her phone and scrolled through her contacts. "Call the plumber from my phone. I know you'll feel better if you get something scheduled."

That was true. He'd forgotten how well Sage had known him once upon a time. They had lived in the same house for months, and he knew what it was like to resist her. He mentally straightened his spine. He could and would get through this next challenging situation. Everything would be just fine.

And if he repeated this phrase enough, could he will it into truth?

"I think I will make that call to the plumber, and then we can pack a few things and head out to your ranch."

Fingers crossed that Loren wouldn't be a brat in front of everyone, especially since they were imposing on the whole Dalton family.

Sage's fingers brushed against Grayson's as he took her phone. A tingly warmth moved through her, and she questioned her invitation to have him on the ranch. She was going to enjoy having Loren there, but with Gray so close, it would be both wonderful and a slow kind of torture.

He walked into the dining room with the phone to his ear.

"You have a farm?" Loren asked.

"We have a horse ranch."

"You're married?" She looked eager at the prospect of Sage being off-limits to her dad.

"No, I've never been married." Not that she hadn't tried and failed. "I own the ranch with my twin sister, Daisy. My niece's family also lives there." Speaking of that, she needed to let her family know they'd be having guests. "Do you like to ride horses?"

"I've never ridden. Mama was scared of horses."

"That's right—I'd forgotten that."

"You really knew my mama?"

"I sure did. She was a couple of years ahead of me in school."

"Do you think you could maybe tell me stories about her?"

"Absolutely." She had plenty of stories. They'd had so many fun times together. If only things hadn't gone so incredibly wrong, they could've remained close. "Do you want to pack a bag for a few nights?"

"I still have my suitcase packed from staying at the hotel. I'll go get it." The suddenly energetic teenager practically ran from the kitchen.

Sage leaned against the counter, closed her eyes and inhaled deeply. She was setting herself up for a plethora of problems. It startled her when Grayson came back into the room and handed her the phone and a dry T-shirt. He'd already changed his, but his dark hair was still disheveled, and she had the urge to brush it back from his forehead.

"I got something scheduled with the plumber for tomorrow afternoon."

"That's good. I'm glad he could work you in so soon. Loren went to get her suitcase. I guess I'll change into your shirt and head home. Do you remember the way to the ranch?"

"I do. We won't be far behind you."

*** *

On the drive back to the ranch, Sage called her sister to let her know about the arrival of their guests.

"Where are you?" Daisy's voice said over the Bluetooth speakers of her car. "You've been gone longer than you said, and I've been worried."

"There's no need for worry." But it did make her feel good to have someone who cared about her as much as her twin. Her best friend and ride-or-die partner in life. "Grayson has had a few problems arise with his aunt's old house. Mainly no water. So we're going to have guests for a night or two."

There was a beat of silence over the phone line before her sister sighed. "What are you doing, Sage? You're going to end up getting hurt. Again."

She mimicked her sigh, knowing her twin was most likely right, but what else could she do?

I could've not gone to his house with pizza and then again today.

"How is he acting?" Daisy asked. "Is he being distant, or has he been flirting?"

"He's not flirting, and neither am I."

Liar, liar, panties on fire.

It was true that he hadn't been particularly cozy with her, but she was already opening her heart, and her sister knew her well enough to know it.

"If you say so."

"I need to stop for gas. We can talk about this later tonight."

"Okay. But I'm keeping my eye on him."

Just like his daughter would be doing. "I'm sure you will. Bye, sis."

"Be careful."

She chuckled at her twin's motherly tone and lifted the

collar of the navy-blue T-shirt she was wearing. The faintest scent of Grayson's cologne lingered in the fabric, and it made her head swim.

She slowed to pull off the road and up to the one gas pump in front of Zimmerman's. The old-fashioned general store had been here as long as she could remember. The elderly couple who owned the place had only modernized the bare minimum over the years, leaving the pale green wooden building with a back-in-time look and feel that Sage loved. Summer daisies swayed in the breeze in window boxes under the row of windows on both sides of the door, and a big black cat dozed under one of them.

"Evening, Sage." Mr. Zimmerman was sweeping the wooden deck that sat to one side of the building and held a metal bistro set and a couple of rocking chairs.

"Hello. I'm glad I got here before you closed. How are you?" She started pumping gas into her silver sports car.

"Can't complain. The kids are coming for a visit this weekend."

"That's wonderful. Tell them hello."

"Did you hear that we have returning residents? Tilly De-Luca's nephew and his family are moving into her house."

Channing being the talkative small town that it was, it didn't surprise her a bit that he already knew. Did he also know that Grayson had returned as a widower? "Yes. Grayson and his thirteen-year-old daughter, Loren."

With a hand propped on his broom handle, he shook his head. "Is that so? Divorced?" he asked in a hushed tone as if saying it too loudly would be inappropriate.

She couldn't have him start a false rumor that Grayson was divorced. "No, sir. He's widowed."

His expression fell, deepening the lines bracketing his

mouth. "That's real sad, and I'm sorry to hear it. I can't imagine not having my Ruth all these sixty-five years."

"Wow. You've been married for sixty-five years?" She twisted her gas cap back into place. How old was this active man who still worked and got around like he was years younger?

He chuckled. "Not quite. But I count from the day I first saw her at a junior high school dance when I was twelve years old. Most striking girl I've ever seen."

"That's a lovely story. Someday you must tell me your secret for making a relationship last."

"No secret. Just listening and loving through the good and bad."

"That's great advice. I'll remember it."

"Do you need anything from inside?" He gestured toward the door with the bristles of the broom.

"No, sir. Just the gas."

"I'll put it on your tab."

"Thanks. Give my love to Mrs. Z."

Back on the road, she turned up the radio and sang along with a Carrie Underwood country song in an effort to calm her anxiety and clear her mind. She only sang when she was alone because she unfortunately didn't have the singing skills her niece had been blessed with.

When she caught sight of Grayson's black SUV in her rearview mirror, her nerves sprang back into a ruckus dance. She hit the button on her rearview mirror to make her entrance gate swing open, and he followed her down the long driveway of Dalton Ranch.

Daisy was outside on the back patio when he parked his SUV beside her sports car.

There was a somewhat awkward handshake between Daisy and Grayson. Her twin wasn't rude to him, but she also wasn't overly friendly. The tension from past events was still hovering between them.

"This is my daughter, Loren."

"Hi," the teen said. "You really are identical twins."

"We certainly are," Daisy said with a smile. "It's very nice to officially meet you. The last time I saw you was through the window of a hospital nursery."

Grayson cleared his throat and then coughed rather loudly, and at the same time, Sage shot her sister a slightly panicked expression.

"You were there when I was born?"

Daisy's eyes darted briefly to Sage's, having a quick silent twin conversation. "I just happened to be in town and stopped by to…congratulate your parents."

"Let's go inside and show Loren where she'll be sleeping," Sage said, quickly ending this conversation before it went wrong.

He and his daughter followed her through the kitchen and then into the wide hallway that led to the staircase at the front of the house. Upstairs, she took them into the extra bedroom.

"Will this work for you?"

Loren turned in a circle. The shiplap walls were painted white, and the gauzy curtains were the color of a sunny day. "Yes. This is a really cool room. Thank you very much for letting me stay in your house. I'll be a good guest."

Sage shared a brief smile with Grayson over the top of Loren's head. She had a strong feeling they must have had a discussion about manners on their drive to the ranch. "You're very welcome. Why don't you settle in while I show your dad the cabin. Or do you want to go with us?"

Loren put her suitcase on the white chenille bedspread. "I'm good here. I have a book I'm reading, and I could *really* use some time to myself."

She kept herself from chuckling but couldn't stop her smile. "Sounds like a very good plan."

"Call me if you need me, kiddo."

"I'll be fine, Dad. Goodbye." She turned from them and unzipped her bag.

"I think we've been dismissed," Sage whispered as she followed Grayson into the hallway.

"You are correct."

They didn't talk much as they walked out into the backyard. A warm wind tossed her curls across her face and carried with it the scent of her own herbal shampoo and his cedar-and-spice cologne. The combination made her lightheaded.

She'd set herself up for a wild ride and predicted there would be twists, sharp turns and sizable speedbumps ahead.

His daughter was settled in a guest room at Dalton Ranch, so he walked with Sage out past the very impressive horse stable and around an old red barn to the little rustic log cabin. They were both lost in their own thoughts until they reached the front porch that was covered by a wood-shingled roof.

"This is where my niece's husband, Travis, lived until a tornado damaged it. Then he moved into the farmhouse. But honestly, I think Lizzy had about as much to do with him moving up to the house as the tornado, or likely more." Sage opened the door and led the way inside.

The log walls were hand-hewn and lightly varnished with a matte clear coat. He put his laptop bag on the brown leather couch that faced a stone fireplace with a television mounted on the wall above the cedar mantel.

She flapped her shirt away from her body, making her curls sway in the current of air. His heart beat a little faster. Seeing her in his T-shirt was moving toward a familiarity that should worry him, but he couldn't seem to drum up much concern. "This is a great cabin."

"I should've told Daisy to come turn on the air conditioner."

"I can handle a little heat. Bring it on, sweetheart." The instant the words left his lips, he regretted using an endearment, especially when her slow grin became a wide smile that made a different kind of warmth flash inside of him. He shouldn't be adding fuel to the slow burn building between them.

Sage started adjusting the thermostat on the wall beside the bedroom door. Where he could see a bed. And she was standing right between him and the soft mattress. How would she react if he swept her into his arms and carried her in there? From the vibes she was sending out, she would be a willing partner.

What am I doing?

He turned in a jerk to stare at the stone fireplace. He shouldn't be flirting and absolutely should not be considering taking her to bed. This was exactly the kind of interaction he didn't want Loren to see and get worked up about.

"It's a new unit that we added when the roof and kitchen were repaired, so it should cool off pretty quickly. Why don't you put your things in the bedroom, and then if you want, you can come back up to the house while it cools off."

Cooling off was exactly what he needed to do.

How in the hell am I supposed to be around her and pretend I don't want more?

When she stepped aside, he took the rest of his things into the small bedroom and put them on the double bed. He had two important reasons to keep his relationship at nothing more than a chill friendship level with Sage—his promise to Britt and his daughter's feelings.

Loren wasn't ready to see him with someone else, and forcing it upon her during such a big transition seemed selfish and unnecessarily cruel. It was one of the main reasons he'd brushed off all the invitations from the women in Houston over the last couple of years. It hadn't been that hard, but none of them had made his whole body feel alive in this way.

"Sage, you don't have to entertain me," he said on his way back into the living room.

"Right. I'll get out of your hair and leave you alone." She turned and walked quickly out the door.

"Wait." He followed her outside into the watery evening sunshine. "I didn't mean for you to leave. I'd like to talk to you about something."

She stopped and slowly turned back to face him. "It's about what Daisy said, right? About being at the hospital when Loren was born?"

"Yes."

"I'll talk to my sister. It won't be a problem. Promise."

"Do you have time to sit and talk for a minute?"

"Sure."

He motioned for her to sit in one of two rocking chairs positioned to look out over a wooded area and then took the one beside her. The view was beautiful and very peaceful. Staying here a few nights might be the mini vacation he hadn't realized he needed. He internally laughed. That was a poor attempt to convince himself because he needed a vacation in the worst sort of way.

But it wasn't time to completely relax. Not yet. First, he needed to resolutely express the seriousness of keeping the secret that Sage had been their surrogate.

Chapter Eight

The front porch rocking chair creaked as Grayson leaned back and settled in for what would likely be an emotional conversation.

Nothing good would come from revealing their secret. The truth would only hurt people, including a woman who was gone and couldn't defend her side of things. Keeping the whole truth of their child's birth would honor Britt's memory and the wonderful mother she'd been.

"I made a promise to Britt that I would never tell Loren that she didn't give birth to her. She can't know that you are the one who carried her for nine months and went through hours of labor to deliver her. And I'm sorry about that because you did a truly remarkable thing."

She nodded and swallowed a few times. "I understand. As you'll recall, I moved to Houston with the two of you so that no one here in Channing would know I was your surrogate." Sage's hands went to her stomach, and her expression clouded. "Around here, if people had seen that I was pregnant there would've been all kinds of rumors. It never would have stayed a secret."

He would never forget her huge part in all of this. Her part in helping him become a parent. Britt had been out of town when Sage had gone into labor a couple of weeks early. He'd been the one who'd held Sage's hand through hours of labor. They'd both cried when Loren had been laid upon her chest seconds after birth, screaming and messy and absolutely perfect. They had laughed and smiled at her first yawn and the way she'd splayed her tiny toes when they'd rubbed the silky soft bottom of her foot.

But then one of them had gone home, crying and alone. He could only imagine how hard it must have been for Sage. Even though the baby wasn't biologically hers, she'd bonded with her, the same way he had bonded with Sage. How could he not while living in the same house and watching her belly grow?

At least that was what he'd thought at first, that his feelings for her had only been out of gratitude. But it had been more. Toward the end of the pregnancy, the feelings had sneaked up on him and grown as his child had, and he hadn't known until shortly before she'd gone into labor that Sage had felt the same. They'd developed a special bond that had been sealed during the birth. He'd never acted on the attraction, and neither had she.

But the temptation…

It had been real and had filled him with guilt. Britt hadn't known about their budding feelings…until she had. At the worst moment possible.

If only Britt hadn't walked into the hospital room while Sage had been nursing Loren and he'd been sitting on the bed beside her with an arm around her shoulders and smiling at both of them. Britt had been furious, and he completely understood why. She'd missed the birth of the child she'd so desperately wanted. And when she'd said she wanted the baby to have breast milk, he hadn't realized she'd meant pumping the milk and putting it into a bottle.

But even after the unfortunate incident, against Britt's

wishes, Grayson had made sure a nurse had taken Loren back to Sage one more time so she could say goodbye.

Sage hadn't known he'd been there watching their tearful goodbye. She'd cried, her tears falling onto the top of Loren's little bald head like a christening. He could still remember the word she'd said in a soft, sweet, trembling voice.

I'll love you forever, my sweet darling girl. I'll think of you on every birthday, and I hope some part of you will remember me.

That day at the hospital was why his family had remained in Houston, Britt making him swear that he would never go near Sage Dalton or Channing, Texas, again. He'd already broken both of those promises.

"Grayson, why was it so important to Britt that the surrogacy be kept a secret?"

Sage's question brought his thoughts back to the present. He was the one who had asked to talk, but he wasn't saying anything.

"There's no shame in needing to use a surrogate. And after all these years…"

"I know." Grayson sighed.

He'd asked his wife the same thing many times, but she'd cried and pitched a fit, only saying it wasn't negotiable. He'd loved her enough to go along with her wishes and done what he could to make her happy. And now that she was gone, he was more determined than ever to make sure her wishes were honored. When it came to this one thing, he could not tell his daughter they'd used a surrogate.

"I don't know for sure why she wanted it to remain a secret, but it was one of several important promises I made to her."

He winced and bit down on the inside of his cheek. He

didn't want Sage to know one of the promises was never to see her again.

She cleared her throat. "Loren has never had any suspicions or asked questions?"

"Not that I know of. Who else knows other than you, me and Daisy?"

"That's it. Neither of us has ever told anyone."

"And you promise she'll keep the secret, too."

"Yes, Grayson. I promise."

The way she was gritting her teeth was one of her tells that suggested she was getting irritated with him, so he changed the topic. "I don't guess there's Wi-Fi here at the cabin?"

"There is, actually."

"That's good. I have some work I should get done later."

"Are you going to continue doing architectural work here in Channing?"

"Yes. Freelance for now."

"Were you working for a firm in Houston?"

"I had my own company, but I had to sell it."

"So you could move?"

"Not exactly. It's a lot more complicated than that, but I guess the only positive is good timing for this move."

"What happened?" She leaned toward him on one arm of her rocking chair, giving him her full attention.

He inhaled deeply. It still made him furious to think about the three employees he'd trusted who had gone behind his back to plot and scheme against him. "There was a small group of employees who tried a hostile takeover."

She gasped. "They tried to take your company from you? Why? I can't imagine you being a horrible boss."

"More like too trusting. I trusted a few greedy people I thought were friends, but someone tipped me off to their underhanded plan, and I sold the whole company before they even knew what was happening. Now they're all out on their asses and the employees who stood by me work for the family who bought it."

"Wow. Corporate espionage and everything. I'm so sorry that happened to you. I'm sure you worked very hard to build your business."

He had, and without it he was floundering, not to mention jumpy and bored. But as soon as he started work on turning the grist mill into office spaces and adding on a couple of apartments in the back, he'd have a project to focus on.

"Can I ask you one more question?"

"Go for it," he said.

"Will you tell me what happened to Britt?"

He'd forgotten she didn't know the details because he didn't like talking about it. It always came with a fog of darkness that twisted his gut and heart.

"She had an aneurysm."

Sage laid a hand on his forearm and squeezed, comforting and encouraging him to continue without saying a word.

"I kissed her goodbye one morning and got a call from the hospital a few hours later. She'd collapsed at a charity event and been rushed to the hospital."

"Oh. What an awful shock. One of those things that happens to someone else."

"Exactly. Telling Loren…"

He couldn't bear to dig into those memories right now. It had been such a horribly painful moment that the memory was tucked away tight.

"After that, Loren was getting into trouble and started hanging around with the wrong crowd and running away. I thought having her in a private school would prevent some of that, but it didn't. Then with everything that was happening with my business, it felt like the perfect time to get her out of Houston."

"Sounds like you made the right decision."

He chuckled humorlessly. "Let's hope so. But that's in the *yet to be determined* column. You've seen my daughter's attitude and the state of the house I thought we could just move right into with no problem."

"And it's all fixable."

"I don't have the reports from the plumber or electrician, so you might be jumping the gun."

"I'm not worried. I have faith in you."

Some of the pressure eased from his chest. Sage had always been supportive and easy to talk to, but now…she was entirely too tempting.

Grayson went up the straight staircase of Sage's 1920s farmhouse. Being an architect, he noticed details of a structure that others didn't. His wife had loved new, sleek and modern, and for her, that's what he'd built in a fancy neighborhood in Houston, but he'd missed living in a house with history and character. The creak of the old wooden floorboards as he walked. Woodwork that was worn and faintly blemished by years of use and countless hands smoothing over the surface. A house with history felt more alive with its happy memories and remnant vibrations of its inhabitants.

Hopefully his daughter would grow to appreciate their new home once it was restored to its original beauty. Grayson stopped in front of the half-open bedroom door at the end of the hallway that his daughter would be using while at Sage's house. He knocked with the back of two knuckles.

"Come in."

Loren was stretched out on the double bed reading a book. Her black boots, that were way too hot for summer, were in a pile on the floor beside the bed, and he noticed her toenails were also painted black. Where was his little girl in a pink frilly dress who used to beg for rides on his back?

She lost her mama and has drifted away from me bit by bit.

"Just checking in with you, kiddo. You'll be okay here tonight?"

"Of course, Dad." She rolled her eyes and laid her open book on her chest. "I'm not a baby. And what do you think I'm going to do? Run away?"

The mere suggestion made his blood chill. If his daughter had the faintest idea of how truly agonizing the fear of her running away had been... "No. That's not what I meant."

She lifted her book and continued reading, but he didn't leave. He crossed the room to a window that looked out over one side of the house. With no tall buildings in the way, he could see all the way to the ranch next door.

He hated that their father-daughter relationship was so strained. He'd been trying to make it better over the last couple of years, but he was fumbling time and again. He hadn't been the parent who enforced the daily rules, and a lot of the time he'd been too busy to read a bedtime story or not even home. He should've been a more hands-on father when she was little, knowing the small details of her daily routine, when her ballet class was held or that she'd out-grown shoes and countless other things. Not just a weekend dad who was the fun guy.

He turned back to face his daughter. "You don't know any of the Daltons, and I want to make sure you're comfortable with that."

"Yep. The twins are pretty cool, but I haven't met the rest of the family yet." She sat up. "Sage is only a friend, right? Just friends?"

"That's right. She's an old friend of mine and your mama's." His chest constricted enough that he rubbed the heel of his hand across it.

This was another slap-you-in-the-face kind of reminder he needed, because even disheveled and mud splattered, the moment he'd seen her standing there in the mill, attraction had resurfaced and hit him hard and fast. It had thrown him, but not giving in to his attraction was the right choice. For the sake of helping his daughter adjust, he would resist the allure of Sage Dalton.

Grayson would focus on starting a new life in an old town. "What do you think about going to see if we can help with dinner?"

"I guess so." She put her book on the nightstand, and he followed her downstairs.

In the kitchen, Daisy, Sage and a young woman who must be their niece, Lizzy, were cooking. Daisy gave him a brief nod that told him she understood the full weight of the secret, but she eyed him in a way that said she'd also be watching him and how he treated her sister. He had no idea how much Sage's twin knew about their past, but knowing the two of them, it was everything.

"A baby," Loren said with more excitement than he'd seen or heard from her in a long while. She immediately sat cross-legged on the floor to be on the crawling baby's level.

"This is Davy, and I'm his mom, Lizzy," said the woman with long blond hair.

"I'm Loren, pronounced like Sophia Loren, but you can call me Ren. How old is he?"

"He's just about to have his first birthday, and we're planning the party."

The baby boy crawled to Loren, and she held out her arms to welcome him onto her lap. "He's so cute."

Lizzy extended her hand to Grayson. "It's nice to meet you."

"You, too. Your aunt Sage has told me you're a very talented opera singer."

"They like to brag too much."

Loren adjusted the baby on her lap. "Sage and Daisy are your aunts?"

"The best aunts ever," Lizzy said.

The teenager looked between the three women and then to the baby. "That means you two are this baby's *great*-aunts?"

"Way to make us feel old," Daisy said with a laugh.

Grayson wanted to both palm his forehead and laugh along with her.

Loren's mouth formed an O. "I didn't mean you look old. I'm super surprised you are great-aunts because you look so young."

"Good answer. I love this girl," Daisy said.

Grayson watched Sage hold a hand to her heart. The look on her face was wistful and sad as she gazed at his daughter. Was she haunted by the memories of their shared past like he was?

"We have a brother who is a lot older than us, and he is Lizzy's father," Sage said. "There's only ten years between us and Lizzy."

"How…" Loren pressed her lips together, stopping herself before asking their ages.

But Daisy seemed to know what his daughter had been about to say. "Lizzy is twenty-six and we're thirty-six."

This time, Sage's face fell even further, and she ducked her head.

Was she concerned about her age? She was just as beautiful as she'd been the last time he'd seen her. It wasn't lost on him that she had a tender heart, and he'd have to remember that Sage was fragile when it came to the topic of their past. From what he remembered, she wasn't as tough as she liked people to believe, but she had a lot of love to give. He couldn't understand why she didn't have a family of her own.

The kitchen door opened, and a tall cowboy walked inside and hung his hat on a hook by the door.

The baby clapped his hands and scooted off Loren's lap. "Da-da."

"Hey there, my little man." The cowboy scooped up his son and held him above his head, making the baby giggle, and then he settled him on one hip. "Sorry to ignore everyone else. This guy can be very demanding."

Lizzy went close enough to give him a kiss. "Trav, this is Grayson and Loren DeLuca."

"Welcome. I'm Travis Taylor," he said and offered his hand to Grayson.

"Nice to meet you. I appreciate you opening your home to us."

Ice clinked in tall glasses as Sage filled them. "They're going to be staying here for a few days while a plumber works on their house. Grayson is going to be in the cabin, and Loren will be using the extra bedroom upstairs."

"Happy to have y'all here," Travis said.

"Dinner is ready." Daisy held up a bowl of salad.

They moved into the dining room where all seven of them sat around a rectangular table set with blue-and-white dishes and a pitcher of wildflowers in the center. Davy was in a high chair between his parents on one side, Grayson and Loren sat across from them, and the twins were on opposite ends of the table. They began filling plates with spaghetti and meatballs, salad and garlic bread.

"Do you like to ride horses?" Travis asked them.

"I haven't ridden in about fifteen years," Grayson said as he passed the basket of bread to Sage. When their hands touched and their gazes locked, an awareness tingled up his arm.

"Travis is a rodeo cowboy." Lizzy lovingly smiled at her husband.

"Ex-rodeo cowboy," he said.

"I've never ridden a horse. Can you teach me?" Loren asked Travis.

"If it's all right with your dad, I'd be happy to."

"Can I, Dad? I'm not scared of horses like Mama was."

He liked seeing her so excited about something. "Sure. That sounds like a good idea."

After that, his daughter blushed when the cowboy spoke to her. Grayson was having his own set of difficulties. Being here on Dalton Ranch was going to be even more challenging than he'd anticipated.

Chapter Nine

Sage left Loren upstairs entertaining Davy and found Grayson on her front porch. He was looking out over the ranch with a serious expression. She held out a steaming mug. "Do you still drink coffee after dinner, or does the caffeine keep you awake now that you're an old man?" she said playfully.

He smiled and took the mug of coffee. "Don't they say forty is the new thirty?"

"Sure. Let's go with that." She walked past him and took a seat on the front porch swing.

"Caffeine or not, I don't sleep very well." He turned to face her and leaned back against a post with his feet braced wide. "It started after we lost Britt and got worse the first time Loren ran away."

She ached for him. It was hard enough for her to watch Loren struggle, and she couldn't imagine what Grayson was going through. "Are you worried about leaving her here with me?"

He took a sip of coffee before answering. "No. I don't think she'll go anywhere. It's me she's running from. Not you."

"She's still wary of me and keeping a very watchful eye. Your daughter is very protective of you."

"Yet she wants to be wherever I'm not. She immediately liked it here, unlike our heap of a house."

Sage thought on that for a minute. "I have a theory. I bet liking it here has something to do with the fact that staying at my house is only temporary. That makes it feel okay to like it here and not like she's… I don't know exactly how to say it. Maybe like she is cheating on her old house or life."

He flinched and rubbed his temples. "That I can understand."

He'd said it so quietly she almost hadn't heard him. As she'd suspected, he was having some of the same feelings about moving on. She might've been describing him as well as Loren. "Being here for a few nights might be a good transition to living in a new town. It puts off the time when she'll finally have to accept the fact that she has a new home. One that isn't the house she grew up in. Give it time."

He came to sit beside her on the swing, but not close enough to touch. "You could be right. I hadn't thought about it like that. I hope once our house in town is all put to rights that she'll be more accepting."

"I bet she will. A welcoming house will make the transition easier. I can truly sympathize with Loren. You know better than almost anyone the lengths I went to in an effort to hold on to this ranch."

"Yes, I do."

"Let's walk for a minute." Not wanting to be accidentally overheard, she stood and went down the front steps. Once they were out of earshot, she continued. "Without you and Britt, I wouldn't have had the money to save my home."

"And I wouldn't have my child. I'd say it worked out for both of us." He grimaced. "I'm sorry, Sage. That was insensitive. I know it didn't go as planned and you got hurt."

What could she say to that? She remained quiet, staring up at the night sky as they walked. At least being their surrogate—combined with Daisy's sacrifice—had saved their family ranch. But unfortunately, she'd allowed herself to fall in love with the baby she'd been carrying because the plan had been for her to be a part of Loren's life.

He sighed. "But maybe it's not such a good idea to let her spend too much time here with you."

A sudden flash of anger made her jaw clench. Just when she was getting a chance to know her, Grayson wanted to end it? Again.

"You owe me, Gray," she said with more emphasis than she'd intended.

His steps faltered, and he rearranged his mouth several times as he searched for the right words.

She'd surprised herself with her hastily spoken declaration, but she didn't wait for him to figure out what to say. "I was supposed to get photos and updates and visits with Loren, like an aunt might. And I know it's partially my fault, but I got nada. Zip, zero, zilch."

"You're right." He nodded and lifted a hand as if he would touch her, but the moment passed.

She started walking again, and he fell into step beside her. A barn owl swooped silently across the treetops and landed before calling to his mate.

"I'm sorry, Grayson. I shouldn't have said that. I was out of line."

He clasped her hand and gently pulled her to a stop but then immediately let go. "Hey, you have every right to be upset. It didn't go as planned."

It sure hadn't. Britt had written a detailed birth plan that Sage had agreed to, but when her water had broken while Britt was out of town, Grayson had taken her to the hospital. He'd been the one to sit with her, feed her ice chips and let her squeeze the crap out of his hand. They'd shared a magical once-in-a-lifetime moment. Together.

"I can understand why she was so upset," Sage said. "She missed the birth of her daughter."

"After Britt walked in and saw us together, looking like a family, she kind of lost it. I'm more sorry than you can know that we went back on our words to you, but my marriage was on the line. I couldn't see any other way at the time."

"I know. I understand why you did it, but…" Her words faded away as more memories washed in like a wave.

When Britt had rushed into the hospital room after missing the birth, Sage had been nursing Loren with Grayson sitting right beside her. Breastfeeding had caused Sage to bond with Loren even more, leaving her that much more broken after the three of them had left the hospital. She had not bound her breasts to stop the flow of milk like they'd told her to do, and they had swelled, hot and hard and excruciatingly tender, causing both physical and emotional pain. She crossed her arms over her chest to soothe the phantom ache.

Turning around, they walked slowly back toward the farmhouse. "I'm sorry that I caused problems in your marriage."

He shook his head. "You have nothing to apologize for. You did nothing wrong."

That's not how she had felt about it all these years. That moment when Britt had come into the hospital room, Sage had been about to lean in and kiss Grayson. A man who hadn't been hers to kiss. She'd just been so overcome with emotions and hormones and the afterglow of giving birth to a perfect little human. Thank God Britt had interrupted just in time. But she'd seen enough to cut Sage from their lives. Completely.

"I carry part of the culpability. I truly hate how we ended things."

Grayson finished off his coffee and let the mug dangle

from his fingers. "Loren asked me earlier this evening if we were just friends in a way that made it clear she thinks that's all we should be. I don't think she's ready for her mama to be replaced."

"I think you're right. It's a good thing we have plenty of practice being nothing more than friends." She hadn't forgotten how much it had sucked to be secretly in love with him while living in the house with him and his wife. The temptation being so close but completely out of reach. She was so glad they had never crossed that line.

"Here's what I'm worried about. Introducing someone else into her life and her getting attached and then it not working out and her being hurt by it all because I couldn't make it work." He stopped and faced her. "I have to show her that she comes first…and that you and I are just friends."

"Agreed."

The reality of their situation burned like lemon juice on a fresh cut, but they both had to take steps to help Loren's transition to small-town life be as smooth and pain free as possible. That's what a parent did.

The next morning, Grayson wanted to get up to the main house before his daughter woke up, but since she loved sleeping late, he wasn't in a huge rush. He made coffee in the tiny kitchen that had granite countertops and rustic cedar cabinets. He dressed in jeans, a dark green short-sleeved Henley and boots that were more comfortable than his dress shoes.

As he approached the farmhouse's back door, he could hear voices, and one of them was his daughter's—surprising for it being only eight thirty in the morning. He stepped into the kitchen, where the scent of bacon and something baking made his stomach rumble. Loren was sitting on the floor beside the round table in one corner, entertaining the baby with a set of wooden blocks.

"Good morning," he said to everyone.

He received a chorus of responses before everyone returned to their jobs.

"Hi, Dad." She tossed a wave his way and went back to playing with Davy.

"Welcome to Sunday family breakfast," Sage said from beside the stovetop where bacon sizzled in a cast-iron skillet.

"What can I do to help?"

"Everything is under control. Just grab a cup of coffee and relax."

Her smile was sweet but held a note of sadness that he recognized. They'd come to an understanding last night. For his daughter's sake, they would remain only friends, and because of how things had gone down after the birth thirteen years ago, he would give Sage some time to get to know Loren. The child she'd given birth to and then never seen again.

He poured a cup and added a dash of cream to cut the coffee's bitterness and then sat at the table to observe this extended family work like a team to prepare a meal.

Travis was flipping pancakes on a griddle, and Lizzy was slicing fruit. But there was no sign of the other twin. She was probably somewhere plotting his doom because he'd hurt her sister all those years ago—and wasn't doing much better now. But after Britt had seen them cuddling with her newborn, cutting all ties with Sage had been the only thing he could do to save his marriage.

Loren restacked the colorful wooden blocks, and Davy knocked them over and then clapped for himself. It was pretty darn cute, and it made Grayson ache for a time when his daughter had been small enough to cuddle. On nights when he'd had insomnia, he had gone into her nursery and rocked her just so he could look at her perfect little face. When she'd still been too young to remember and Britt hadn't been around, he had occasionally told Loren stories about Sage. The woman who'd lovingly carried her and given her life. What would she think of him telling an infant about her?

He looked away from Loren and Davy and caught a glimpse of Sage watching him before she quickly turned her head. She'd been so protective over the baby growing inside her, and he had admired the way she'd watched every bite she'd put into her mouth to make sure she would be healthy and strong.

Something tugged on the leg of Grayson's blue jeans, and he looked down into the baby's smiling face. "Hello, Davy." The toddler pulled himself up a bit unsteadily, and Grayson lifted him into his lap. He didn't think he'd held a baby since Loren, but it all came back to him.

Up close, he realized that the child had been born with Down syndrome. He'd never personally known anyone who had, but it sure didn't seem to be holding this little one back. Davy doing so well likely had something to do with all the love and support surrounding him.

"Dad, I got to squeeze the oranges with an old metal tool that Sage and Daisy's grandmother used to use." Loren got up from the floor and sat in the chair beside him.

"Excellent. I love fresh-squeezed orange juice." He shifted the baby, who was playing pattycake on his knees. "What about you, Davy? Do you like to drink juice?"

Davy held up a hand and imitated squeezing something.

"That's sign language for milk," his mother said and came over to them with a bottle.

"I'll feed him," Loren said and took the bottle and the baby.

"Davy knows sign language?" Grayson asked.

"We're working on it," Travis said. "He knows about five signs already."

"That's impressive." Had Britt done the same thing with Loren when she was this age?

Lizzy pulled a tray of cinnamon rolls out of the oven, and the room filled with a delicious aroma. "We usually have breakfast at the kitchen table, but it would be too crowded for seven of us, especially with the size of the high chair. So, we'll use the dining room again."

Everyone grabbed dishes and plates of food and took them into the dining room, where they had another family meal. The kind he and his daughter were not used to, and the way Loren was responding to it made him both happy and sad.

He had no siblings, a mother who lived abroad most of the time and no living father. He couldn't give his child this kind of big family.

Chapter Ten

Sage had woken with the determination to look on the bright side of things and enjoy every little happiness she could, and so far, it was going well.

After breakfast, Grayson insisted on cleaning the kitchen since he hadn't done any of the cooking. Everyone was happy to let him and went off to do whatever they had planned for the day. Lizzy and Davy had gone to their weekly playgroup at the park in town. Daisy and Travis were helping Finn Murphy with something on the ranch next door. Four Star Ranch was owned jointly by Travis and all three of the Murphy brothers.

Sage was sweeping the kitchen as he finished loading the dishwasher and Loren wiped the stovetop. Grayson had grown quiet during their meal, and she knew he was overthinking something. She'd seen him do it many times before.

Since she'd seen them at the mill, she'd been watching Gray and Loren interact and had recognized a few things. They had a complicated and cautious kind of relationship. He didn't want to upset his daughter more than she already was—which had led to her getting away with too much—and Loren was testing her limits every chance she got. They'd talked about so many big issues last night that she hadn't wanted to bring it up. They hadn't yet renewed their friendship enough for her to question his parenting.

This beautiful, grieving child was acting out for multiple reasons. The pain of losing her mom was an obvious one, but as far as Grayson was concerned, it was more complicated. Loren seemed to want his attention but, at the same time, did not want it.

Telling herself to stay out of their lives and mind her own business was useless. The child she'd thought about so often over the years was right in front of her, and she couldn't resist the opportunity to connect with Loren. Plus, there had to be something she could do to help improve their father-daughter relationship.

Loren rinsed the dishrag, hung it over the sink and then turned to her. "Where's the cabin Dad is staying in?"

"It's on the other side of the horse stable," Sage said. "Want to see it?"

"Sure. I guess I could do that." The teenager's tone of voice said she was chill and indifferent, while her eyes gave away some of the excitement she was trying not to show. Because of course she couldn't have anyone believing she was excited about it. She wasn't done punishing her dad for moving her to Channing.

"We can go as soon as you're ready."

"And after we see the cabin, can we see the horses? Please."

"Sounds like a good plan." This child's eagerness to see the horses reminded her of herself at the same age. A sweet but painful emotion settled over her. She might have carried her for nine months, but it wasn't like Loren had inherited any of her traits.

"I'll go get my shoes," Loren said and dashed from the room.

This was a perfect opportunity to start improving their father-daughter relationship. "Grayson, are you coming with us?"

He turned off the water. "Where are we going?"

She internally winced, glad he hadn't proven he wasn't listening while his daughter had been in the room. That would do nothing to help the situation. He'd been so in his head that he hadn't even heard the conversation going on around him, but not hearing his daughter was a problem. Although she should cut him some slack. He was dealing with a tough situation the best he could.

"Loren wants to see the cabin and the horses. She went to put on her shoes."

"Oh, sure. I did hear y'all saying something about horses."

Loren's quick footsteps on the old wooden floor slowed as she neared the kitchen, and then she strolled in as if to say *There's no rush or eagerness to see here, folks*. "I'm ready."

"Let's go see the horses," he said and opened the back door and followed them outside. "When did you put in the patio and grill?" He pointed to the area under the cluster of shade trees. The large red-brick patio was laid in a herringbone pattern and had a built-in grill and a polished concrete counter beside it. An outdoor dining table and six chairs were in the center, and a firepit and four rocking chairs were at the other end.

"Just a few years ago. Around the time we built the new horse stable."

"Dad had an outdoor kitchen back home. Barbequing is the only way he can cook."

He grinned. "It's true."

"In Houston, we had an outdoor refrigerator and a pizza oven, too."

"Sounds really nice," Sage said. "I've always thought a pizza oven would be cool. Especially since we can't get it delivered out here."

They walked past the horse stable and then the old red barn to reach the cabin on the tree line.

"It's practically in the woods," Loren said. "Is it scary in the middle of the night?"

"Only when I heard the scratching and howling," he said.

Loren gasped. "What was it?"

"You are teasing about the scratching, right?" Sage opened the cabin door. "I don't want a pack of coyotes after the horses."

"Yes, I'm teasing. I only heard an owl."

It didn't take long to show her the one-bedroom cabin. When they went into the horse stable, Loren stopped and turned in a circle. "Wow, this is a fancy place for horses to live."

A stall door farther down the row opened, and Travis came out with the naughty white foal.

"Oh my goodness. It's a little baby horse," Loren said.

Mischief tugged on his lead rope and tossed his head, his gangly legs wobbling with excitement, eager to run to greet them, but Travis held him back.

"That's Mischief, the little booger who's responsible for the way I looked when you first saw me at the mill." Sage saw the quiver of a restrained smile on Grayson's handsome face.

"You can come pet him," Travis said.

"He's so cute." Loren went to him, tentative at first but then let the foal nuzzle his head under her arm. Travis began answering the teen's many questions.

Grayson once again seemed far away and lost in his own thoughts.

"Are you worried about her learning to ride?" she whispered. He jerked his head to her as if he'd forgotten she was there. Not very flattering to be forgotten so easily. Even if they could be nothing more than friends.

"She'll be fine. I'm just thinking about some work I need

to get done. A big freelance project I'd like to get the contract for."

"Are you still planning to start another company?"

"Yes, but one that is smaller than the last one. I just need to get the office space built."

"Where are you planning to build it?"

"Dad! Travis said he can give me my first riding lesson right now."

Travis and Mischief approached them. "Only if it's okay."

"It's fine with me. Just be careful," he said to his daughter.

"Cool. You don't need to stay. I'm not a little kid."

"I'll put her on my wife's horse, Misty," Travis said. "She's our calmest mount."

"That sounds good. I'm going to get to work on a proposal for a new project, so I'll be in the cabin if you need me," he said to Loren and then turned to walk out of the stable without a backward glance for Sage.

Her skin grew hot. Grayson was forcing distance between them, and even though it's probably what needed to happen, she didn't have to like it. "If either of you needs me, I'll be in the house."

Where she would be giving herself a strong reminder about the annoying boundaries of friendship.

Sage's thoughts were bouncing around to places they shouldn't, and she needed a distraction to keep her mind occupied, so she went into the home office and opened her laptop. There was an article about a new horse-training technique that she wanted to read, but instead she found herself looking at reviews and testimonials about the sperm bank she was thinking of using. Educating herself and knowing all the facts before making a final plan was always a good idea.

She propped her chin on her fist and sighed. The thought of going through it alone was downright depressing.

"What are you working on?"

She jumped at the sound of her sister's voice. She didn't want to admit to what she was really doing, so she closed her laptop. "Nothing much. I'm mostly just wasting time. What about you? You're wearing your irritated wrinkles."

Daisy rubbed her forehead. "I don't have wrinkles that bad, do I?"

"No, but you will if you keep scowling."

"I'm annoyed with Finn." She sat in the second desk chair that faced Sage and pulled her long braid over her shoulder to take off the rubber band and undo it.

The flash of a memory made Sage sigh. She had loved watching their parents work across from one another at this old partners desk. It had made everything feel so stable and safe. She missed both of them so much. Especially at a time when she was struggling with a decision.

"What did Finn do? Or not do, as the case may be."

"Being best buds with a guy can be challenging. Especially when it's one you're attracted to. Men really are from Mars."

"I completely understand what you mean. Just when you think you have them figured out, you don't." Grayson being a perfect example. "Have you revisited the idea of you and Finn taking things beyond friendship?"

Daisy tipped back her head and sighed, her strawberry-blond hair swinging as she shook her head. "Nothing has changed. He doesn't have any romantic feelings for me. Also, he doesn't believe in marriage and doesn't want any kids. I want both, and I really do value his friendship. We can talk about almost anything."

"And you don't want to lose him by inserting more into the mix."

"Exactly. I need to meet someone I can have a romance with, and then it will become easier to deal with my attraction to Finn." Sage opened her mouth to say something, but Daisy held up a hand. "I know. Don't say it. I realize it's not just going to go away."

"So, what did Finn do that has you so annoyed?"

"He doesn't want to take my advice about some things that need to be done inside of their ranch house. And I might be a wee bit touchy because he went out on a date that he said went really well and he's thinking about asking her out again."

"Could he be doing it to make you jealous?"

Daisy shook her head. "No. He thinks of me as a buddy, not a desirable woman. Maybe I should let you give me that makeover you're always wanting to do."

"Any time you're ready."

A door closed in the distance, and the sound of Travis's and Loren's voices could be heard as they came closer.

Daisy got up and stuck her head out of the office. "If you're looking for us, we're in here."

Loren came into the office, followed by Travis. "I got to ride Misty around in the arena behind the stable."

"She did great," he said. "She's a natural."

Loren gazed at him like he'd hung the moon, and Sage could see a little teenage crush brewing. Davy came cruising around the corner, crawling at top speed with his mama calling after him. He was wearing a green-and-white striped T-shirt and nothing else.

Travis scooped him up. "Where are your pants, squirt? Are you running away from your mama?"

"Mama," he said and clapped his hands on his dad's cheeks.

Lizzy came rushing into the crowded office holding a toddler diaper. "I turned away for one minute, and he took off. He heard his daddy's voice and had to see what's going on."

Travis laid his son on the leather love seat under the office windows and quickly secured the diaper.

"If everyone has work to do, I can play with him for a while," Loren said, her eagerness endearing and showing her sweet nature that she tried to hide behind black clothes and a scowl.

"That would be great," Lizzy said. "You can play with his toys in the living room before his nap."

Everyone filed out of the office, leaving Sage alone with her thoughts and worries once again. She didn't see Grayson for the rest of the day, and when Loren made a trip to the cabin, she came back to report that he'd gone to the grocery store and would not be coming up to the house for Sunday-night supper.

He was avoiding her. But what had she been expecting? *Too much, as usual.*

She could not let fanciful daydreams get in her head. But…could it be that he was avoiding her because resisting the temptation was just as hard for him as it was for her? She felt a little guilty about hoping that was the case.

Later that night, Sage went down the hallway to see if Loren needed anything before she went to bed. The door was open, but she stopped before going in and admired the sleeping child. A book was open on her chest, but she was sound asleep. Sage tiptoed in, missing all the squeaky spots on the floor. Carefully, she picked up the book, marked her page with a *Twilight* bookmark and put it on the bedside table.

Loren rolled onto her side and tucked her hands under her cheek.

Sage smiled as happy tears gathered in her eyes. She

looked so young and vulnerable in sleep. There was no frown or sadness on her sweet face. She pulled the blanket up to Loren's shoulders, kissed her forehead and then quietly left the room for her own, where she'd likely toss and turn.

Halfway down the hall she stopped and looked back. Could it be that Grayson was staying away to give her the time she'd asked for with Loren? Because he felt guilty about keeping her from her all these years? That was certainly a better thought than him just not wanting to be around her.

Chapter Eleven

Sage and Daisy's prized stud horse, Titan, was in high demand, but they were always looking for new business, so on Monday, she had several prospective client meetings. They had kept her busy enough not to think about Grayson—for a few minutes at a time.

The day once again went by without seeing him. She was no expert, but Sage could tell he was hiding his own pain and struggling more than he would ever admit. He'd always been that way. Strong and steady. The kind of man who took care of others ahead of himself. She needed to remember that he was likely still grieving his wife and leaving their home and his whole life in Houston was harder than he was ever going to admit.

"Maybe I've been pushing too hard for a renewed connection," she whispered to herself.

She wanted so badly to pull him into a hug and comfort him. Friends did that, right? But she would give him time.

A heaviness settled over her. *Time.* Her time to become a mother was limited.

She found Loren in the living room slumped in the pink chair, staring at the television as if she wasn't actually seeing it. "Ren, would you like to help me make dinner? I'm using one of my mama's recipes."

She sat up and studied Sage with a child's curiosity. "You called her Mama like I do?" She swallowed hard.

"Yes, Daisy and I both."

"I had some kids tease me for calling her Mama. They said it sounded like something a baby would say."

"Well, they are completely wrong," she said with an exaggerated huff and a hand on her hip. She liked that it made Loren smile. "Come with me and I'll let you choose what we should make."

The teen trailed behind her. "Because you called her Mama, you wouldn't be able to call any other person by that same name, right?"

"I never thought about it, but now that you mention it, I don't think I could. It's a good thing there are lots of other options for people to use."

"Like Mom and Mother and Mommy. If you have a baby, what do you want them to call you?" the teenager asked innocently, having no idea of the pain that question caused.

"If I'm lucky enough to be blessed with a child, they can call me anything they want."

They picked a recipe for taco casserole because they had all the ingredients, and as they cooked together, they compared stories about their childhoods.

Sage pulled out a stack of dinner plates from the cabinet. "Ren, do you know if your dad wants to come up to the house and eat with us?"

"I'll text him and see." Loren clicked away at her phone and then put it down on the marble top of the island. "Dad said he won't be coming up to the house for dinner because he's right in the middle of something. He also said I can stay here if it's okay with you or I can go there if I want to eat a sandwich for dinner because he's working. Figures," she mumbled.

"Of course you can stay here. You're always welcome. Does he work a lot?" Sage asked and put the casserole into the oven and set a timer.

"Not as much as he did when Mama was alive, but he still works a lot."

The disappointment on Loren's face made Sage want to march down to the cabin and tell him he was upsetting his daughter and needed to get his butt up to the house.

Or maybe I should butt the hell out of his life.

He was already avoiding her, and Sage wasn't a hundred percent sure why. She hoped it was to give her and Loren time to bond, but an annoying inner voice kept whispering that he was staying away from her to avoid dealing with the guilt that accompanied their mutual attraction. She knew all about the kind of guilt that could flash hot enough to burn.

Instead of going to talk to him, she started washing the dishes they'd used while cooking. "Want to know what I think about why your dad is spending a lot of time at the cabin?"

"Sure. I guess so."

"I know he wants to be really strong for you, but I think he is struggling with the move like you are."

"Really? But it was all his idea to leave our home in Houston."

"True, but he did it because he wants more than anything to keep you safe and for you to be happy."

The teenager pushed herself up to sit on the end of the counter near the door and then grimaced. "He's probably staying away because I've been a brat."

"No, honey." She let the soapy sponge drop into the water and gave Loren her full attention as she dried her hands. "It's not that. I'm just guessing, but I think it's because he wants to be strong for you and doesn't want you to see that he's also struggling. He probably just needs some time to himself."

"But…" She sucked in a breath and ducked her head. "Leaving Houston was my fault."

Sage moved close enough to stroke a hand over Loren's long hair. "It's not your fault, honey. He just wants to give you both a fresh start. And do you know what? You have a chance to do something I never got to do."

"What's that?"

"You have a chance to reinvent yourself in a new place. I've always lived here in this house in the same small town, and I didn't have that opportunity. But I dreamed about it."

"You didn't go away to college and have that chance?"

"No. We lost our mama, and we almost lost the ranch, too. Daisy and I stayed here, and together we saved it."

"Like in that movie we watched last night about saving a family restaurant with a fundraiser."

"That's a pretty good example." If only it had been that easy for her and Daisy. Their journey to keep the ranch had been much more difficult than a feel-good movie.

"Was it hard to save it?"

Sage took a deep, steadying breath. "Yes, it was very hard. But everything I went through was absolutely worth it." If only she could tell this sweet, sad child that giving birth to her was her proudest accomplishment. Worth all the pain and sadness that came after losing the opportunity to watch her grow up.

Loren slid off the counter to pet the cat who was winding through Sage's feet. "Why didn't you and my mama stay friends?"

A sick feeling engulfed her. She couldn't tell her the truth, and that bothered her. If it was up to her, Loren would know how she'd come into the world. "I guess it was a combination of distance, career goals and the day-to-day grind, like I was doing to save the ranch. I think sometimes adults get too busy with their lives and unfortunately let friendships slip away."

Or burn them to the ground, like she had done.

"I guess that makes sense." She sat cross-legged on the floor. "Do you think when school starts that I should tell people to call me Loren or Ren?"

"Both are beautiful, but which name feels right to you?"

"I can't decide."

"Well, I think you're pretty perfect just the way you are, but if it feels right, starting at a new school in the fall is a good opportunity to be who you most want to be. Maybe something as simple as a new hairstyle and a nickname."

With one hand, Loren tugged at the collar of her black T-shirt and then looked at the ends of her hair. "I haven't had a haircut in a really long time."

"I can help you with that whenever you're ready. Maybe you can try out a new sport."

"I suck at sports."

"Travis said you are a natural horseback rider. That's a sport."

Loren grinned, probably at the mention of Travis more so than the compliment. "So, starting over small-town style."

"Exactly. I love that expression."

The cat settled in Loren's lap, and she cuddled the animal. "I'll think about it."

A few hours later, Loren was watching a romantic comedy with Daisy and Lizzy, and Sage couldn't resist walking down to the cabin. She knocked on the door, and Grayson called out for her to come in.

"Hey, kiddo— Oh, I thought you were Loren."

"Nope. Sorry to disappoint. It's just me." She closed the door behind her. He was wearing faded jeans that rode low on his lean hips and a maroon V-neck shirt that she knew hadn't been cheap.

"I'm not disappointed." He smiled, but it was hesitant. "I'm happy to see you."

"Does Loren knock on the door when she comes down here?"

"She does—now that she walked in while I was standing in the kitchen in a bath towel. I believe she said something like, 'Really, Dad? Why?'"

His imitation of Loren's voice made her laugh. "That sounds about right."

"Even though I was more covered than I am in a swimsuit, it was completely egregious."

Why couldn't I have been the one who caught him in a towel?

"What is Loren doing now?"

"She's watching a movie, and I wanted to talk to you about something."

"Have a seat." He hitched a thumb at the leather couch, and he took the chair. "Is she behaving?"

"She's been great. I'm really enjoying spending time with her." Sage fiddled with her ring, a curvy silver band that matched up like a puzzle piece to the one her twin wore. She was having second thoughts about interfering, but he needed to know how his child was feeling.

"Loren was disappointed that you kept working and didn't come up to the house for dinner."

He propped his elbows on his knees and tunneled his hands in his hair. "Damn it. I'm always screwing this up."

"This?"

"Being a father."

"Not true. You're dealing with a lot. Cut yourself a break." She hated to see him doubting himself. "I hope you won't be mad at me, but I told her you were probably struggling with the move like she is but don't want her to know."

He smiled sadly. "I'm not mad."

"Is it really work that's keeping you down here?" When he went completely still, she thought he wasn't going to answer.

"No." Grayson leaned back in the chair and met her gaze. "Loren seems to want time away from me, and I'm trying to give her that."

"She might act like she doesn't want to be around you, but she does."

"There's one more reason I've been staying away."

Chapter Twelve

Grayson admired Sage sitting across from him, so lovely with her hair curling around her face. He'd almost gone up to the farmhouse at dinner time. He had wanted to so badly, but he didn't want his daughter to pick up on his attraction to Sage before he got a handle on it. But how to do that was the billion-dollar question.

"Well…what is it?" she asked. "What is the other reason you've been staying away?"

"It's because of you." She gasped and looked so hurt that he got up and went to sit on the couch beside her. "Not in a bad way."

"What other way is there?"

He took hold of her clenched hand, sliding his fingers under hers and gently unfolding them, enjoying the way she shivered in response to his touch. "In the way that I'm having a hell of a time resisting you."

Her fingers squeezed his, and she met his gaze. "Truly?"

"Yes, ma'am." He casually let go of her hand. "It's been hard to stay away, but I have because…"

"Because of Loren," she finished for him.

"Exactly. I've been down here trying to figure things out, but I'm having more trouble than usual making a plan, and I'm afraid Loren will pick up on more between us than casual friendship."

"She's a smart girl, and you could be right."

"I'm glad you understand." Having her support would hopefully make this easier.

Some of the tension eased from her posture. "I do. And I'll do what I can to help. I also understand the hard-to-resist part. I've had a lot of practice."

"You've had to resist that many guys?"

She chuckled. "No. I'm talking about you. Ever since the first day I saw you."

"No way."

"Yes way. But you were almost four years older, so at the time, it's no surprise you didn't notice me. I was just a kid to you."

She was no kid now. She was a smart, accomplished, vibrant woman, and knowing how she'd always felt about him wasn't going to help his wavering willpower. "We've agreed to stick with friendship, for Loren's sake, and that means both of us sacrificing our desire to explore our attraction."

"Gray, she is so worth whatever we have to do."

The following day, Grayson was feeling a little more in control of his emotions and ready to rejoin the world. This wasn't a time to feel sorry for himself. He was a father, and that was his number one priority. That evening, he was in the living room watching television with Sage and Loren.

His daughter checked her phone and gasped. "They're having a pool party."

"Who?" he asked.

"My friends. Back home." She jumped up from her spot beside the coffee table where she'd been sketching a picture of the sleeping cat and pointed her finger between him and Sage. "You already have friends here. My social life is over.

It's over!" She ran from the living room, up the stairs and slammed her bedroom door.

Grayson winced. His teenager's mood had gone from good to tortured in a few seconds flat. "I'm sorry about that. Is that normal for a girl her age?"

Sage gave him a sympathetic smile. "Yes. I'm afraid to tell you that it is completely normal."

He groaned. "I'm in way over my head." He couldn't believe he'd said that out loud. He never admitted weakness or doubt in his ability to anyone. Why did he keep telling her?

Maybe it was because telling Sage his worries felt a bit like talking to an imaginary friend—as juvenile as that sounded. But that was almost what she'd become in his mind. Someone not quite real who'd faded into a ghost of a memory. Something he'd had to do to move on with his life. Letting her go completely had been a part of his plan to do the best thing for his wife and child.

Sage leaned back with her hands linked around her drawn-up knees and got that faraway *I'm thinking* face. Even as a teenager, she'd been thoughtful about her words and decisions. "Every parent feels out of their depth at some point." Her brow crumpled, and her throat bobbed as she swallowed. "Or so I'm told."

"I can attest to that being true. Especially for a single parent like me. The waters can be unknown, turbulent and murky."

"I'm sorry it's been so rough. Tell me how to help."

He shook his head. "I wish I knew, but I have no idea."

And there he went again, admitting a shortcoming. She was just so easy to talk to. This lovely woman wasn't an imaginary friend who he could only speak to in his mind. She was real and had real feelings and emotions and suggestions that were already starting to help him and his daughter adjust to a new way of life.

* * *

Sage was brushing their best stud horse, Titan, when Grayson walked into the stable. Her heart fluttered like it always did when he was near, but the lines of worry bracketing his mouth made her tense.

"What's wrong?" she asked.

He propped his arms on the chest high stall door. "I just got off the phone with the plumber."

"Oh, no. Bad news?"

"Most of the plumbing needs to be replaced."

"Yikes. That sounds like a big job."

"That's not all. Shortly before that, I got the report from the electrician. The fuse box isn't up to code, and part of the house needs rewiring. And if I do move forward with remodeling the kitchen and bathrooms, this is going to take way longer than I thought. I need to start looking for an apartment or house to rent for a while."

"Not on our account." When she put her hands on top of his on the stall door, he stiffened, and she removed her hands, hurt that there had to be this forced distance between them. "You can stay here as long as you want. No one else is using the cabin, and Loren is a pleasure to have in the house." She came out of the horse stall, and they started down the aisle.

"We can't impose—"

"Gray, I know you remember our discussion about you owing me a little time with Loren."

He inhaled deeply and then nodded. "Yes. I do."

"So, back to your situation with your house in town. Do you really want to make Loren pack up again and move into some rental only to move again after that? I think you should stay here. Loren seems pretty happy, and I'm enjoying getting to know her."

"She has been happier than usual. Ever since she hasn't

been stuck with only me. And the longer we stay here…" He shoved his hands into the back pockets of his jeans. "Being here has just got me thinking. I can't give her a big extended family like you have, and I'm worried that she'll be disappointed when it's just the two of us again."

She stopped walking and so badly wanted to pull him into a comforting embrace, but the possibility of it turning into more than a friendly hug was too great. "She does want to be with you. It's why she does these things to get your attention. If she wanted to be left alone, she would be trying to go unnoticed and not calling your attention to her."

"I hadn't thought of it that way."

A white horse stuck his head out of a nearby stall, and Sage patted his neck. "I wasn't going to say anything about this because I figured I should mind my own business, but if you're willing, I would like to help you and Loren improve your relationship."

"It can't hurt. Thanks."

As they neared the back of the farmhouse, they paused to watch Loren and Daisy planting herbs in the flowerbed under the kitchen windows.

"Gray, I realize being around me makes you feel guilty. I know Britt wanted you to stay far away from me, but it's a different time now, and getting to know Loren has been wonderful," she said in a soft voice, hoping he could understand her longing. "Since she's happy here, most of the time, this seems like a good place to heal your relationship. But that means you can't seclude yourself at the cabin without her."

"She does look happy with her hands in the dirt, and I have to do whatever it takes to keep her smiling. She is the most important thing in my life and comes first."

It made her happy to know how much he loved his daughter.

He turned to Sage. "We'll stay here on the ranch while our house is made livable."

A sense of relief washed over her, but she needed to remember that although their stay on her ranch had been extended, it was still only temporary. During this time, she'd continue to find ways to bring this father and daughter closer and help improve their relationship while she could.

Chapter Thirteen

Loren dangled a long purple ribbon in front of the fluffy white cat, laughing as the animal made sounds more like a chirp than a meow while leaping for it.

Sage came into the living room and put her cup of coffee on the little round table between her and Daisy's chairs. Except for that first day, Sage was always so put together, like her mama had been. Hair, makeup and carefully chosen fashion. Her twin was just as pretty, but Daisy was more natural with her long hair, minimal to no makeup and casual clothes. She had also noticed that Sage didn't have dimples, but Daisy had one dimple low on one cheek.

"Now that Travis has taught you the basics, would you like to take a horseback ride with me? I need to check a few areas of the ranch, and it's more fun on horseback rather than driving a truck around."

She dropped the purple ribbon onto the floor, and the cat grabbed it in her mouth and ran off. Loren hadn't completely made up her mind about Sage yet. She was nice and she'd discovered yesterday that she was easy to talk to, but Loren still worried that she might think it was okay to take her mama's place. But she really did want to ride in more than the fenced-in area Travis had made her stay in.

Riding was something she'd never done with her mama,

so it wouldn't be like cheating on her memory. Doing this with Sage seemed okay.

Sage was casually picking up Davy's toys and dropping them into the basket to one side of the fireplace and not forcing her to answer. It was pretty cool that she wasn't too pushy and usually asked her instead of telling her what to do.

"I think that would be okay." She looked down at the over-sized black men's T-shirt she was wearing as a sleepshirt. "Guess I should put some jeans on."

"What size shoe do you wear?"

"Six and a half. Why?"

"I thought you might like to borrow a pair of cowboy boots so you don't mess up your pretty black ones. I wear a size seven, so with a thick pair of socks, a pair of mine should be okay until you can get some of your own."

"Do you have a black pair I can wear?"

"I sure do. Have you always liked black clothes?" Sage sat on the edge of the blue velvet sofa.

Why was she asking this? No one had asked her about her clothes since... Her stomach got that hot twisty feeling that made her want to throw up. "Not always."

"I go through different style phases, too. Daisy says that I shop too much, but it's so hard to resist cute clothes and shoes."

Loren always got sad when she thought about the last time she'd gone shopping with her mom. Over the last two years, she'd outgrown all those cute clothes, but she'd kept them. They were too special to ever give away. Without her dad even knowing, she'd also packed up some of her mom's clothes, waiting for the day they would fit her. Mostly pretty dresses in fun colors and designer shoes. But for now, she'd stick to her boring black clothes. They made her feel like she had a layer of protection from the world. Plus, the big shirts hid the fact that she needed her first bra.

Loren picked at a loose thread on the hem of her T-shirt. "It's easier when everything is black."

"I know exactly what you mean. Sometimes you just need something in your life to be simple. And clothes are something you can control."

Her stomach felt a little better when Sage smiled in a way that seemed understanding. It wasn't fake or like she was after something. Maybe she should give Sage more of a chance. As long as she stayed in the friend zone with her dad.

Loren ended up wearing the only pair of black jeans she had that still fit and a pair of Sage's cowboy boots. Out in the stable, Sage talked about what she was doing as she put the saddles and bridals on the horses. She would be riding Lizzy's horse, Misty, because she was the calmest on the ranch. Everyone was way too worried about her getting hurt, and it made her want to scream. Why couldn't everyone understand that she was not a baby?

Once she was on the horse and they started moving, Loren felt more relaxed. "How old were you and Daisy when you first rode a horse?"

"I don't remember exactly. But we were small enough to ride in front of our dad in his saddle."

The horses walked side by side as they came out of the shade, following a trail that wound through the woods and came out at a pond.

Sage motioned to a small wooden dock that stuck out over the water. "I'm not much for fishing myself, but if you like it, I'm sure someone will bring you out here with the fishing poles."

Loren wrinkled her nose at the memory of the fetid smell

of fish and bait and all the gross things that went along with it. "Dad used to go fishing in Galveston, but Mama and I never liked it."

"Maybe you could bring your art supplies out here and set up on the dock to draw or paint while he fishes."

She looked at the line of trees to one side and a clear shot to the horizon on the other. "This would be a good place to work on landscapes. I had a room at our old house that I used as my art studio. It looked out over our backyard."

The sharp ache that had become way too familiar, burned in her throat. She would never ever stand in that room or see that view again.

"Want to tell me about your house in Houston?"

Loren hesitated because thinking of the house where she'd grown up usually made her want to bury her head under the covers and cry, but right now, she had the urge to describe it as a way of pretending she was walking through its rooms, if only for a few minutes. Remembering would help keep the details alive in her mind.

"We had a big modern house with a pool, the outdoor kitchen I told you about and a guest house almost as big as our new *old* house here in Channing. Mama's kitchen had stainless-steel appliances, not the ancient weird-colored ones that were Aunt Tilly's."

Sage smiled. "Avocado green was once very popular. Along with a mustard color called harvest gold."

"That sounds…terrible." She scrunched up her nose. "I hope Dad doesn't think we're keeping them. That's something that definitely needs to change."

"You've had a lot of change all at once."

"It's a way lot. We're going from having a housekeeper and gardener and a cook to doing it all ourselves. And then there is the whole school thing. In Houston, I went to a private school with tons of options for electives like my art classes. But here, there is only one school. And I just know they aren't going to have the classes I want."

"It sounds like it was a wonderful place to go to school."

A gust of hot wind blew Loren's ponytail around behind her. "At my private school, I had to wear a boring uniform. That wasn't so great."

"You won't have to wear a uniform at Channing High School. That's a part of what we talked about before. You can express yourself however you want, for the most part."

"I can't believe I have to start my first year of high school in a new town."

"At least it will be a new experience for all the freshmen, and you won't be the only one who is starting high school."

"But in this tiny town, they've probably all known each other forever. I don't know anybody." A panicky feeling made her stomach tremble.

The horses skirted around the pond, and a flock of birds took off into the air.

"I might know a few people for you to meet. I'll check with a few friends. And I'll tell you a secret."

"What is it?"

"Because Channing is small and you're new to town, everyone will want to meet you."

Her chest got tight. "Like I'm a freak or something?"

"No, honey." Her smile was comforting. "They'll just be curious. I guess there's always the possibility of there being a mean kid, but most of them will be excited to have someone new who comes from a big city and knows cool things."

"You don't think they'll make fun of me or not let me sit at their lunch table or something? There were definitely some mean girls at my old school."

"I'm sorry to hear that. You know, your mama was a new kid in town at about your age, and she did just fine."

"Really?" She sat up taller in the saddle.

"Yes."

"You mean I'm like her?"

"You sure are, and you're having the same type of experience."

"I wish she was here to tell me what to do."

"So do I, honey."

Talking to her mama in her head wasn't enough because she could only guess at what she'd say. Would Sage know the advice she would have given? Her dad might know, but she didn't know how to talk to him about that kind of thing.

Sage steered her horse around a huge tree, and they started back toward the house. "You look like her, and your laugh sounds like hers, too."

She remembered her mama's laugh, and she missed it. She hadn't felt like laughing much lately. In fact, the only laughing she could recall was with baby Davy. "Did you become friends with my mama right away when she moved here?"

"She was a couple of years ahead of me in school, so it took a little time for us to get to know one another but not too much. I remember how pretty and stylish she was. I went shopping with her a few times, and she helped me put fun outfits together."

A feeling of pride swelled inside Loren. Her mama had been great, and it made her feel good that Sage remembered good things about her and how she'd helped her. "She was really good at that kind of stuff."

"She sure was."

"She taught you about fashion like she did me," Loren said. "That's kind of cool."

"It's definitely cool."

"So, you were friends with her, and friends don't do anything bad to the other one, right?"

"That's right." Sage looked down at her stirrups and brushed dirt from the leg of her jeans.

"They don't talk bad about them or steal their boyfriends." She hoped Sage would pick up on the hint that she shouldn't try to date her friend's husband, even if she was dead.

"That's a good rule. If you want any help with back-to-school clothes shopping, I'll be happy to help."

Loren supposed it would be okay if she was her dad's friend, but she'd keep reminding Sage that she had also been a friend to her mama.

Chapter Fourteen

The morning was sunny but not too hot, and Grayson told himself it was going to be a good day. He was headed toward the farmhouse when Travis came out of the horse stable.

"Good morning," the cowboy said with a nod of his head. "Are you looking for your daughter?"

"Yes. Have you seen her or Sage?"

"They went on a ride. Loren takes to riding like she was born for it."

"She didn't get it from me or her mom." The words *born for it* echoed in his head, making him think of Sage. She might love fashion and makeup and all the girly stuff, but Sage also knew horses and riding.

"I understand you're an architect?"

"I am. I'm doing freelance until I can get a new company up and running."

Travis propped his folded arms on the top rail of the wooden fence that surrounded the corral. "Lizzy and I have been playing around with a drawing of the house we want to build on our ranch next door."

"You own the Four Star Ranch next door?"

"Yes. I bought it not long ago with the three Murphy brothers, Finn, Riley and Jake. They got the part with the stone ranch house, and they already live there. I got the barn and a few other structures. So, Lizzy, Davy and I are living here until we can build a house."

"You're lucky to have family right next door."

"That's for sure. We put in a gate between the two properties so we don't even have to get out on the road to go between them. I can train horses on my ranch and still help out around here."

Another cowboy with red hair and a short stocky build came out of the stable, and Travis returned his wave. "I'll see you tomorrow."

He turned back to Grayson. "That's a new Dalton Ranch employee. I'm helping get him up to speed on how things run around here. I used to be the ranch manager, but now that I have my own place, Daisy has taken on that official title."

That roll seemed fitting for Sage's tomboy twin. "Does Sage have a job title?"

"I guess it would be client relations or something like that. But that doesn't mean she doesn't get her hands dirty. She's a hard worker and quite capable."

"That I believe." Something bumped his ankle, and he looked down to see the fluffy white cat staring up at him. She headbutted him once more and then bounded away.

"That cat is a pain but mostly harmless. Just watch out for her to jump out of hiding places when you least expect it."

Grayson chuckled. "I'll remember that. If you want me to take a look at the house plans you and Lizzy are working on, I'd be happy to."

"That would be great. We'd really appreciate it. You can tell us if our idea is reasonable or not."

Grayson liked helping families build their dream house and had really missed it since he'd sold his company. Helping Travis and Lizzy would occupy his mind and, if he was lucky, keep him from thinking about Sage. Constantly. It would also be a chance to help out the family who was making them feel so welcome.

"There they come over the rise." Travis pointed to Loren and Sage off in the distance, still too far away to make out their features.

The scene before him was so different from the kinds of things he'd seen Britt and Loren do together, and although there was still sadness that came along with the memories, he was happy to see Sage and his daughter getting along.

"Did you and Sage used to date?" Travis asked.

"No." The muscles along his neck tightened. Were they being that obvious? If so, that was a problem. "We've never been a couple."

"But you have feelings for one another."

Grayson hooked his thumbs into the front pockets of his jeans. "What makes you think that?"

Travis held up both hands in a *never mind* gesture. "Sorry, that was way too personal. Forget I said anything."

Had one of the women said something to him, or was this guy just that observant? If Travis was picking up on it, his daughter might. "Are we that obvious?"

"No. Well…" He glanced toward the girls off in the distance. "I can sometimes see it in the way Sage looks at you, but it's not totally obvious. She works hard to conceal it. And correct me if I'm wrong, but with you, I recognize something I went through myself with Lizzy. An inner battle about why you shouldn't be with her or love her."

Damn, but this guy is right on target. "Can you keep all of this to yourself, please?"

"Of course. Whatever you say stays between us."

"I don't know what your reasons were for staying away from Lizzy, but my main one is my daughter. She's not ready for me to be with someone who isn't her mother. She has made her opinions and wishes very clear."

"From my hard-earned knowledge, I'm going to give you some unsolicited advice that you are welcome to take or ignore," Travis said. "Don't punish yourself for something that isn't your fault."

Grayson grinned and shook his head. "How old are you? You sound like a much older man."

Travis laughed and propped one boot on the bottom rung of the wooden fence. "I get that a lot. I'm thirty-two, but I was raised by my grandfather and great-grandfather. Guess some of their wisdom rubbed off on me."

Loren raised an arm and gave them an enthusiastic wave as they approached.

Grayson walked toward them as they stopped their horses beside the big sliding stable door. "Look at you, cowgirl," he said to his daughter.

Loren dismounted so gracefully that you'd think she'd been riding for years. "I'm even wearing cowboy boots. Sage let me borrow them."

"That was nice of her." He smiled at the object of his temptation but quickly looked back to his daughter. "You can get a pair of your own if you want."

"I know just the place to get them," Sage said and led the horses into the stable. "Ren, I'll show you how to brush down your horse."

"Do they need a bath?"

"Not today, but you can help me do that on another day. And I'll let you bathe Mischief so you'll understand why I looked like a walking disaster the first time you saw me at the mill."

Loren grinned. "I thought you were living in the abandoned building and Dad had discovered you."

He barked a laugh, and Sage turned to shoot him a murderous glare but then stuck out her tongue, while Loren laughed behind her hand.

Loren's good humor made something loosen deep inside his chest. She was coming back to him a bit at a time with the help of a little horse therapy and spending time with... a mother figure.

This time the sensation in his chest was a jolt. If she grew close to Sage, there was a chance she'd change her mind and be more open to the possibility of them dating. But also, he worried that Loren *would* bond with her, and if things didn't work out between him and Sage, his daughter would lose another mother figure. He needed a flashing sign that reminded him to proceed with caution.

Could Travis be right about not punishing himself for something that wasn't his fault?

That night, Sage had to go check on a horse, and as she was coming out of the stable, she could see lights on at the cabin and hear music as he stepped out onto the front porch. Sage thought of her and Loren's conversation about being the new kid in town and what she might wear to school in Channing. She got the feeling that the teen's current too-big and drab fashion choices were partly mourning and partly not wanting to shop without her mom.

She could sympathize with missing a mom. She'd been twenty when she lost hers, but it had still been a difficult adjustment. Especially with the added stress and drama of almost losing the ranch. It was the reason she had agreed to be a surrogate. She and Daisy had both made really hard decisions and sacrifices that would forever stay with them.

Instead of going back to her house—as she should—she turned the opposite direction and walked down to the cabin to tell Grayson about her conversation with Loren while horseback riding.

"Evening, neighbor," she said.

He turned her way as she came out of the shadows. "What brings you out this late?"

"I was checking on a horse and saw your light on."

"Come in." He held the door for her.

"I wanted to tell you a bit about my conversation with Loren while we were riding."

"Oh, boy. Do I want to know?"

"Yes. It's all good. She told me about your old house, but she was smiling as she did. We discussed school and making new friends here in Channing like her mom did when she moved here. And even a bit about fashion. You've mentioned not knowing what to do about her only wearing black clothes, and I think I have an idea about why she's doing it."

"I'd love to hear it."

"Who helps her shop?"

"I've asked her about getting new clothes many times, but she always says she only wants to order things online."

"She used to shop a lot with her mom, didn't she?" She took a seat on the couch.

"Yes, they…" He rubbed a hand against the back of his neck. "Oh. Of course. She doesn't want to shop for clothes without her mama. I should've realized that."

"I offered to take her shopping for school clothes, but she didn't say one way or the other. So, we'll see."

"You're pretty awesome," he said.

"You're only just now figuring that out?" She stretched out on her side and propped her head on one hand like she was Cleopatra.

"No. I've known it for a long time." He chuckled and grabbed two bottles of beer from the refrigerator. "Want one?"

"Please." She sat up to give him room to sit and was glad when he did. The bottle hissed as he twisted off the cap for her.

"I have another favor to ask," he said.

"About Loren?"

"No. I noticed you've remodeled the bathrooms in your house. They look great and still fit the architectural style. Do you think you could help me pick out materials for mine?"

"Sure. I love doing that kind of stuff."

"Can you also recommend a good contractor?"

"We were very happy with the one we used for our bathrooms and for this cabin's repairs after the storm. She's really good."

"That's great. If I like their work, I can use her company when I start work on the mill in Old Town."

She paused before taking a drink and put her bottle on the coffee table. "I've been meaning to talk to you about the mill. What are you planning to do? Just some minor repairs?"

"No. A whole lot more than that."

"Like what?" she asked in a drawn-out, worried tone of voice.

"Now that Old Town is being revitalized, I'm going to turn it into office spaces and maybe a couple of small apartments in the back."

She gasped. "You can't do that."

"Why not?"

"Because your great-great-grandfather helped build the grist mill, and it needs to be restored, not ruined."

"I'm not going to ruin it. The outside will remain basically the same and only the interior will change."

She stood and began to pace around the small room. Office and living spaces were not at all what she'd hoped for. That would put her back at square one for a place to reestablish and host Old Town Christmas.

"Is that why you showed up at the mill the other day? To make sure no one ruined it?" he asked.

She stopped in front of him. "I wanted to meet the new owner and convince them to restore it enough to use as a community center. A place to bring back the Old Town Christmas celebration."

"I remember that being a fun event. All the back-in-time costumes and decorations."

"The church where we used to hold a lot of it burned down years ago, but I've been wanting to bring the festival back. I thought the restored mill would make a good place for that and lots of other events in Old Town, for the same reason you mentioned. When I saw you and Loren at the mill that day, I kind of forgot about my original mission."

"I don't see how I can make any money off it if it's a community center."

"Oh." She dropped onto the couch cushion beside his. "I hadn't thought about it being a money-making venture for you. Maybe I can help you think of an idea to make money without chopping it up into boring offices."

He laughed and stretched his arm out on the back of the couch behind her. "You think my architectural skills are boring?"

She winced. "No. I didn't mean it that way. I'm sure you can make offices that are very beautiful. I just hope you'll keep your mind open to all the options for the mill."

"I'll do that."

Sage noticed a remnant of blue painter's tape on the ceiling, got up and then jumped to try and reach it.

Grayson chuckled behind her. "What are you doing?"

"Trying to get that piece of blue tape. Give me a boost, please. I don't want it to leave a mark on the new paint."

Although putting his hands on Sage and lifting her into the air sounded very appealing, it was a bad idea. "I'll get it." He got up to help her even though he was enjoying watching her jump up and down.

"You can't reach it, either. These are taller than normal ceilings."

Grayson raised an arm and stretched and could just barely touch the tape but not enough to be able to peel it off.

"Just lift me up, and I'll grab it. I know you can do it because I saw the furniture you lifted while moving into your house."

"Of course I can lift you. That's not in question." Grayson was hesitating because touching her in such an intimate way would be the most exquisite kind of torture. The kind he should resist. He really should. But Sage backed up to him and raised her arms, so he clasped her around the waist and lifted her high enough to peel it off.

"Got it," she said.

As he lowered her, she leaned back and her body brushed against the front of his. A rush of heat flashed through his blood. Her feet were back on the floor, but he hadn't let go of her. Why wasn't he just taking his hands off her waist and stepping away? It was such a simple thing, but at this very second, it felt monumentally impossible.

She relaxed her weight against him and tipped back her head to smile, but right when he was about to turn her in his arms, she stepped away from him.

"See? That wasn't so bad. We can be friends. No problem."

Clearly she didn't know what was currently going through his head.

His phone rang from its place on the coffee table, and he picked it up. It was the client he'd been working so hard to get. "I'm sorry, Sage. I need to take this call."

"Of course. No problem. See you tomorrow," she said on the way to the door.

"Hi, Susan. It's great to hear from you."

Sage flashed a pinched expression before she closed the door behind her. Was she jealous? He kind of liked that idea. A lot. Even with all of his talk about keeping romance out of their relationship, he was starting to wonder. Was it possible...

Could they privately explore what was between them and not let anyone else know?

Chapter Fifteen

Sage's stomach turned over, and she quickened her pace toward the house. Grayson had certainly seemed eager to talk to whoever the woman was on the phone.

"I'm being completely absurd." There was no reason to believe the woman on the phone was a lover. But she could be.

Back at the house, she went upstairs to Daisy's room, closed the door so they wouldn't be overheard and flopped onto the bed beside her. Her twin had her back propped against the headboard and was reading a book.

"Cheer me up."

"Tell me," Daisy said, of course already knowing her mood likely had something to do with Grayson.

"It's nothing you didn't warn me about."

"Oh, no."

"Oh, yes. When I get jealous over him taking a phone call with someone who just happens to be a woman, I know I'm in big trouble."

Daisy dropped her book on the bed and put an arm around her sister. "I'm sorry. Who was he talking to?"

"Someone named Susan, who he seemed very eager to talk to. I didn't stick around to hear more."

"It's probably his buddy's wife or something totally innocent."

"I know you're right. I'm aware that I'm being ridiculous."

"We could ask the fire chief to dinner. He has the hots for you, and it will make Grayson jealous."

Sage laughed. "Let's not."

"It made you laugh, and that was my goal," Daisy said. "When they first came back to town I would've told you to stay away from him."

"You *did* tell me that."

"But now that I've seen him around you, I'm going to reluctantly suggest that you don't give up. Your relationship with Loren is good, and maybe given time, there can be something more between you and Grayson."

"I hope you're right." She stretched out on the bed and flexed her feet. "We definitely can't just jump into anything because Loren's feelings are still fragile. And I think his are, too."

"Don't pin all your hopes on it, but at the same time don't lose all hope, either."

"Very helpful." Sage chuckled. She could always count on her sister to lift her mood. "Since he's her father, until he tells me different, I'm going to follow his lead and continue to be what they need me to be—a good friend."

"Smart idea. Go take a shower and put on your pajamas, and I'll see if Loren wants to watch a movie with us."

Grayson tossed and turned and finally gave up and got out of bed at midnight. He needed to do something physical, and since it couldn't be anything fun in bed with Sage, he'd settle for a run. He pulled on a T-shirt, shorts and slipped on his running shoes before going out onto the tiny front porch of the cabin. He started off at a jog but slowed to a walk in only a few feet. Just taking in the night at a leisurely pace was more appealing.

The moon was only a crescent, and the night was clear,

making the stars seem extra bright. Britt had liked astronomy, but he couldn't do much more than spot the Big Dipper.

"If you can hear me, darling Britt, please know that I'm doing my best. I'm sorry I broke my promise about staying away from Sage. I had to get our girl out of Houston. A small town is safer, and I own the house here, and...it's hard to explain. There was something that drew me here like it could be the home we need. Even though I broke the other, I promise to keep the secret of Loren's birth."

He scanned the dark sky from one side of the horizon to the other. A dome of stars surrounding the world. "If there is any chance that you're okay with what I'm doing and me letting Sage help us through this transition, please give me a sign."

A shooting star zipped across the sky, and he sucked in a sharp breath as a feeling of weightlessness raced through his body. The chances of that being a coincidence were high, but he was choosing to take it as a positive sign that Sage was what Loren needed. Was it possible it was a sign for him too?

Even though everyone would be asleep, he suddenly felt the need to be close to his child. Normally he could walk down the hall and check on her, but tonight he'd settle for sitting outside. He started toward the house. None of the lights were on, so he took a seat on one of the patio chairs like a sentry. A barn owl hooted in the distance and was answered by another, their communication echoing in the cool night air.

The kitchen door opened, and Sage came outside. His heart instantly beat faster. With no makeup, hair a bit mussed from sleep and a pale pink silk robe that came to mid-thigh, she was like a midnight fairy no one was supposed to see, but he was lucky enough to catch sight of the illusive beauty.

"What are you doing up?" he asked and rose from his chair.

"Something woke me, and I couldn't get back to sleep." She ran her fingers through her hair. "What about you?"

"I never got to sleep. How did you know I was out here?"

"I didn't. Not until I got up for a drink and saw you through the window. Need some company, or would you rather be alone?"

"I could use the company. Want to take a walk?"

"Love to. Since I'm only wearing flip-flops, we'll have to stay on the gravel road."

As she came forward, the soft fabric of her robe swished around her toned thighs, parting in the center to give him a peek of white pajama shorts. They fell into step along the road that led to the front gate of the ranch.

"I got that freelance job I was hoping for."

"Oh, that's wonderful. When did you find out?"

"When I took that phone call right before you left the cabin earlier tonight."

"I'm so happy for you." She played with the silk tie on her robe and kept her eyes straight ahead. "I thought maybe the call was from one of the women you were dating back in Houston."

"I haven't dated anyone."

"Oh. When Loren said something about all the other women, I just thought…"

He didn't try to hide his amusement. "Is someone jealous?"

"Not me."

"Liar."

Her cheeks turned a lovely shade of pink. "Okay, you caught me. Maybe just a wee bit. What were you thinking about when you were sitting in the dark by yourself on the patio?"

"You." He grinned when her steps faltered. "You are the reason I couldn't sleep."

"I'm not sure if I should say sorry or take it as a compliment."

If he'd learned anything it was that life could be cut short, and he didn't want to waste any more of it. "Are you up for an experiment?"

"Depends." She stopped to face him with her head cocked inquisitively. "Tell me your idea before I commit to being your guinea pig."

Am I really going to do this?

His hands grew damp and he wiped them on his shorts, but he decided to go for it. "What if we can find a way to start slowly exploring what's between us in private, but when we're around anyone else, we're just two good buddies."

"That's a very intriguing idea, but first—" she pinched his arm "—I'm checking to see if you're sleepwalking and won't remember this tomorrow."

He chuckled. "I'm fully awake, sweetheart." In fact, all of him was starting to wake up.

"So, public friends, but sexy buddies in private?"

He took her hand in his and kissed her knuckles. "That's what I'm thinking."

"All right, Mr. DeLuca, how do you suggest we go about exploring the what's-between-us part of the experiment?"

He shrugged good-naturedly. "I haven't worked out all the details."

"Wow. You don't have a list and a plan?"

"Nope. You caught me early in the planning phase."

"Then let's start with something easy." She laced their fingers. "Holding hands seems like a good start."

"Perfect."

Walking in the shadowy moonlight with her touch warm and comforting, the harsh guilt he usually felt around Sage suddenly didn't seem so oppressive. The long curving driveway was lined on each side with oaks and redbuds and some kind of flowering vines growing along the cedar fence. Summer leaves softly rustled in the breeze, carrying the scent of the hot day.

"What comes after hand holding?" he asked.

"I guess hugging."

"Is that like getting to first base—as we used to say back in the day?"

Her laugh was soft and sweet. "No, I think kissing is first base, followed by different types of touching being second and third, and then the main attraction is home base. At least that's the way I remember it."

He was grinning from ear to ear at her description. *This is going to be a fun experiment.*

When they got to the gate at the end of the long curving driveway, they turned back.

"Will you tell me stories about Loren? What was she like when she was little?"

"She was a happy baby and walked when she was only ten months."

"Wow. That's early."

"We had to do some extra baby proofing in a hurry." Thinking about all the great memories made him smile. "She loved unicorns and was scared of clowns." He told Sage about the time when she would only eat red foods and her no-shoes phase.

She squeezed his arm and smiled. "Do you have home movies? I'd love to be able to hear her sweet little voice."

"I do. And about twenty-five photo albums Britt put together."

"That sounds like her. She was always good about documenting events with photos. I hope you'll let me look at them."

"Loren might like to show you the photo albums."

"Oh, I would love that."

As they neared the house, she yawned, and he knew it was time to let her get back to bed.

"I guess this is where we say good-night, sweetheart."

"Before we do, we should practice how we'll hug in public. You never know when it might come up," she said.

"Like an experimental 'test' hug?"

"Exactly."

"I have a feeling we're going to be a good scientific team." He opened his arms, and she nestled against his chest with hers banding his waist. She smelled so good, like a sugary treat he wanted to eat. His head was swimming. He slipped one side of her robe down her arm, and next to the thin strap of her top, he pressed his lips to the delicate curve of her shoulder.

She shivered under his touch. "I don't think friends do that." She giggled when he nipped lightly at her skin, but she didn't take her arms from around him.

"I'm sure some do."

Their simple embrace became gentle caresses, and he couldn't resist exploring and learning the shape of her. Sliding his hands over her silk-covered back and then dipping down to the curve of her hips as he kissed the side of her neck, tasting her skin in a way he'd only ever fantasized about.

She moaned softly and tipped her head to give him better access. "Friends definitely don't to this," she whispered. "But I don't want you to stop."

"Since I've already failed tonight's simple task of practicing a public hug…" He cradled one side of her face, and his heart raced when her lips parted on a soft sigh. "Want to see how we do with first base?"

In answer, she rose onto her toes and met his kiss with a feather-soft gentleness that threatened to undo his plan to go slow.

"Good night, Gray," she whispered against his mouth.

"See you in the morning, sweetheart."

Sage's lips tingled in the best way possible as she raced upstairs and straight to her bedroom window. Grayson had been her first big crush, and she felt like a teenager who'd just had her first real kiss. It had been gentle and filled with longing but exceeded her expectations. The touch of his lips, implying he'd be careful with her heart. A promise of tenderness.

She held back one of her new icy-blue velvet curtains and watched Gray disappear into the night, knowing he would reappear in the security lights of the stable.

She sighed when he once again came into view. The artificial light glinted off his dark hair. He was even more attractive in his maturity, with fine lines that proved he'd laughed and smiled over the years. Grayson dressed in a suit was a striking, distinguished image. In jeans, he was ruggedly sexy. But dressed down like tonight, he was approachable and made her think of the young man he'd been when she'd first met him.

She loved getting to know the man he'd become, but keeping her eyes and hands off him in public was going to be a test. She'd always had trouble hiding her emotions, but for Loren, she would do whatever it took to protect her.

The next day, Sage needed to go into town to run some errands, and Grayson and Loren wanted to go with her and eat at the Rodeo Café. They followed Loren into the restaurant that sat at one end of Main Street in the historic section of Old Town. She should be exhausted from her late-night walk with Gray, but she was riding on such a high, it would be a while until she floated back down to Earth. Even being in public where they couldn't touch or share a special smile wasn't interfering with her good mood.

The booth she wanted was available, so she led them to it because she knew Loren would like the framed pictures on the wall. Sage sat on one side of the booth. "Ren, look at these two photos."

The young girl slid across the red vinyl on the other side and leaned in to look. "Oh, wow. Is that Travis?"

"It is. Back in his rodeo days."

She saw Grayson momentarily debate whether to sit beside her or his daughter, and he wisely chose to sit across from Sage.

"So cool. Is there something on the menu that is named after Travis?" Loren asked.

"No, but that's a good idea. You should suggest it to the owner." She handed them menus from the metal rack that was pushed to one side of the tabletop and also held condiments. "Thanks for coming into town with me this morning to run errands. It's given me the perfect excuse to have a stack of pancakes."

"Happy to help," he said and slid his foot forward to rest beside hers, touching her in the only way he could.

"Dad, they have candied bacon. We have to get that."

"You know I never turn down bacon. How about you, Sage?"

"Count me in. I have a cookbook that includes bacon in every recipe. I'll get it out, and we can make something from it."

Loren flipped over her menu. "We better buy some bacon on the way home."

Sage caught Grayson's gaze, and he winked. Today was a good day.

After their late breakfast, they walked down the street to the courtyard behind the row of shops.

In a black T-shirt dress that went to her knees and a pair of red flip-flops Daisy had given her, Loren looked over her shoulder as she walked ahead of them. "Lizzy told me there's a legend about the fountain, and that's why her and Travis will be together forever."

"Did they toss in a coin and make a wish?" Grayson asked.

"No. They kissed beside it." She moved ahead of them toward the rock-and-crystal shop.

Once she was far enough ahead of them that there was no chance of overhearing, Grayson leaned closer to Sage. "I'm surprised she's letting us go anywhere near the fountain."

Sage chuckled. "Me, too."

Inside the store, Sage excused herself from them when she saw a couple of teenage girls who she knew from when Travis gave them riding lessons. "Hello, girls."

"Hi, Ms. Dalton," they said.

"I have someone I want to introduce you to." She pointed to Loren across the store. "Loren is new to town and will be starting school with you this next year, but she doesn't know anyone yet."

"Want us to show her around?" asked Joanna, the petite one with a deep olive complexion and long, shiny black hair.

"She can hang out with us. We're meeting up with some other kids down at the picnic tables near the water," said Tina. Her red curls were held back from her heart-shaped face with a yellow headband.

"That would be very nice of you to ask her. She might be a little bit shy."

They followed her around a display of geodes. "Loren, I'd

like to introduce you to a couple of girls who you'll be going to school with."

"Hi, I'm Tina."

"And I'm Joanna."

"Hi. You can call me Ren."

"Cool name."

Sage could see the worry on Grayson's face, and she pulled him away from the trio of teens. "They're really sweet girls, and they want to take her to meet some other kids."

"And you think I should let her go?"

"If you're comfortable with it, yes. We won't be far and can even stay within eyeshot if you want."

Loren came over to them. "Can I go down to the creek and meet some other kids?"

"Sure, kiddo. That's a good idea."

His daughter looked slightly surprised by his response. "Thanks."

"Sage and I are going to walk down to the mill so I can make some notes about my ideas for the place. Text me when you're ready to meet back up with us or if you need me."

"Okay. See you later."

"Are we really going to the mill?" Sage asked, because she had some ideas that she wanted to float past him.

"After I see the group of kids she's hanging out with."

They followed the girls at a good distance. The three of them stopped at a picnic table occupied by a group of local kids. There were boys and girls as well as families at nearby tables. Once he was satisfied with the look of the group of teens, they walked along the water's edge to the mill.

"Why haven't you had any kids of your own?" he asked. "I know from personal experience that you loved being pregnant and had no trouble giving birth."

An unpleasantly familiar ache started in her belly and

wound its way up into her chest. "I did love being pregnant. It's not for a lack of trying that I'm not a mom."

He stopped walking and tucked one of her curls behind her ear. "You couldn't get pregnant again?"

"There's a lot more to it than that. First, I spent years waiting to fall in love, get married and have a baby. That obviously didn't happen." She switched her purse to the other shoulder. "Then I fostered a newborn in hopes of adopting her, and that ended with my heart breaking."

Again. Like saying goodbye to Loren in the hospital.

"I'm so sorry, sweetheart."

"Her mom changed her mind and wanted her back, and I don't blame her, but I'd fallen in love with the sweet baby girl."

"And this was all after we went back on our promise to let you see Loren."

She wanted to argue, but there was no reason because he knew the truth. "A while back, I was engaged…." She sighed deeply. "Even knowing how much I want a baby, he had a vasectomy."

"You're kidding."

"I wish."

"He just said he was doing it whether you liked it or not?"

She scoffed. "Worse. He went behind my back to do it and wasn't going to tell me. I found a medical bill in his pocket when I was washing his jeans."

"Oh, sweetheart. Damn. I'm glad you found out and didn't marry the jerk."

"Me, too." He hadn't wanted to have a family with her, but her ex-fiancé sure had wanted her money and lifestyle. After that, trusting her own judgment had suffered.

Grayson pulled his keys from his front pocket, unlocked a side door of the grist mill and ushered her inside ahead of him. "I'm sorry I brought up something that's so painful to talk about."

"It's okay. We need to be able to talk about all of it. Don't you think?"

"Yes, I think you're right. Communication is important." He leaned in to give her a quick kiss, but one wasn't enough.

The touch of his tongue was electric, and their gentle, teasing kisses became deep and searching as they tried to discover what made the other one sigh or moan with pleasure.

The clatter of metal against the concrete floor made her heart leap into her throat as they sprang apart.

Chapter Sixteen

A Willie Nelson song was playing on the radio as Grayson neared the back door of the farmhouse. He couldn't wait to see Sage again. He smiled every time he thought about the day before when the raccoon scurrying out from under a pile of corrugated tin and dashing across the floor of the mill had scared the pants off them. After the relief that it was only a wild animal who'd been spying on them, they'd laughed about being caught like mischievous teenagers. And they'd vowed to be more careful.

He went into the farmhouse through the kitchen door, just like he was family. He paused to fully take in the domestic scene before him.

Sage held on to the edge of the sink and leaned to her side so far that one leg lifted into the air as she turned down the volume on the radio. It wasn't the modern voice-activated kind that connected to the internet. Just a plain old-fashioned radio with dials. Her twin scooped batter into muffin tins, and her niece, Lizzy, measured ingredients. But the absolute best part was the smile on Loren's face.

She was wearing a pink apron over her black clothes and stirring something in a large yellow mixing bowl. It was a hopeful glimpse of the happy little girl he remembered from a couple of years ago.

Please let her come back to me.

If only he had a guardian angel who could advise and guide him through this time in their lives. He so badly wanted to get it right and not make any mistakes that might hurt his child.

"Hi, Dad."

"Hey there, kiddo. What's going on in here? It sure smells good." Measuring cups, glass canisters of ingredients and batter bowls were scattered about the countertops.

"It's baking day," Lizzy said. "I'm making cupcakes for a friend, and Daisy is taking cookies to the hospital."

"Who's in the hospital?" he asked.

"I go there to hold babies who need extra attention," Daisy said.

"Baba," a little voice said from under the table, and Davy crawled out with a toothy grin no one could resist.

"That's how we got lucky enough to have this precious angel in our lives." Daisy scooped him up and kissed his cheeks until he giggled.

Sage was making a concerted effort to feign indifference about his appearance, but he'd seen the secret smile she flashed when no one was looking, and he appreciated her willingness to protect his daughter.

He made the first move and crossed the kitchen to her. "Are you still up for going with me to take measurements at the house?"

"Absolutely."

Grayson tugged playfully on his daughter's long ponytail. "Loren, are you coming into town with us?"

"Can I stay and bake instead of going to the haunted house?"

"Very funny." He put an arm around her thin shoulders. "If you'll save some cookies for me, then yes."

* * *

Of course, the front door of Aunt Tilly's house stuck, and Grayson had to give it an extra shove to open it. "That's one more thing to add to the list of repairs."

Sage went inside ahead of him. "The door is an easy fix. We can use a planer to slowly take off the part that's rubbing against the frame."

"We?" He chuckled. "You know how to do that?"

She dropped her purse onto his emerald corduroy sectional that was too big for the room. "I grew up on a ranch with a dad who fixed everything himself and thought his daughters should know how to do the same."

"Like your plumbing skills?"

She feigned outrage but couldn't maintain it and then laughed as she pulled the tape measure out of her purse. "Good point. But I'm pretty sure I can take measurements without causing another disaster."

"Hey, the kitchen sink was what I needed to realize I had to make some repairs and for Loren to get out of sleeping in a rundown house."

"Glad to be of service. I'll send you my bill."

"You'll have to show me your preferred payment method." He stroked a finger slowly across her cheek and leaned in close enough for a brief brush of lips.

She let out a breathy sigh and swayed forward.

"But we can discuss that later," he said and started up the stairs to hide his grin. He'd never been one for openly flirting, but with Sage it came so naturally. They could be fun and playful, and he loved teasing her the same way she liked to do with him. "Let's start measuring upstairs," he called over his shoulder.

She mumbled under her breath about exasperating men

and then started up behind him, which made him smile even bigger.

They started taking measurements in the upstairs bathroom, jotting down notes and discussing remodeling options.

He rubbed his hand over the woodwork of the doorframe. "What do you suggest I do in here?"

"I think you need to get a new clawfoot tub and add a walk-in shower, but try to keep the sink because the style is beautiful and it's in good shape."

He had to put extra force into turning the hot-water knob, but the water was still off. "We need all new fixtures."

"For sure, but they can still look retro." Sage held up her hands and then spread them wide as if he could see what she envisioned. "I picture Carrara marble and robin's-egg blue paint next to the craftsman woodwork that has been restored to its rich color."

"Sounds good to me. I trust your judgment." He put an arm around her waist and pulled her close.

"As you should." She tipped back her head and pressed a soft, lingering kiss on the underside of his jaw before stepping away with a saucy smile. "We have work to do downstairs. That other bathroom isn't going to measure itself."

He chuckled and followed her down the switchback staircase, taking the opportunity while they were alone to admire the way her jeans fit her curvy hips. Back downstairs, Sage went past the half bath and into his bedroom.

"I don't think there is anything to measure in here," he said.

"I was just looking to see if there's a way for you to expand it into a full bath that can be accessed from your room."

He stood back and studied the corner. "Sure. I could draw up a plan for that with no problem."

She turned in a circle, taking in the bare mattress on the

floor, several stacks of boxes and a hanging clothes rack. "I noticed you put your bedroom furniture upstairs. Are you planning to sleep up there or down here?"

"Downstairs. I just thought it was time for some new furniture." Her smile was understanding, and he knew he didn't have to explain why.

"New furniture is a good idea. A fresh start can be very good for the soul."

They took more measurements and ran through ideas. While she took a call from her sister about a business decision, he wandered into the kitchen. The contractor Sage had suggested would be starting the renovations in a few days. He'd hired her on the spot when she'd talked about saving all the historic details and keeping everything as original as possible. The added time to restore and not just rip out and replace everything would make this job take even longer than he'd anticipated.

And that meant extending their stay with the Dalton family. Grayson couldn't believe how fast Sage had once again become a part of his life, and in only a short time, Loren had grown to like her—even if it was still a bit cautious. His daughter was happy out at the ranch, and he hoped staying longer would help her transition to their new town.

But what if it made her never want to come back to this house and it just be the two of them again?

Where's that guardian angel when I need some answers?

Sage's yelp of alarm was followed by a thump, and he ran into the living room.

"Just when I said I wouldn't mess anything up." Sage was in front of the windows with her hands on her cheeks and was staring down at something on the floor.

But all his attention was on the woman before him. Late afternoon sunlight bathed her in a soft golden glow that made her strawberry-blond curls dance with color. She looked like an angel.

Is Sage my guardian angel on Earth? He briefly glanced upward as if Britt would be there to give him an answer. Or scold him.

Sage's expression clouded. "Sorry."

He realized he'd hadn't said anything, so he smiled. "Don't worry about it for a second."

"I thought it would be a good idea to test the window blinds and see if they still roll up and down, and I'm sorry to say, this one does not." She turned back to look up to where the metal brackets had come loose. "I can't believe I caused another disaster."

He came up behind her and wrapped her in his arms. "This is hardly a disaster."

Her soft sigh was accompanied by snuggling her body against the front of his, her bottom moving just enough to make him groan. It had been so long since he'd been with a woman, but Sage Dalton wasn't just any woman. And sleeping with her would mean so much more than scratching an itch.

While she'd been pregnant, he'd fought his attraction. He'd buried his feelings for Sage deep down because he'd truly loved his wife and wanted to save his marriage, but his feelings had always been there, just waiting for the right time to resurface. And boy, had they. Being around her made him feel like a teenager.

He reached past her and slowly pulled the second shade down and then kissed the side of her neck, loving her little shiver. "At least there's still one to give us some privacy."

She turned in his embrace, linking her arms around his neck. "What do you have in mind?"

Her skin was like silk under his thumb as he traced the

curve of her jaw. "I can't go on wondering and wanting. I can't be so close to you and resist you any longer."

Her fingers played through his hair, and her sweet smile was his answer. "Once we do this, it can't be undone."

"I know." Given time, surely his daughter would come to see that he had to move on with his life at some point. "If we tend to our needs when we're in private, then maybe we won't be like horny teenagers when we're around other people."

"We can satisfy our desires behind closed doors and protect Loren at the same time."

"We'll be cautious until she's ready and more accepting of the idea of us. Have we now thoroughly convinced ourselves that we're doing the right thing?" he asked.

"I'm convinced," she whispered against his lips, then swayed forward and claimed a kiss that had them both breathing harder.

Walking backward, Sage smiled at him with dreamy half-lidded eyes and pulled him across the room and down onto the sectional. It didn't matter if the couch was too big for the room because it was just right for a spur-of-the-moment make-out session.

They hadn't removed a single piece of clothing, but it was one of the most sensual experiences of his life. After waiting so many years he'd worried their time together wouldn't live up to the fantasy, but waiting so long only added to the excitement. He wanted more of her. All of her, but...

"Sweetheart, I'm afraid I'm unprepared for this."

She stroked her hand across his chest, and it came to rest over his heart. "If you're not ready, I understand. We said we'd go slow."

His chuckle ended on a groan. "It's not that. I'm a guy without any condoms. I don't suppose you have any?"

"No, I don't, and I'm not on the pill."

He was disappointed but at the same time glad they wouldn't be rushing what was between them. It was too precious, and they had to be careful. "I guess we'll have to stick to first and second base for now."

"It's more than I ever thought to have with you, so I'll take it."

Just as her hands slid beneath his shirt, a hard knock on the front door startled both of them, and when Sage tried to sit up, he rolled too far and fell off the couch. They started laughing so hard they were barely making a sound, and he couldn't get up.

"Are you hurt?" she asked between giggles.

"No."

The knock sounded again, and he grumbled before getting off the floor and going to answer it. A tall, thin woman about his age stood on his porch. Her pale blond hair was in a blunt cut that brushed her shoulders, and her wide set blue eyes raked over him in a way he'd grown accustomed to.

"Hello. Can I help you?"

"Hi, I'm Betsy Phillips, from two doors down. You must be Mr. DeLuca?"

"Yes, I'm Grayson DeLuca. It's very nice to meet you." He moved to hold out his hand and shake hers, but she was holding a large covered casserole dish. "Come in, please." He stepped back and gave her room to enter.

"I wanted to express my sympathies for your loss," she said as she stepped inside and then held out the dish. "This is a lasagna."

"Thank you. I really appreciate this." He'd known the condolences would start rolling in as the word spread. He'd only been spared more because they were staying out at the ranch.

"I'm a widow myself, so I understand some of—" She

saw Sage sitting on one end of the couch. "Oh, hi. I didn't see you there at first."

While Sage introduced herself, he set the lasagna on the coffee table.

They chatted for a few minutes about people who lived on their street—all of which he felt could've waited until a time when he wasn't so anxious to start learning the details of Sage's body.

When he finally closed the door behind his neighbor, Sage was smirking at him.

"What's so funny, missy?"

"That must be what Loren was talking about."

"What do you mean?"

"About women throwing themselves at you. It's quite fascinating to watch, and now I understand a little better where she's coming from with making sure my motives are good."

"I have no idea what y'all are talking about." He did know, but admitting it didn't feel right. "This lasagna looks like enough to feed everyone tonight. We should get back to the ranch."

"Nice subject change."

"I can't help it. I'm hungry, and since I can't have what I really want, I'll have to settle for food."

"Let's lock up and go tend to your tummy."

Before he opened the front door, he stopped to kiss her once more. "What do you think about making a stop at the drugstore on the way home?"

"I think that's a fabulous idea, and that you'll have to go in alone because people talk in a small town."

He grimaced. Gossip was one of the small-town things he had *not* missed. "How do you feel about coming to hang out at the cabin tonight once everyone is asleep?"

"I'll give you one guess what my answer is."

Chapter Seventeen

Once Sage was sure Loren was sound asleep, she slipped on her prettiest lacy pink bra-and-underwear set and then covered them with a wrap-style dress in a silky black fabric that felt good against her skin. Covering her nervous excitement was harder to do. After years of daydreams about intimacy with Grayson, her fantasies were becoming a reality. She had worried the real thing wouldn't live up to the fantasy in her head, but so far, it was better. Who could've known that the touch of his big, warm hands would bring her so much pleasure?

The night was brighter than the one before, and she didn't need a flashlight. Right past the stable she paused so she wouldn't startle a mama armadillo and three babies crossing the gravel road. They had always reminded her of her older brother's remote-controlled army tank, their hard shell and a tail that swung around like the tank's gun.

Grayson was sitting in one of the rocking chairs on the cabin's front porch. When he saw her, he stood, and his smile was so warm and welcoming that most of her nervousness faded into the night. The mellow strains of a Tim McGraw song drifted on the breeze.

"You're like a goddess materializing from the darkness. Strong and brave and breathtaking."

His compliment gave her confidence a nice boost, and

a distracting warmth was building in her core. She nestled into his embrace, his scent making her want to drink him in. "You smell delicious."

"It's just soap."

"It's you." She smiled up at him and met his eager kiss. "Yum. You taste good, too."

"I just ate a piece of caramel candy." He swayed them in a slow dance to match the beat of the country song.

"You've always liked those. I thought I was so special when you'd give me a caramel back when you were a cool high school guy."

"I was pretty cool."

Sage laughed and let her hands roam across his wide shoulders. "And always so modest."

"Hold on to me, sweetheart." He lifted her by the hips and carried her down the two steps to the flat grassy yard. As soon as her feet hit the ground, he twirled her around and then back into their moonlit dance.

"You always did such a good job of pretending you didn't know I had a crush on you when we were in high school."

"I really didn't know." He followed her lead and let his hands explore her back and then lower to the swell of her hips.

His touch made her skin tingle, and she pressed her body more closely against his broad chest. "You mean I wasn't making a fool of myself for years?"

"Not at all. You hid it well. I didn't even know how strong your feelings had become until the very end of your pregnancy."

"Well, I guess we're both good actors."

"That will come in handy for our current predicament."

"Let's hope we haven't lost that skill."

"I can think of a skill or two I can show you." His fingers slid into her hair, and he cradled the back of her head.

His kiss was deep and sweet and everything she could ask for. Gray made her feel like a desirable woman and like he was a man who knew something about the art of passion. This time he lifted her off her feet, cradling her in his arms as he carried her inside the cabin.

And closed out the world.

Sated and happy, Grayson held Sage half draped across his chest as they caught their breath.

Her fingers trailed lightly over his arm. "I don't want to get out of bed, but I should get back to the house. I can't fall asleep here and blow our secret on the very first night."

"Talk to me first," he surprised himself by saying. His hand paused on its slow path over the curve of her bottom.

She rolled onto her back and stretched like a very satisfied cat. "I'd love to. What do you want to talk about?"

Shifting onto his side, he let himself drink in her beauty. "Nothing specific. I just want…" What did he want? "I want to know this wasn't a one-time fluke or a dream."

"And talking will make it feel more real. I get it."

He trailed a finger across her bare stomach. "You don't have a single stretch mark on you."

"I had a few, but they've faded over the years. Still, I loved being pregnant." Occasionally she still dreamed about the baby moving inside of her and always woke wistful.

"I could tell. You had that pregnancy glow people talk about."

"I did?"

"You sure did. There were also a few times I heard you talking to the baby in your belly."

"I wondered if anyone ever caught me doing that. Sometimes late at night, I'd read to her. I had several children's books that I would read over and over. Especially those last few weeks when she was particularly active late at night. I would read, stop to for a bathroom break when she danced on my bladder and then read some more."

He smiled and wrapped one of her curls around his finger. "Do you remember what books you read?"

"I still have them in a box under my bed with other mementos. Some were short books like *If You Give a Mouse a Cookie* and Dr. Seuss books, and some were longer chapter books."

"That story about the mouse and the cookie was one of her favorite books."

"Are you just saying that to make me feel like I had a hand in part of her life?"

"I'm serious. It really was her favorite." He brushed soft curls from her beautiful face and fanned the silky strands across the pillow. "I wouldn't have Loren without you, sweetheart."

She shivered. "Even with all the heartache, I'd do it all over again. My high school crush was one thing, but then when I got pregnant, I don't know if it was the hormones or all in my head, but while we were all living in the same house in Houston…my crush grew into more."

"Sweetheart—"

She put a fingertip to his lips. "Let me finish before I chicken out, please. Having you by my side when Loren was born…" She choked up. "It was so beautiful and emotional that I lost my head and good senses. Maybe if I hadn't been gazing at you like a lovestruck fool when Britt walked in, maybe I could've had Loren in my life all these years. I blame myself for the mess I caused all of us."

He cupped her cheek and stroked her lips with his thumb. "Don't. It wasn't just you. Britt saw the look on *my* face, too."

"I'm still haunted by your devastated expression as you

followed your wife out of the hospital room. That's the last time we saw one another."

"Sage, I saw you one more time after that."

"After Britt came in and freaked out—understandably, I might add—I know I never saw you again."

"Do you remember when they brought Loren to you that last time? I was the one who told the nurse to do it."

"Did Britt know?"

"No." And he'd paid for it later when she'd found out. "I knew you needed to say goodbye. You had just given birth and were a bit emotional. When I peeked into your room, you were holding her close with your cheek against her head and crying as you told her that you loved her. Your tears were wet on her little bald head like you were christening her."

A single tear ran down Sage's cheek. "That moment is a precious bittersweet memory."

"I can remember almost exactly what you said to her through your tears."

"You heard me?"

"I did. And it broke a piece of my heart. You told her that you would always love her and you were so happy to be part of her life, if even for a little while."

"I'm so glad to be part of her life again."

"I'm glad to have you back in it, and this time, it can be different."

"We just have to wait for Loren to understand that I only want the best for her and don't want to take her mother's place."

He rolled her onto her back and brushed soft curls from her beautiful face. "It will all work out. I can feel it."

She moved her hips and giggled. "I feel something, too."

He groaned and kissed her, and when her long legs wrapped around his hips, he knew she was not leaving his bed any time soon.

Chapter Eighteen

"Sage, wake up sleepyhead."

She groaned and cracked open one eye. The first rays of sunrise filtered in around her velvet curtains, and her twin's smiling face came into focus. "Why are you waking me up so early?"

"Because I can't wait to hear what happened with Grayson. Why else?"

Just hearing his name put an instant smile on her face, and she was wide awake, even after only a few hours of sleep. "Last night was…" She sighed and hugged a pillow to her chest.

"Oh, that good?" Daisy chuckled, knowing the answer simply by seeing which smile her sister used.

"Better. So much more than my imagination could conjure up."

"I'm happy for you, sis." Daisy stretched out on the bed. "Did you talk about what comes next?"

"We talked about all kinds of things. The day of the birth and things that had been haunting both of us. I'm so glad we have good communication."

"What happens between you two now?"

"Well, until Loren is ready to accept her father with someone other than her mama, we'll be keeping the depth of our relationship hush-hush."

"Understood. You might want to talk to Lizzy about it because she's aware there is something going on."

"Good idea." She rubbed her fingertips across her lips. "Because there is definitely something going on."

The sun was shining, the sky was blue and Sage's heart was filled with happiness. She was so tempted to hook her arm through Grayson's as they walked toward the stable, but she was a good girl and resisted. Playing the part of daytime friends and nighttime lovers was challenging but also exciting, and the anticipation of waiting on a touch or kiss was exhilarating.

He was looking extra rugged in old jeans, one of the T-shirts that hugged his broad torso, a cowboy hat and boots. Just watching him walk was a treat. "I'm glad you're riding with us today."

He adjusted his tan Stetson to shade more of his face. "Me, too. It'll give the three of us time to work on our relationship."

From around the back of the stable, Loren ran toward them. "Mischief got out!"

Sage groaned. "Of course he did. It's always something with that horse. Hence his name."

His daughter came to a stop in front of them and paused to catch her breath. "I barely had the gate open a crack, and he dashed right out and toward the pond. I'm so sorry I let him escape."

"It's okay, honey." Sage hugged her and was so glad Loren didn't instantly pull away. "He can't get off the ranch. It's all fenced in."

"Let's saddle up and go after him." Gray gave Loren's ponytail a playful tug. "Now it's more than a ride. It's an adventure."

"Dad, wait until you see how I can saddle a horse all by myself."

"Excellent. You can help me because I've likely forgotten all the proper steps."

Father and daughter were talking and joking, and it was a beautiful thing to see. She pulled her phone from her back pocket and snapped a photo of them. Today was a good day, and she planned to enjoy every second of it.

Sure enough, the runaway foal was frolicking at the edge of the pond. His white coat was splattered and smeared with mud.

"Let's dismount just in case the little demon spooks our horses." Sage swung down from the saddle and the others followed. "The way he likes mud, he's more pig than horse."

"I'll bathe him so you don't end up looking like you live in the abandoned mill," Loren said with a big grin and couldn't hold back her giggle.

"Very funny, little girl." She was excited to be part of their teasing, and she loved how happy it was making Grayson. His smile was easy and natural.

"Mischief," Loren called. "Come here and be a good boy, please."

The foal pranced toward her, but right before she could grab hold of his halter, he turned and darted back for the water as if hoping she'd give chase.

The way Loren perched her fists on her hips with her head tilted to one side, she looked so much like her mother. "I see a lot of Britt in her," Sage said to him, and quickly wished she hadn't. Bringing up his deceased wife was not the best tactic for advancing their relationship.

Thankfully, he smiled and nodded. "I see it, too. Thank you for helping bring Loren out of her black phase—both clothes and mood."

"I've only slipped a few new items into her wardrobe."

"It's a start."

Mischief splashed into the water, kicking up his hind legs and having a grand time while Loren watched from the edge of the pond.

"He likes apples, right?" Grayson asked.

"They're one of his favorite treats. I should've thought to bring some."

"There are a couple of those small ones in our picnic lunch." He went back to his horse and grabbed an apple from his saddle bag. They left the horses to graze and moved closer to the pond.

Sage stretched out her arms. "Spread out and we might have a better chance of catching him."

He stood at the edge and waited for the next time the foal came out of the water. "Look what I have, Mischief." Grayson wiggled the shiny red fruit in the air. "One of your favorites."

The foal calmed and walked right toward him, but once he took the apple in his teeth and Grayson tried to grab the halter, Mischief tossed up his nose and knocked off his cowboy hat.

"You little monster." Grayson turned around to grab it out of the water.

"Gray, watch out because he'll—"

Before she could get the warning out, the horse head-butted Grayson square on the butt and sent him flying face first into the water.

Sage and Loren burst into laughter and then laughed even harder when he rose from the water dripping wet and scowling. The horse trotted over and stood calmly beside Loren as if nothing had happened, and she was able to clip on the lead rope Sage handed to her.

"I have a few new suggestions for alternate names for that

animal. Not all of them fit for public usage." He gave them a playful scowl. "You two think this is funny?"

"Yes," they said in unison and laughed harder.

"Which one of you is going in first?" He shook his head and sprayed them with water.

"Not in my new boots," Loren squealed and took off running with the foal trotting along beside her on his lead rope.

"And what about you, cowgirl?"

"You would really toss me into the pond?" she asked in mock surprise.

"Toss? Of course not." He pulled her against his wet body before she could react. "But pulling you in with me isn't off the table."

She liked being in his arms, even if he was getting her new shirt all wet with pond water, but they weren't alone and she knew they couldn't stay this way. Loren's back was still to them as she ran with the horse, but he let go of her before she could turn around.

"Do you want to go back to the cabin to change out of your wet clothes?"

"Maybe later." He pulled off his T-shirt and started wringing out the water.

She made a whimpering sound that made him smirk. A wet shirtless cowboy in the sunshine was a magnificent sight. "You're a tease, Grayson DeLuca."

"Takes one to know one."

"I'll get you back," she said.

"I'm counting on it."

Over the next few weeks, they spent their days taking care of business but also leaving plenty of time for fun. The three of them had gone to the zoo, a museum and other summertime activities. Loren's mood was up and down but lately had tended to be more up, and Sage felt a closeness growing.

Most nights, Sage went down to the cabin to see Grayson. The one night he came up to the house, he almost got caught coming out of her bedroom when Loren made a late-night visit to the bathroom. That was the last time they tried risking that. The cabin had become a special place for them where they could close out the rest of the world, if only for a few hours.

He had become friends with Travis and started going to poker night with him and the three Murphy brothers at their house next door on Four Star Ranch.

More and more every day, Sage felt like they were getting to a point where Loren would accept her as more than just a friend to Grayson, but he didn't think his daughter was ready. She couldn't help but worry that it was Grayson who wasn't ready.

On a Sunday afternoon there was no work going on at Grayson's house, so the three of them went into town to check on the progress and get some things done. The remodel was coming along nicely. Now that the electricity was back on and the new air-conditioning unit was cooling the summer air and the upstairs bathroom had at least a working toilet, it was easier to be here.

Loren had helped Sage mix up a batch of witch's brew and thought it was totally cool that she knew the Dalton family's secret recipe. While Grayson was buying a whole list of items at the hardware store, they were using the oil on the woodwork in his bedroom. Sage shook up the bottle, unscrewed the lid, poured some onto a rag and handed it to her surprisingly eager helper.

"I'll start on the bottom shelf, and you can start up high where I can't reach," Loren said.

"Excellent. That will save me from crawling around on my old knees."

"Oh, please. You're not *that* old."

Sage chuckled at the teen's inflection. "I'm glad you think so." At age thirteen, she'd thought her mid-thirties would never arrive. But they had, and they were slipping away fast.

Loren braced herself on one arm and reached to the back of the shelf with the other. "Why is this shelf so deep? You wouldn't even be able to see the books."

Sage bent down to look. "I think those lower shelves are meant for storing things other than books."

"I have a cool idea. Dad should put a false back on it and make it secret storage."

"That's a fabulous idea. He'll totally be up for that." She went back to polishing the top shelf.

"You know him pretty well, don't you?"

Sage's throat tightened, and she was glad Loren couldn't see her face because she wasn't sure what might be revealed. Some level of guilt? Love?

She had to be very careful with this kind of question so she wouldn't accidentally give away the fact that she'd lived with Britt and Grayson in Houston for months. "I guess I do know him pretty well in some ways. I know what candy he likes. Soft caramels."

"I like them, too."

She expected a string of further questions from the teen, but they worked in silence for a couple of minutes. "Have you talked to any of the kids you met in Old Town?"

"I've been texting with Tina and Joanna." She was finished with the bottom shelf and moved even lower to the wide baseboard along the bottom of the built-in. "You were right about them being curious about my life in the city. They've only lived here in Channing. I've been telling them stuff about city life."

"I'm so glad you've already made friends. They can teach you about small-town life. It will also make the first day of school not feel so overwhelming."

Loren rubbed the oiled rag extra hard on a scuffed area of the woodwork. Something clicked and the molding sprang slightly forward. "Oh, no! I broke it."

Sage sat on the hardwood floor beside her. The section of wood that had moved away from the wall had perfectly smooth sides…like a drawer. "Ren, I don't think you broke it. I think you've discovered a real secret compartment."

"Oh, man. That's slap," she said, using a teenage slang she'd picked up from her new friends.

Sage wedged her fingers in the small space between the base molding and the built-in bookcase. It was stuck from years of disuse and temperature fluctuations, but with a little jiggle and strong pull, she was finally able to pull open a wide drawer. A poof of dust particles swirled in the sunlight streaming in the windows.

Loren gasped and then grinned from ear to ear. "I actually discovered a secret compartment."

"You sure did."

"What's all that stuff inside of it?" Loren asked. There were stacks of paper, an almost-flat rectangular box and a leatherbound portfolio.

"Do you think we should find out?" Sage asked.

"Yes. For sure." Loren pulled out the portfolio, and the dry leather threatened to crack along the spine as she opened it to lay it out flat on the floor. "Oh, wow. It's artwork."

"What a wonderful discovery for someone who loves art."

Loren began to carefully flip through them. It was filled with page after page of sketches and watercolors. "These are really good. I hope I'm this good someday. Was Dad's aunt Tilly an artist?"

"Not that I know of. The only thing I really know about her is that she was a high school English teacher. Look right here." She tapped the bottom right corner of a watercolor of a flower garden and a woman in a white dress. There was a swirl of letters almost hidden among the folds of the woman's skirt. "There's a signature, and it looks like the name Ken."

"Oh, yeah. It does. Wouldn't it be cool if he's someone famous?"

"Totally cool." While Loren looked more closely at the artwork, Sage pulled out a thick stack of three-ring bound pages. The cover page read *The Earl's Reluctant Bride*. That title piqued her curiosity, and she flipped to the middle and started reading. It had been typed on a typewriter—so major kudos to this author—and had editorial markups handwritten here and there in fading red ink. It didn't take long to recognize a Regency romance novel. The writing was really good, so she kept reading, and then her eyes widened.

She glanced quickly at Loren. It was a good thing the teen was completely focused on the artwork because this book was very spicy and not something she needed to see. She flipped back to the beginning and found the author's name and a date of 1980.

"What is that?"

Sage snapped it closed. "An old book manuscript. Do you like historical fiction?" she said in hopes of discouraging the teen's interest.

Her little nose wrinkled. "Not so much. I'll leave those to you. I'm going to go lay out all this artwork on the dining room table."

Thank goodness. Loren was years away from being able to read this.

The second she was alone, she pulled out several more ring-bound manuscripts and the rectangular box. She lifted the box's lid, and on top were faded photographs of a newborn and a bunch of papers. She'd study the contents later, but right now, she wanted to dig a little deeper into the book manuscripts. Curious about the titles, she used her phone to see if they'd been published.

Oh, wow.

They had not only been published as a series but had been bestsellers. And she was looking at what were probably the original manuscripts. There was only one reason she could think of for them to be here in this house. Had the straitlaced Tilly DeLuca written these spicy books?

When Grayson got back from the store, Loren caught him at the front door. "Dad, you will *never* guess what we discovered."

"A ghost?"

His thirteen-year-old rolled her eyes. "I said something you *won't* believe. Come see." She went into the dining room where artwork was spread across the table. "Look what we found."

"Wow. In this house?"

"Yep, it's really good and it's all signed, but I don't know the artist and don't know why someone would hide it."

"Where was it?"

"That's the killer part," she said with a wide grin. "Come see something totally cool."

This time he followed her into his bedroom where Sage was sitting on his mattress reading something. She flashed a smile and put down a thick stack of old yellowed pages that were tattered around the edges.

"Let's show him," Loren said to her.

They both got down on the floor, and with a dramatic

countdown that made him smile, they simultaneously pushed on the wide baseboard. It sprang away from the wall a crack, and they pulled it out the rest of the way.

"Damn, that's the coolest thing I've ever seen." He kneeled beside them for a better look at the hidden drawer.

"We knew you'd like it. I have an idea for another secret hiding spot on the bottom shelf, but I'll have to tell you about that later," Loren said and used his shoulder to push herself up. "I'm going back to study the artwork."

The ways she almost skipped out of the room made his heart happy. His little girl was coming back to him, just like Sage had said she would.

Sage went back to sit cross-legged on the mattress. "Come see what else was in there."

He sat beside her and stole a quick kiss. "I'm glad you two had fun while I was gone."

"I'm afraid we also stopped working when we made our discovery, so we didn't get much done."

"I don't care about that. I just like seeing her happy. Thank you."

"My pleasure." She shot a quick glance toward the open doorway and then kissed his cheek. "Now, take a look at this."

He took the bound pages she'd been reading. There were four typed words on the cover page. *The Earl's Reluctant Bride.* "What is this? A book?"

"Oh, yes." She giggled. "Quite the book. Open it to page thirty and read some of it."

He flipped to that page and started reading. And quickly knew why she was grinning so wide. It was a bedroom scene that was definitely of the erotic variety. "This was in my prudish aunt Tilly's house?"

"Yes. And there are more of them."

"Did Loren see this?"

"No. Definitely not. I told her it was historical fiction, and thankfully she was completely uninterested. I looked up all the titles, and they were bestsellers in the early nineteen eighties."

"Who is the author?"

"Brace yourself. I think these were written by your aunt."

"Tilly?" He barked a laugh. "No way. She was the most prim-and-proper woman I've ever known."

"I don't know what to say about that, but I think I have proof. First, remember that collection of old typewriters you put on consignment at my friends' shop? A writer might have a collection like that. Especially an author who actually used one to write her novels."

"I don't think a typewriter collection is enough proof for me."

"I thought you might say that. The author is Bett Lucas, but I think it's a pen name. I found payment receipts from a major publishing house, and they're made out to Matilda DeLuca."

"I'm in shock." He lay back on the mattress and laughed.

"Don't faint on me yet because there's more."

"Do I even want to know?"

She handed him a birth certificate. It was pristinely smooth with no crimps or folds, as if it had been lovingly handled. He scanned it and sat straight up. *Matilda DeLuca.* The birth mother of a baby girl was his aunt Tilly. "I can't believe it. I guess I didn't know her at all. Did the baby live?"

"Yes. There are adoption papers for her baby girl."

"But no marriage, divorce or death certificates? Like maybe there was a husband or any hint as to who the father was?" None of this fit with what he knew about his great-aunt.

"Not that I've found. There's the artwork, manuscripts, a record of royalty payments in an envelope and the stuff about the baby. I might've missed something among all the pages in this box." She started flipping through the adoption papers.

Grayson studied one of the black-and-white photographs of a newborn wrapped in a blanket and another one of them in nothing but a cloth diaper.

"There's no birth father on the birth certificate or on the adoption papers." Sage held up the stapled papers and gently shook them to see if anything fell out. At the very bottom of the box under a sheet of tissue paper was a thick piece of cardstock. She flipped it over to reveal newborn footprints.

Sage's expression clouded over in an instant. "Oh, Tilly," she said on a pained breath, and she clasped a hand to her chest.

The sorrow on her face made Grayson catch his breath.

A full body chill splashed across Sage. She'd forgotten how sharp the stab of pain had been as she'd kissed Loren goodbye, a piece of her heart gone off into the world. Out of her life. Forever. It had been the hardest thing she'd ever done, and she hadn't even been the biological mother like Tilly.

"Sage? What is it? Talk to me, please."

She continued staring at the tiny footprints. "Gray, I know how she felt. Poor Tilly. I know what she went through when her baby girl was adopted." She looked up into his handsome, concerned face and caught a brief glimpse of what she thought was love before he pulled her against his warm chest.

"My sweet Sage. I had no idea how hard it was for you. Go ahead and let it out, sweetheart." He stroked her hair. "I'll hold you while you cry."

But she didn't need to cry. Her separation from Loren—and Gray—hadn't been forever after all. She was getting a second chance.

Chapter Nineteen

Grayson hefted another fifty-pound bag of horse feed from the bed of the truck and stacked it with the others in the old red barn that sat between the stable and the cabin.

"Hey, Grayson," Daisy said from behind him.

"Good morning."

"Thanks for unloading the truck. I really need to hire another farmhand. At least another part-timer. The last one we had didn't work out."

He lifted his cowboy hat to wipe sweat from his forehead. "I'm happy to help out where I can."

"I have a thought I want to run by you." Daisy propped her folded arms on the side of the truck bed.

"What's on your mind? Is this my periodic sisterly warning?"

"We'll get to that part." She smiled big enough to show her one dimple.

Grayson chuckled and sat on the open tailgate. "Forewarned. And I would expect nothing less. I'm glad Sage has you to watch her back."

"She watches mine in return."

He wanted to be that person for someone and have them do the same for him.

Is Sage my person?

His heart beat a little faster. Not so long ago, it was a future he'd never let himself consider. Forbidden fruit.

"I think you and Sage could use some uninterrupted, not-having-to-sneak-around time alone."

"I certainly can't argue with that, but I don't really have a choice right now."

"I think I can help you with that. I'm making a quick trip to San Antonio for a horse show and thought Loren might like to go with me. What do you think?"

"How quick is quick?"

"Two nights. I'm planning to drive there on Friday, the show is on Saturday and home on Sunday."

He scratched his chin with the back of his hand. A horse show was something Loren would enjoy, and it would give him and Sage some real time alone. They could even take a quick trip of their own. Maybe something romantic or adventurous.

"If Loren wants to go with you to San Antonio, then I'm fine with it."

"Really? Well, that was easier than I thought."

"I trust that you'll keep your eye on her at all times?"

"I will. Like she's family." Daisy put a hand to the center of her chest, as if to say there was room in her heart for his child. And maybe for him—if he played his cards right.

"You know about her propensity for running away when she gets upset, right?"

"Yes, I do, and I'll certainly keep that in mind." She studied him, but not in the slightly hostile way she'd done when he'd first arrived. There was compassion in her big green eyes. "Don't take this the wrong way, but doesn't she only run from you? I mean, because you're her parent, and kids like to use that against their parents."

An unexpected chill spread across his back and shoulders. He was the only parent she had left. He hadn't been able to stop her mama from being taken, and he was the one to blame for ripping Loren's familiar world out from under her. "I guess you're right."

"I won't let anything happen to your daughter. I care about her, too. Along those same lines of caring, here comes the warning. Please, be careful with my sister's heart." She squeezed his shoulder and walked away.

Careful. Like he hadn't been the first time.

An hour later, Grayson found Sage in her office and closed the door behind him so they couldn't be overheard. She looked up from the open file-cabinet drawer and smiled in a way that had begun to soothe the most wounded parts of him.

He slipped an arm around her waist. "Do you have any plans for this weekend?"

"I do not. What's up?"

"Loren is going to San Antonio with Daisy for the weekend."

She turned to wrap her arms around his neck, letting her fingers tease up into his hair. "When did this happen?"

"Just a little while ago. Daisy asked me, then I asked Loren if she wanted to go, and she was excited."

"That will be fun for them. And you're staying here?"

Her hopeful expression was adorable and just what he'd counted on. "I am. I bet Lizzy and Travis would like to have the house to themselves. How would you like to get away for the weekend? Just you and me."

"Oh, I like the sound of that very much." Her lips were soft as satin against his, brushing softly before she pulled back with a satisfied smile.

"I hoped you would."

"What do you have in mind, Mr. DeLuca?"

"I'm open to suggestions. But I'd like somewhere that isn't too far of a drive so we don't have to spend all of our time in the car."

"I have a perfect idea. It's a place that's very close and private, and now that I think about it, it's where I really want to go most." The tip of her tongue ran back and forth across her top lip, which told him she was thinking out a plan.

"And that place would be…"

"The cabin."

That surprised him. "The one I'm currently living in?"

"Yes. I always have to get out of bed and go back to my own, and I'd like to be able to sleep beside you and wake up together."

He hadn't even thought to suggest that, but he was loving the idea. "Sounds perfect. We can get some groceries and seclude ourselves at the cabin."

"I'll start making a list, and I'm going to put plenty of junk food on it. Everyone knows that calories don't count when you're on vacation."

Sage had packed a ridiculous amount of stuff to spend the weekend at the cabin on her own ranch, but she couldn't make up her mind. Her suitcase was stowed in her closet until the coast was clear. From the kitchen counter, she grabbed the bag of snacks she'd prepared for Daisy and Loren's trip and then went outside to say goodbye. Everyone was gathered beside her sister's red truck.

"What are you going to do while we're gone?" Loren asked her dad.

"I'm going to take care of some business."

Sage handed the snack bag to her sister. "Well, I'm not doing any work at all this weekend. I'm going to rest and relax."

Gray pulled cash from his wallet and held it out to his daughter. "Take this, kiddo."

"Thanks." She took the money, hugged him and climbed into the passenger side of the red truck. "Did you know Daisy's seats have built-in massage as well as the heat-and-cool features?" she said through the open window.

"I didn't, but that should make your trip very comfortable. Stay with Daisy at all times and do what she says. And have fun."

"I will."

Daisy pulled Sage into a hug. "You two have fun. Call me if you need me."

"I will. Be safe, sis."

As soon as they'd waved goodbye and it was just the two of them, an unexpected shyness steeled over her. "What should we do first?"

"Do you have anything you want to bring down to the cabin?"

"One suitcase." He was going to laugh when he saw the size of it. "I'll go get it from my room."

"I'll come with you. I have a feeling you're going to need help."

Delighted that he knew her so well, she laced their fingers. "Why would you automatically think that I'll need help with my stuff?"

"Just a hunch." He kissed the top of her head. "After we get you settled, do you want to go fishing?"

It wasn't an activity she'd normally choose, but she'd be happy doing pretty much anything with him right now. "Sure. Sounds fun."

Once her things were put away at the cabin, including setting out her beauty products in the small bathroom, she changed from her favorite turquoise maxi dress into denim shorts and a pink tank top.

When she came out of the bedroom he whistled. "Wardrobe change number one. Very nice."

"Proving my need for a gigantic suitcase. You just never know what occasion might arise."

"Those are your special fishing clothes?"

"They are now." She sat to pull on her sneakers.

He picked up a tackle box and two fishing poles that had been leaning against the wall near the door. "Did you fish a lot growing up?"

"No. Daisy sometimes went with Daddy, but I don't really know much about fishing. Will you teach me?"

"You bet."

They set off toward the pond, talking and laughing the whole way. The day was hot, but the sky was filled with puffy white clouds that thankfully blocked some of the summer sunlight. She took off her shoes and sat on the end of the wooden pier and dipped her feet into the cool water.

"You should put your feet in. It feels great."

It surprised her when he took off his boots and joined her. Travis always teased her, Daisy and Lizzy about walking around outside with bare feet, but this man hadn't hesitated. The last of her unexpected nervousness flew away like the mama and daddy blue jays that were darting back and forth with food for their nest of babies in a tree beside the pond.

"We're just using fishing lures, so there's no messy bait to put on a hook." He demonstrated how to cast the line out into the middle of the pond and then handed her the pole. "Reel it in nice and slow and give it a little jerk now and then so it moves in the water like an insect the fish want to eat."

She did as he said while he got his own line out into the water. Nothing went for her hook, so she tried casting it again, but it only plopped a couple of feet away. "Oops. Show me what I did wrong."

"You need to push the release button at the right moment." With his big hands over the top of hers, they cast the line. "If you hate fishing, we can find something else to do."

"I don't hate it at all." She leaned in for a kiss. "I'm going to catch the biggest fish."

"Game on."

Once she finally got the hang of it, she caught a small fish, while he caught three, all bigger than hers. Determined to get her line all the way out into the center of the pond, she put extra effort into her next cast.

"Whoa!" Grayson's cowboy hat was jerked off his head and dangled from the fishing hook.

She covered her mouth but couldn't hold back her laugh. "Sorry."

He was also laughing as he retrieved his hat from the end of her line. "How come everyone is determined to toss my hat in the pond?"

"At least I didn't push you in like a naughty horse. Are you hungry? Because I am."

"Starving."

"Let's go back to the cabin and have lunch before I hook you somewhere that will hurt."

He stole a quick kiss. "I think I'll have you for dessert."

When they stepped into the cool of the cabin, he hung his damp hat on a hook by the door. "Bless the soul who invented air conditioners."

There were several rolled-up blueprints on the coffee table beside his open laptop. "You told Loren you were going to take care of business this weekend. Do you really have some work you need to get done?"

His slow crooked grin made a shower of tingles dance across her skin.

"My business is finding out if you snore or are a bed hog. And connecting with you. You know what I just realized? We've never made love during the day."

"You're right." Feeling so much bolder than she was this morning, she pulled off her tank top and tossed it behind her. The flare of desire in his eyes emboldened her to unsnap her shorts and let them fall to the floor, leaving her in a lacy pink underwear set. "What would you like to find out first?"

"Let's start with daytime lovemaking."

He lifted her, and she wrapped her legs around his waist, the press of his mouth hot against hers. His scent and touch filling her head and her heart.

Heaven help me now. I'm completely in love with Grayson.

Grayson watched the splash of late afternoon sunlight move slowly across the soft skin of Sage's back. She was asleep, and now he knew she didn't snore, but he couldn't take his eyes off her. They'd made love. Twice. First quick and eager, burning off the lust between them. Then slow and exquisitely tender, tugging at his heart.

He pressed a hand to the center of his chest where a new feeling had begun to ease some of the pressure he'd been living with for too long. This lovely woman was helping him to put some of his broken pieces back together.

They could tell one another their secrets and dreams and know that they would be safe. He wanted more of her, and it scared him. But not enough to keep him from spending time with her.

She rolled onto her back and sighed before a long leisurely stretch. "Hi, handsome."

"Did you have a nice nap, sweetheart?" He trailed his fingers through her silky soft hair.

"I did. You exhausted me in the most delightful way."

"The feeling is mutual. What should we do now?"

When she slid her hand across his stomach, it growled, and they chuckled.

"Let's eat," they said in unison.

After dinner, Grayson sent her out onto the cabin's front porch to stargaze while he opened a bottle of wine. Spending the weekend here at the cabin had been a brilliant idea. There was no time wasted on travel or dealing with other people.

When he stepped outside, Sage held a finger to her lips, and he followed the direction she pointed. A gray fox was leaping around in the moonlight as he chased something they couldn't see.

"I love watching the wildlife play," she whispered. "He's so cute."

The delighted smile on her face was what he found cute. "It's a nice night for it." He handed her a glass of wine before sitting in the rocking chair beside hers.

"It's a perfect night."

Her cheeks were pink from their time at the pond and her hair a bit wild. And he didn't want to stop admiring her.

It was time to take a deeper look at his life and admit the truth.

I'm in love with Sage.

Chapter Twenty

Sage tied another blue balloon to one of the back patio chairs and watched Loren play with Davy in the grass beside the patio.

"Lala, Lala," Davy called over and over.

"What's he saying?" Sage asked her niece.

Lizzy paused to watch them. "Lala is what he has started calling Loren."

"Oh, that's so cute. He's given her a nickname."

"Loren and Grayson fit right into our family," Lizzy whispered.

The simple comment made her flinch, and she lost her grip on the string of the next balloon she was tying, and it floated up into the sunny sky. "Oops. Sorry about that."

"No worries. We have plenty more."

She thought the same thing about them fitting in, but she couldn't allow herself to get her hopes up too high. She knew very well how things could take a quick downward turn in the wrong direction. It had happened after Loren was born and then again with her ex-fiancé. Happy one minute and crushed the next. *Caution* should probably become her middle name.

She looked around the yard for the man of her desires. He was hauling bags of ice from Travis's truck to the coolers lined up under the shade of the trees. His muscles flexed enough to strain the sleeves of his black T-shirt. Combined with his worn-in jeans, a black cowboy hat and boots, he was giving off a bad-boy vibe, and she loved it. He was one good-looking man. It wasn't until Lizzy giggled and patted her on the back that she realized she was staring.

Good grief! I'm going to end up blowing this whole secret-relationship thing.

The birthday party was in full swing with music, food and lots of laughter. Sage stood off to the side, taking in the whole scene. Having a first-birthday party was something she thought she'd never have in her backyard, but now that she had, she wanted to have another one for her own child. At some point soon, she needed to talk seriously to Gray about what she wanted.

"What are you doing over here by yourself?" Grayson's deep voice came from behind her.

"Just taking it all in."

"Tell me about the guests I don't know."

Sage chuckled. "You're going to think I'm making some of it up."

"This should be good." He raised his hand as if he would touch her but crossed his arms instead.

She knew the feeling of wanting to show their affection in public and being forced to hide their attraction. After their weekend together, it was even a million times worse.

"That young man over beside the grill with Travis is John. He is Davy's biological father, and with him is his mom and younger brothers."

"I didn't realize it was an open adoption."

"That's a whole story in itself. The short version is Davy's mother passed away, and we were already fostering him before John even knew he had a son. There was a time when we thought he would take him, but it worked out in the best way for everyone."

"What about the older man and woman with Lizzy?"

"That's my older brother, Joshua. He's Lizzy's father, and the woman is Travis's mother."

"Oh, I saw them kiss earlier and thought they were a couple."

"They are a couple. The oddest, most unlikely couple you could think to put together, but it seems to be working."

"No one can say your family is boring."

"That's the truth."

"Dad, come look," Loren called to him.

"I better go see what she needs. Are you coming to join the party?"

"I will in a few minutes." She watched him walk away, enjoying the way his powerful body moved.

Imagine if my and Daisy's secrets were out in the open.

That would certainly give people a lot to talk about.

The birthday party had been a huge success, everything was cleaned up and the birthday boy was worn out and sound asleep. Since the guys wanted to watch a game and the women wanted to watch a romantic comedy, Grayson and Travis went next door to his ranch.

Travis only gave a cursory knock on the front door before going inside. The house on Four Star Ranch was bigger and grander than Grayson had expected, and it had surprised him the first time he'd come over to play cards with the guys. It had a two-story stone fireplace that drew your eye up to the vaulted ceiling, cross-braced with huge timbers. The place was clean, but the furniture was something you might see in the apartment of a college kid. Their worn denim sectional sofa and two mismatched recliners were clustered to face a big-screen TV and surrounded a coffee table where no one had ever used a coaster.

Finn raised a hand in greeting. "Pick a seat, and I'll grab y'all a beer."

Grayson chose one of the recliners, and Travis took a spot at one end of the couch.

At age thirty-one, Finn was the oldest, tallest and blondest of the three, and the one he saw most often over at Dalton Ranch—usually with Daisy. He'd seen them arguing good-naturedly and thought there might be a romance brewing under the surface. When Daisy wasn't looking, Finn often watched her with a smile Grayson was familiar with.

Jake Murphy, the jokester brother who smiled and laughed a lot, came in through the front door, followed by a short-haired black dog who jumped over the back of the couch and settled onto the middle like it was his special spot.

"I thought you had a date tonight," Travis said and scratched the dog's head.

"That fell through." Jake flopped onto the other end of the couch. "Aren't we a bunch of sorry excuses for single guys. A Saturday night and we're all sitting around with no dates."

"Hey, I'm married," Travis said. "I don't know what's wrong with the rest of you."

Finn came back in from the kitchen, passed out cans of beer and then kicked back in the second recliner.

"I'm thinking about asking out Sage's friend Emma," Jake said and sat forward to pull off his boots. "She's the one who owns that store in Old Town. Glitter and something."

"It's called Glitz and Glam," Travis said. "I ought to know because I see enough of their shopping bags around the farmhouse. You might want to get the name of her business right if you're going to make a decent impression on her."

"Noted."

"Grayson, why aren't you and Sage dating?" Finn asked. "There seems to be something heating up between you two."

"Why aren't you and Daisy dating?" he volleyed right back at him.

The rest of the guys hooted with laughter, and his brother threw a pillow at him.

Finn shot them a finger gesture that told them what he thought about that. "Daisy and I are only friends."

Grayson knew that excuse, and he wasn't buying it. He wanted to say more, but if he did, it might tip them off to his own secret situation. The more people who knew, the chance grew of something accidentally being said.

"Friends who spar and flirt," Jake said. "Big brother is just scared of being turned down."

Finn cracked open his beer. "If you'll remember, she used to be our boss when we worked on Dalton Ranch, and that was a good reason not to screw things up and lose our jobs."

"And now what's your excuse?" Travis asked.

"Daisy isn't my type."

"Big brother likes party girls with lots of makeup and short skirts."

Finn ignored Jake. "She's the only woman I've ever been friends with. If I let it become more than that, I'll end up breaking her heart like I always do and then be minus a friend and have to live next door to a woman who hates me forever."

They all made different sounds of understanding and agreement. Grayson knew Finn's concern firsthand. He had his own worries about ruining a friendship. And his relationship with his daughter.

"Is that why you're holding back with Sage?" Jake asked.

He debated how much to tell them. He'd gotten to know

them fairly well over the weeks, but would they keep what he said in confidence?

"You can trust them," Travis said as if he could read his mind. "If you tell us it can't go farther than this group, this is where it will stay."

Grayson took a long pull on his beer. "It's because my daughter isn't ready to see me with someone who isn't her mom."

"Respect to that," Finn said.

The dog put his head on Jake's lap, and he rubbed the animal's head. "I second that. Worrying about our feelings is definitely not something our father—or mother, for that matter—would've done. Quite the opposite, in fact. They paraded people in and out of our lives and set a poor example."

"Poor?" Finn sneered. "They were downright crap as parents."

The front door opened, and the middle brother and quiet one, Riley Murphy, came in with a case of beer under one arm and plastic grocery bags in each hand. "What's up?"

"They're all trying to figure out women," Travis said.

"Is that a real thing?" Riley asked on his way to the kitchen. "I haven't figured them out and don't imagine I ever will."

Grayson felt like he knew Sage pretty well. But did he really?

Sage carried two large bowls of popcorn upstairs and stretched out on one side of her king-size bed. It had been a long time since they'd had a pajama movie night, and after a busy week getting ready for Davy's birthday party, she needed the downtime.

Daisy came in with a bag of chocolate candy and climbed

up onto the center of the bed. Lizzy came in behind her and got in on the other side.

Sage reached into the bag for a piece of candy. "Where's Loren?"

"She was right behind us with the water," Lizzy said.

A few seconds later, Loren hovered in the doorway with four bottles of water in her arms and paused as if unsure what to do.

Sage patted the bed beside her. "Saved you a spot."

The teenager's tense expression eased into a sweet smile, and she climbed in beside Sage. "I wasn't sure if there was room for me."

"There is always room for you, honey." Happy tears welled in Sage's eyes. Everything was falling neatly into place. Very soon, they would be able to talk to Loren about their future.

"Which movie are we watching?" Lizzy asked.

"Loren gets to pick." Sage pointed to three DVDs on the nightstand. "Which one sounds good?"

"Let's see." She began to read the titles. "*Leap Year*, *The Holiday* or *The Proposal*. I haven't seen any of them. What do y'all think?"

Everyone said a different movie, and they all laughed. After giving the teenager a brief synopsis of all three, they ended up watching *Leap Year* because it was set in Ireland.

Halfway through the movie, Davy woke and ended up in bed with them, but after giving kisses to everyone, he fell back to sleep within minutes. Daisy was the next one to succumb to sleep, followed by Lizzy and then Loren.

There were no doubt pieces of popcorn that had made their way under the covers, and she was pretty sure there was a chocolate stain on her pink comforter, but Sage had rarely been happier.

Her bed was crowded with the people she loved most. The

only one missing was the man she'd given her heart to. But she hadn't told him that she'd fallen in love. She was still wary from her broken engagement, but she'd find the right time to tell him—soon.

In her sleep, Loren curled against Sage, and she eased her arm around the child, enjoying the moment as the movie played in the background. She mentally crossed her fingers that Loren was ready to accept her into their lives on a deeper level.

Please don't let me lose them again.

Back at Dalton Ranch, Grayson got out of Travis's truck. "I'm going to come inside and say good-night to my daughter before I go down to the cabin."

"I know Lizzy will be asleep by now, and I hope my son is, too. What do you want to bet that they all are?"

"Loren's kind of a night owl, which is something we need to work on before school starts." At the foot of the stairs, they heard the drone of a TV but no voices as they went up quietly so they wouldn't wake the baby. Grayson turned for his daughter's room, but Travis quietly called his name.

"Come look in here."

He stopped beside the other man in the doorway of Sage's bedroom and smiled. Three women, a teenager and a baby were all sound asleep in the king-size bed. It gave him hope that Loren was almost ready to accept someone new into their lives.

Travis went into the room and woke his wife with a kiss and then lifted his sleeping baby boy. Lizzy got up, whispered good-night to Grayson and the little family left the room.

His daughter was snuggled against Sage the way he remembered her doing with her mama. His throat tightened and burned, but he held back the tears. This was a good thing. A really good thing. But Britt…

She had loved their daughter with all her heart, and he ached for her that she didn't get to experience this beautiful stage of Loren's life. He remembered a time when he would've carried their child to bed and then fallen asleep beside his wife. But that was then. The future was wide open to possibilities.

Sage's hand was so protectively cradling Loren. She'd stepped right into the role of a mother. He wanted to crawl into bed beside her like he'd done their weekend at the cabin, but she was being guarded on one side by his daughter and on the other by her protective twin. Even though he would be the only one sleeping alone, this was still progress.

Sage opened her eyes and smiled a heartachingly sweet smile.

His past relationship was behind him, and this was a different time and place. A different woman.

A woman I've fallen in love with.

But telling her would have to wait until Loren was ready and had accepted their relationship.

Chapter Twenty-One

Loren couldn't believe she was going to babysit for the first time. It would only be for an hour or less while her dad went with Lizzy and Travis to Four Star Ranch to the site for their house, but it was a start, and it made her feel more grown up.

"Be a good boy." Lizzy kissed her son's forehead and put him on the living room floor in front of his basket of books and toys. "There's a bottle of milk in the refrigerator. Davy will probably want it soon and hopefully be ready for a nap."

"Got it," Loren said. "I have your phone number and Travis's, too."

"Very good. Call if you need anything or have any questions. We'll be right next door."

"I will. And we won't go outside or do anything dangerous." Loren sat on the floor in front of the one-year-old. "We're going to play and get ready for a nap. Right, Davy?"

"Lala." He reached for her, and she settled him on her lap.

"Lizzy, are you coming?" Travis called from the front door.

She sighed and shrugged. "Guess I better go. See you in a little while, Ren. Bye, sweet angel boy. Mama loves you."

"Mama." He hooted like a little owl and waved his chubby hand.

She helped him blow a kiss. "Bye, Lizzy. We'll be fine."

The second the door closed behind her, Davy crawled off

Loren's lap and began banging on his toy drum. They played with toy horses and stacking rings, and then she read one of his favorite books about a grumpy hippopotamus. It was only a few minutes before he started to yawn.

"I'll go get your milk. Stay right there, and I'll be right back." Loren left Davy playing on the living room floor and went to the kitchen to get his naptime bottle and made herself a glass of ice water in a big pink plastic cup. When she went back into the living room, her heart plunged into her stomach.

The baby was gone.

She dropped the bottle and her glass of water, splashing her legs and the rug.

"Davy, where are you? Oh my God. What if somebody kidnapped him?"

She couldn't breathe, and her blood pounded in her head. She'd told them she could handle babysitting while they went to the ranch next door for an hour, and they hadn't even been gone for twenty minutes.

"Davy! Please, God, let him be okay." She started looking around the room and then heard clapping and found him behind the couch.

She crumpled to her knees and pulled him into her arms. "Don't scare me like that ever again."

He pulled her hair and gave her a wet kiss on her cheek. "Lala."

The panic and fear that had seized her body left her nauseous and trembling. Was this how her dad had felt every time she'd run away? If so, she suddenly felt very guilty. She'd wanted to get his attention, but she hadn't meant to make him miserable.

Maybe it was time to cut him a break. It wasn't his fault her mama was gone.

* * *

Grayson was in the home office at the farmhouse, adding some details to the plans for Travis and Lizzy's house. He wanted a log cabin, but she wanted elegant touches, so he was doing his best to combine the two.

"Dad?"

He looked up from the house plans to see his daughter hovering in the doorway. "Hi, kiddo. What's up?"

She came all the way into the room and closed the door behind her. She still wore a pair of black shorts, but her T-shirt was sunny yellow with daisies around the collar. "Not too much."

"New shirt?"

She looked down at what she was wearing. "No. It's Lizzy's. Most of my shirts are in the wash. I'm sorry for running away when we lived in Houston."

It took a moment to process the words she'd tacked onto the end. They surprised him. He put down his work and gave her his full attention. "I appreciate that more than you can know. But I'm curious, what's brought on this apology?"

She leaned a hip on the double-sided partner desk and picked at the pink polish on her fingernails. "When I was taking care of Davy, he hid behind the couch, and just that one minute was *sooo* scary." She met his eyes. "I didn't mean to make you feel that way when I ran away."

"I know, honey." He stood and pulled his daughter into a hug, cradling her head against his chest. She was taller than he'd realized. Almost as tall as her mom had been. "You're growing up on me. And I'm very proud of the young lady you're becoming."

"Thanks." Loren lifted her head and then crossed the room to sit on the love seat under the windows. "I guess I thought running away would take away some of the pain of missing Mama."

"I wish you'd felt like you could come talk to me. I'm sorry I wasn't more approachable, and I promise to do better. From now on, know that you can come to me about anything at any time of the day or night."

She nodded. "Okay. Is it also okay if I sometimes talk to Lizzy or the twins about stuff?"

"Of course. Just know I'm always here if you need me. What do you say we agree to work on our communication skills?"

"I can agree to that. Do you think…" She brushed the toe of her sandal back and forth on the hardwood floor. "Can we keep the part about me thinking I lost Davy to ourselves?"

"You bet. It'll be our secret." He'd never tell her that he was glad it had happened to her. It was a good lesson and had hopefully taught her more about empathy.

A few hours later, one of the *Star Wars* movies was playing on the television, and Loren was in the center of the blue sofa between him and her new hero, Travis. Grayson couldn't believe his daughter was sitting beside him watching it. If it had been just the two of them in the house, she no doubt would've said it was too nerdy.

Not long ago he would've taken it personally that she was here because of the other people in the room, and not him. Over the past weeks he'd learned he didn't have to—and honestly couldn't—help Loren through this tough life change all on his own. She was coming out of her depression, and that's all that mattered. It was okay to accept help and lean on others.

Sage and Daisy were across from him in their matching comfy chairs, one pink and one pale blue. In a pair of khaki shorts, Sage's long legs stretched out in front of her. The memory of her wrapping them around him was making it exceedingly hard to focus on the TV screen.

Lizzy walked into the living room and put her wiggly fresh-from-his-bath son on his father's lap. "I have extra tickets for Saturday night's opera performance. Would anyone like to go?"

"Count us in," Daisy and Sage said.

Loren handed a toy to the baby. "I want to go. Can we, Dad? I want to hear Lizzy sing on the stage."

"Sure. I'd love to." If his daughter was asking him to go somewhere with her, he wasn't saying no. This was progress.

"Excellent." Lizzy settled on the arm of the sofa and kissed the top of her son's head. "They're really good seats."

"I have a new red dress I'm eager to wear, and this is the perfect opportunity," Sage said.

Loren plucked at the hem of her yellow T-shirt. "I don't have anything fancy to wear."

Sage and Lizzy smiled at each other and said in tandem, "Girls' shopping trip."

Loren looked from the women back to him and chewed the corner of her lip. "Is it okay for me to go?"

"It's more than okay," he said. He knew she was asking for more than permission or money. She was asking if it was okay if she went shopping without her mama. It both broke his heart and made it sing with relief.

Sage stood and stretched, making her shirt ride up enough to show her belly button. "Daisy, are you going shopping with us, or do you want to be the one to stay home with Davy?"

"I have a meeting and can't do either."

"I'll look after Davy," Grayson said.

"Dad, do you even remember how to change a diaper?"

"I certainly do."

Sage cocked her head and grinned at him. Why did he suddenly feel like babysitting was going to be a test?

Chapter Twenty-Two

The next morning, Sage, Lizzy and Loren walked into Glitz & Glam for a shopping spree. The teenager had been quiet on the ride into town but perked up when she looked into the window and saw the pretty clothes. Sage couldn't wait to get her into some cute outfits. Ones she would feel good about wearing to school.

"Welcome, ladies." Her friend Emma came out from behind the counter. Her gorgeous red hair was in a high ponytail today, and she wore a dress that looked right out of the 1950s. "I've set aside a few things I thought you might like, but feel free to look around as well."

"Mama would've liked this place." Loren fingered a pink floral-print dress with a boatneck collar.

"I think you're right." Sage put an arm around Loren's shoulders. "Britt liked to shop as much as I do, and I think I've told you that I owe some of my fashion sense to your mama."

Loren smiled and then pulled cash out of her purse. "You did. This is how much money Dad gave me. Can I get much with this?" she asked Emma.

From behind Loren, Sage gave her friend a nod and a thumbs-up, acknowledging that she would cover any remaining cost.

"Absolutely." Emma selected one of the pink floral dresses

in an extra small and held it up. "Would you like for me to put this in your dressing room while you look around?"

"Yes, please."

Lizzy motioned to Loren. "Come look over here. I see some shirts that might be perfect for you."

Watching the two of them chatter away while picking out clothes for themselves and for each other made Sage happy. With a large selection, they put Loren in the biggest dressing room, and she started trying everything on. They swapped out sizes as needed and gave their opinions when asked. This was one of those good days Sage vowed to remember.

"How does the white blouse fit?" Sage asked from outside the dressing room.

"Well… I have a little problem." Loren opened the door enough to peek her head out. Her expression unsure and a little embarrassed. "This shirt kind of needs a bra, and I don't have one. I never have."

Sage's heart squeezed. This was something Britt would've done with her. Something a mother would do. She'd bet this was the reason Loren wore oversized black shirts. "I can certainly help you with that. I think I saw some bralettes that will work until we can go somewhere for some more traditional styles that are just the right fit and style. I'll be right back."

As she went to the rack that held a small selection of undergarments, she was smiling, and at the same time, tears were building.

Why am I so emotional about a bra?

It was actually a pretty simple answer. There was something special about being the first one to help Loren with this milestone. It was the joy of getting to know her and spending this precious time together. And sadness that Britt couldn't be here to see her beautiful child growing up.

Sage longed for the friendship she'd had with Britt once upon a time, and she wasn't sure if she could ever fully forgive herself for how their relationship had fallen apart. She closed her eyes and took a deep breath. But going into labor while Britt was out of town had been out of her control.

She glanced out the store's plate-glass window where she could see the cloudless blue sky. *Britt, if you can hear me, please know that I love her, too. All I want to do is help your daughter with the things you would've done for her so beautifully.*

"Sage?"

She turned her head at the sound of Lizzy's musical voice. "Did you ask me a question?"

"Yes. Loren said you're trying to find her a bra, and Emma found this one in a new shipment. What do you think?"

"Oh, good. That might work." She took the bralette, then headed back to the dressing room and held it over the top of the door. "Try this one and see how it fits."

"Thanks."

She stayed close in case Loren needed another size or advice or anything at all.

"It fits! Are there more colors?"

The teenager's excited voice made her chuckle. "Excellent. I'll see about the other color choices. Come out when you have on your next outfit."

She snapped a few candid shots of Loren checking out the different outfits at the three-way mirror. She picked out a few of the best photos and sent them to Grayson. His response was a happy face and a thank-you. When she asked how the babysitting was going, he assured her he was good and they should go to lunch.

"Who wants to go to a late lunch after this?" she asked them.

"I do," Loren said and looked at herself in the three-way mirror. "Can we go to The Rodeo Café?"

"You took the words right out of my mouth," Lizzy said. "I've been craving their fried-chicken salad lately."

After another hour, they all stood back and looked at the options hanging on a rack near the dressing rooms. Loren picked out a few dresses, some jeans, shorts, shirts and a pair of summer sandals in pale pink. It was a great start on a new wardrobe.

The teenager left with three bags of new clothes—none of which were black.

Grayson adjusted his tie as he stood off to one side waiting on the ladies at the opera hall in Fort Worth, Texas. Travis was outside talking to Finn on his phone because all three Murphy brothers were at the ranch house taking care of Davy, and he had promised Lizzy that he'd check in with them. Lizzy was the kind of protective mom Britt had been and, he suspected, the way Sage would be.

The girls all came out of the restroom in a group. Loren was talking animatedly, and it looked as if she was painting a picture in the air. Her white dress with pink-and-blue flowers flared around her legs as she spun to imitate whatever it was they were talking about. He chuckled, and his heart swelled with love for his baby girl who was growing up way too fast.

Sage smoothed down the back of Loren's hair and gave his daughter her full attention. In a silky red dress, she was the most striking woman here. The scarlet fabric draped across one shoulder, leaving the other bare, and he so badly wanted to kiss the soft skin right below her collarbone. There was a spot that always made her sigh and sink her fingers into his hair. He pinched the bridge of his nose and shook his head.

Now was not the time to let his thoughts go down that path. This was a night to build all of their relationships.

Daisy pulled them over to look at the souvenirs, and he continued to watch them. Sage was smiling at his little girl with what could only be real love in her gaze. Loren obviously liked her and the whole Dalton family, and it felt like she was coming around to the idea of him dating someone. Maybe soon he'd be able to talk to his daughter about Sage becoming more than his friend.

Once the whole crew had joined him, they found their seats. When the lights went down and the orchestra began to play, he let his hand touch Sage's, and she hooked her little finger around his.

Lizzy was magnificent in the chorus, and the performance of *La Bohéme* was beautiful and tragic. Most of the women and a few men were wiping away tears. Loren's rapidly changing expressions gave away how captivated she was by the performance, and Grayson foresaw many future nights at the opera. A feeling of weightlessness made him smile.

I think we have a real chance of becoming a family.

Once they were home and Loren was asleep, he and Sage sat on the front porch swing. She'd taken off her fancy dress and wore shorts and a tank top that were sexy enough alone, but with her dramatic evening eye makeup, she was a goddess. Cradling her against him with her head on his shoulder and her fingers stroking his chest, he was relaxed and content. But it was more than that. It felt like everything was falling into place.

"Thanks again for taking her shopping."

"I loved doing it. We had so much fun, and now I know her sizes and favorite colors and styles."

"I'm glad you do, because I know nothing about fashion for today's teenage girls."

"It's always changing."

"I think Loren is coming around to us being together."

She raised her head to look at him. "I think you're right. Should we talk to her about it? Although I think you should probably talk to her by yourself so it doesn't feel like we're ganging up on her."

"That's a good thought. I'll talk to her tomorrow and get a feel for what she's thinking and see if it's the right time."

Sage yawned. "That's a good plan."

"I should let you get to bed, sleepyhead." He tipped up her chin and kissed her.

"I suppose we should get some sleep." They stood, but rather than him saying goodbye, they remained in one another's arms, swaying together with the night sounds and their heartbeats for music.

Chapter Twenty-Three

Loren woke with her heart hammering and tears on her cheeks. She lay perfectly still and took a moment to make sense of where she was and then breathed a shuttering sigh of relief. She wasn't all alone in a dark, empty opera hall calling for her mama, her voice echoing around the cavernous space.

Unanswered.

Her next breath shuddered, and she wiped her eyes. There was enough moonlight streaming in the window to illuminate the bedroom at Sage's ranch. She wasn't lost or alone in a strange place. But she felt alone. Her body trembled with that detached, sick feeling that came after a bad dream.

"I miss you, Mama."

Although dressing up and going to the opera had been really fun, it had made her think of the ballets and other performances she'd been to with her mama. It suddenly felt like she'd done something wrong by enjoying her time with someone else. Someone like Sage.

She suspected that her dad liked Sage as more than just a friend, but she couldn't let all of their old memories be lost or replaced.

She wanted to see her dad but he was down at the cabin, and going all the way down there alone in the dark was too scary. But she had to get the dream out of her head, or she'd never get back to sleep.

Watching TV would help clear the dream fog. She already knew how to step around all the squeaky spots on the stairs and creaky old floors. In the entryway, she caught sight of two silhouettes on the front porch, and she heard faint voices but couldn't make out the words. As she moved closer, she realized it was her dad and Sage.

What are they doing?

A rush of emotions made the leftover nightmare feelings reignite. She stood in the center of the entryway, frozen in place and unsure whether to stay or go.

Sage laughed, and her dad pulled her into his arms. And kissed her.

Loren gasped. *He's cheating on Mama.*

Her dad was kissing someone who wasn't her mama. She'd never seen him kiss anyone else. An ugly feeling twisted her insides, and she covered her eyes, but the image was still there, layered on top of the ache she was already dealing with from her bad dream.

She wanted to be okay with Sage and her dad hanging out and had thought she was, but witnessing them kissing… She shivered. Yuck!

How could he do this?

Is this why he'd taken her away from everything she'd ever known in Houston? Was it all because he'd wanted to come hook up with Sage?

They leaned close and kissed. Again!

"Are you kidding me?" Loren said loud enough for them to hear.

They sprang apart, and her dad yanked open the front door. "Loren, what are you doing up at this hour?"

"What am *I* doing? What about you? Is this why you dragged me away from my life? From everything that was ours with Mama?" she yelled. Her fingernails dug into her palms, but it wasn't enough pain to distract from the ache in her heart.

"No, sweetheart. This isn't why." He stepped inside. Sage followed and closed the door.

"Did you two plan this whole thing before we even moved? Did you?"

"I had no idea I'd reconnect with Sage. I moved us here for a new start. That's it. Not to cause you any pain or distress."

She looked at the woman who had become a part of their lives, but even the sad expression on Sage's face couldn't stop her eruption of feelings. "It's very suspicious the way you showed up everywhere on that very first day. At the mill, then the fountain and then our house. And all the help with cleaning and stuff."

"Ren, I had no idea you were moving back to Channing. I was more shocked than anyone to see you that first day."

"There is nothing to be upset about," he said.

"You were kissing another woman!"

His face paled, and hurt flashed through Sage's eyes right before she looked at her feet.

"Ren, honey, we didn't do any of this to hurt you or your mama's memory." Sage came forward like she'd hug her, but Loren backed away.

"Well, you did!"

"Loren Grace, calm down and listen to me," he said.

She pointed at her dad. "What would Mama think about you kissing Sage?"

He sucked in a sharp breath, and his expression twisted as if she'd hit him.

"I want to go home." She stumbled once on her run up the stairs but stopped at the top. "To Houston."

Her dad was following, so she ran into the bedroom, slammed and locked the door. Davy started crying a few seconds later, and she felt bad for waking him up in the middle of the night, but her world was crumbling out from under her. Sitting on the center of the bed, she drew up her legs and hugged them tight against her chest. Doors opened and closed, and the adults talked in hushed voices in the hallway, and then Davy stopped crying.

There was a soft knock. "Please open the door, kiddo."

"Go away, Dad."

"We said we would talk to one another from now on."

They had said that, but after her emotional dream and the horror show on the front porch…she just couldn't right now. "I need some space. I don't want to talk tonight."

"I'll be downstairs on the couch if you change your mind. I love you, and I'll be here when you're ready to talk."

She ignored him and even considered running away, but she remembered the fear it had caused her to not know where Davy was for only a minute, and she couldn't do it. Besides, it was scary out there in the dark.

"I hate to see her alone and hurting like this," Sage said loud enough to be heard through the door. "I just want to comfort her and make it all better."

Does Sage really care about me, or is this an act to fool Dad?

The caring felt real when she was alone with Sage, but could she trust it, or was it just her seeing what she wanted to see?

"Grayson, can I see if she'll talk to me?" Lizzy asked.

"Sure. It can't hurt to try."

There was another knock. "Ren, it's Lizzy and Davy. Can we come in?"

"Is this a trick so Dad can get in?"

"No. It's not a trick."

She got up from the bed, unlocked and opened the door.

As Lizzy slipped inside with Davy on her hip, Loren saw her dad and Sage hovering outside with worried expressions. It kind of made her feel good that they were so concerned, but was it really because they cared about her feelings or just because they'd gotten caught? Because they should definitely be feeling guilty.

Loren cut off their view as she closed the door. "I'm really sorry I woke Davy up."

"It's okay."

He lifted his head from his mama's shoulder and reached for her. "Lala."

Hugging his warm little body against her chest made her trembling start to ease. She climbed back onto her bed, settled Davy beside her and stroked his hair just the way he liked. "Go back to sleep, angel boy." She liked that nickname for the toddler and had started using it like the rest of the Dalton family.

Lizzy lay down on the other side of him. "Want to talk about it?"

"Do you know what happened? What they were doing?"

"Yes, Sage told me. She hated the thought of you in here alone and upset."

"I had a bad dream about Mama, and I got up and then I saw them."

"I'm so sorry." Lizzy stroked her hair much like Loren was doing to the baby.

It's like Mama used to do. She closed her eyes and enjoyed the sensation.

"It must have been hard to get up needing to find comfort and getting such a shock," Lizzy said.

"It was. They said they were just friends. But they lied."

"I do know that your dad and Sage really did start as friends. That's how Travis and I started, too. Well…actually, Travis and I started more as two people who irritated the heck out of one another. Then it grew into friendship, and we couldn't stop the love that came along soon after. Sometimes you just can't stop it."

"That's really how it happened for you and Travis?"

"It is. When it's meant to be, it's meant to be."

Davy was back to sleep, and now that the panicked feeling from her bad dream and the anger from catching them kissing had faded, she was exhausted. She yawned.

"Will you tell me why you don't want Sage with your dad?"

"It's not because it's Sage. Having him with anyone feels weird. Do you know that there were women flirting with him right after the funeral?"

"Oh, that's terrible. I can see how that would be really upsetting." Lizzy started singing. It wasn't her big opera voice but soft and soothing.

She closed her eyes and let the song lull her back to sleep.

Loren woke enough to crack open her eyes as Lizzy lifted Davy and carried him from the room. Shortly after, the floor creaked as someone came back in. It was probably her dad, so she pretended to be asleep. But when someone kissed her forehead, it wasn't the scent of his familiar cologne. It was Sage's soft cherry-blossom scent.

"Good night, sweet girl," Sage whispered. "I love you."

Warmth bloomed in her chest and spread all the way down to her toes.

Does she really love me? Does she love Dad?

Grayson stared at the living room ceiling. Each breath hurt as it burned through his tight lungs. He couldn't stop thinking about the gut punch Loren had delivered when she'd asked what her mama would think of him kissing Sage. It killed him to imagine Britt's wounded reaction.

He'd more than broken his promise to stay away from Sage, and it had ended up hurting the child he'd been working so hard to protect and heal. Just when everything had been coming together, it was falling apart at warp speed.

When he'd seen the shooting star, he'd thought he'd gotten a sign from Britt that what he was doing was okay, but had he just been seeing what he wanted to see? Maybe this happening because he was selfish and had begun to think they could become a family of three.

His logical mind was battling his emotional side, causing a tornado of emotions. He was second-guessing every decision he'd recently made.

Footsteps on the stairs made Grayson sit up on the living room couch. He hoped it was his daughter, but the person who came in was Sage. The woman he didn't know what to say to. His sweet, beautiful, loving Sage, who was no doubt as upset and confused as he was.

She moved as if she'd sit beside him on the couch, but instead she changed direction and sat in her pink chair. "She's sleeping, and Lizzy said she's okay. I'm glad there was someone here she would talk to."

"I need to thank Lizzy." Silence grew between them. To keep from saying anything he'd regret, he was doing something that had driven Britt nuts. He'd grown quiet, hardly showing any emotion at all. A standard fallback while he adjusted a plan or thought through a problem. Going forward, he had to put all of his focus on his child, not himself.

"How are you feeling about…everything?" she asked.

He rubbed his hands roughly through his hair. That question was more difficult to answer than you'd think. "Guilty. Confused. Unsure of what to do next."

"What can I do, Gray?" Her voice wobbled with emotion. "How can I help?"

"I wish I knew. Maybe things will be more clear in the morning. You should go get some sleep."

She bit her lip, and for a second, he thought she was going to cry, but she nodded and stood. "I'll leave you alone to think. Try to get some rest." She walked close enough to touch him but only blew him a kiss. "You know where I am if you need me."

"Sleep well, sweetheart."

He couldn't allow himself to need and depend on Sage. He watched her go and felt an emptiness settle in as she disappeared from sight. Why did things have to be so complicated? He'd thought Loren was ready to accept them as a couple, but his initial gut feeling had been right. She wasn't ready to welcome Sage into their lives.

The only thing he knew to do was put some distance between them. It was time to move into their house in town, even if it wasn't completely finished. First thing in the morning, he would go to town and assess the progress.

And rather than continuing to run a marathon at a sprinter's pace, he'd slow things way down with Sage.

Chapter Twenty-Four

Sage grabbed a new jar of honey off the top shelf of the pantry. Something rustled behind her, and she turned, expecting it to be the cat who always followed her inside hoping for a treat. Instead of seeing a white cat on the floor, it was a pair of cowboy boots that led up to the stoic face of the man she loved.

"Gray, I thought you were the cat."

"Sorry. Just me." A barely there smile almost reached his mouth. "I'm running into town to check on a few things at my house. Loren is sleeping and likely still doesn't want to talk to me anyway. If she gets up before I get back, please tell her she can call me, and I'll come right back out here."

"I will. Are you and I going to find some time to talk soon, too?" She hugged the jar of honey against her chest.

"I think that would be a good idea." He looked over his shoulder, then stepped farther into the pantry and gave her a quick peck of a kiss. The kind of kiss you'd give a family member, not a lover. "See you in a while."

"Drive safe." She remained in the pantry a minute longer, preparing herself for whatever the day brought her way.

Things had been going so well over the last few weeks, and their future had looked promising. Until last night. When Loren caught them kissing.

She could feel him retreating and feared he'd once more

become the distant man he'd been when they'd first arrived in Channing. The quiet, moody guy he became when he was overthinking something.

She made her coffee and went upstairs to get dressed. Too bad she didn't have a suit of armor to protect her heart. At least he'd found her to tell her his plans, and he'd kissed her goodbye in the privacy of the pantry. He hadn't completely pulled away from her.

It will be okay. It has to be.

Once she was ready for the day, she went down the hall to check on Loren, but her room was empty. Sage searched the house, and when she still couldn't find her, panic began to rise.

What if she'd run away again? And this time under her watch.

"Calm down," she told herself. Knowing Loren, she was probably with Mischief. The cat plopped down in front of her and meowed for attention. "Lady, let's go outside and look for our girl."

As they neared the stable, she saw Loren and Travis on horseback riding away. She'd slipped outside without Sage even knowing she'd left the house. Loren was avoiding her, and it left a huge ache deep inside her chest. She'd grown used to their closeness, and the relationship they'd developed was precious to her, and she couldn't imagine losing it.

To keep herself busy, she checked on the horses, talked to their newest employee and returned phone calls, but no one was back yet. Sage was making herself crazy waiting to see who would talk to her or who wouldn't and what would happen next. And where they went from here.

She grabbed the stack of mail she'd forgotten to bring in from her car and flipped through it as she leaned back to close the kitchen door with her shoulder. She paused on an envelope from the sperm bank that she'd been talking to in Fort Worth. They'd never sent her mail before. Too curious to wait, she put the rest of the mail on the butcher-block counter and ripped open the envelope. The letter gave her a list of new profiles to look at when she logged back into their website.

Since her first kiss with Grayson, she hadn't been opening their emails because she'd been hoping she wouldn't need their service. If she had her choice of fathers for her baby, it would be Grayson. Hands down, no question.

The cat jumped onto the counter and meowed.

She snapped her fingers. "Get down, Lady. You know you're not supposed to be up there."

As she walked closer, the cat ran along the countertop and knocked a jar of raspberry jam onto the hardwood floor. It smashed, and the cat leapt from the counter onto the center island. Another place she wasn't supposed to be.

"Good grief, naughty girl." She dropped the letter on top of the rest of the mail, opened the door and shooed the cat out into the back yard. She needed to get the glass and sticky mess cleaned up because there was a crawling baby in the house. Since her sweet one-year-old nephew Davy had become mobile, she always kept the floors as clean as possible.

An all-too-frequent feeling of emptiness washed over her and left behind the urge to cry. All she wanted was a child of her own giggling and crawling around before she was too old.

Was that really too much to ask for?

Grayson entered the code at the gate to Dalton Ranch and drove down the long curving gravel road. His house had been rewired, replumbed, and the kitchen only needed cosmetic finishing touches and an oven. He had one completely remodeled bathroom upstairs, and the second that he'd expanded into his bedroom was still a work in progress, but he could easily live with that for a while.

What he could not live with was watching his daughter struggle emotionally. Moving into town would keep necessary distance between him and the amazing woman he'd unwisely fallen in love with, and it would prove to Loren that she came first.

Since he rarely cooked, the lack of an oven at his house was no big thing and they could use the microwave until it arrived, but he sure was going to miss the home-cooked meals shared with the Daltons. He and Loren had been spoiled by the food and the family atmosphere. Going back to their old eating habits was going to suck, but until his child was ready to move on, he had to make decisions that were best for her.

He got out of his car and stared at the farmhouse and the flowerbed under the kitchen windows where Loren had helped plant herbs. They'd had fun here. His daughter had smiled and laughed in their kitchen.

Stop it. I've got to slow this thing down before I make everything worse.

The neigh of a horse caught his attention, and he saw Loren in the distance on horseback. Travis was on a much bigger horse beside her. She'd still been asleep when he'd left for town, but he was glad to see she'd come out of her room and was doing something she enjoyed.

This would also give him a chance to talk to Sage in private, but he wasn't looking forward to what he had to say, and he continued to stand by his open car door. He knew what he had to do, but he was so conflicted.

It was hard to make a plan and stick to it when his heart kept trying to lead him off track.

"Time to have a serious conversation."

As he closed the car door, the white cat jumped out from

behind a potted plant, hissed at him and then darted across his path and scrambled up the tree at lightening speed.

"I am not going to miss that cat." But he was going to miss being this close to Sage. Close enough that she could come to him at the cabin at night, where they could be completely alone without fear of being discovered.

But they had been discovered, and that was the problem.

He wasn't a single carefree bachelor who could do whatever he wanted. He was a father first and foremost and would make any sacrifice necessary to protect Loren. Slowing things down would protect everyone.

It wouldn't be so easy to see Sage in private once he was living in town, and that would give them a chance to figure out what came next, and what was best for all of them. His child was finally smiling and laughing and happy, and he couldn't have her reverting back to her dark mood and clothes. He liked seeing her in cute, colorful outfits that fit her.

At some point, Loren would have to realize he had to move on with his life, but he couldn't risk ruining her progress by pushing a new relationship on her too fast. Time apart would show him if what he had with Sage was real and lasting or just something they'd both needed to get out of their systems.

Was their passion just the novelty of them fulfilling a long-ago desire for one another? It didn't feel that way. It felt like more. It felt like love.

He shook his head and kept walking toward the farmhouse. They had no choice but to slow down. There was time to, well…to take their time.

There's no rush.

When he opened the back door of the farmhouse, Sage was on her hands and knees cleaning up some kind of a spill.

"Need help?"

"No, thanks. I'm almost done, but you can hand me another old dish towel from the drawer under that stack of mail."

He pulled open the drawer, grabbed a towel and tossed it to her. Closing the drawer made a piece of paper blow off the top of the mail and float to the floor. He put it back on the stack, but a logo at the top caught his eye. It looked like a little swimming sperm. He knew he shouldn't look, but his curiosity got the better of him, and he read a few lines before he could stop himself from snooping.

List of potential sperm donors.

His gut flipped over and then tightened. "Sage, what's this?"

She looked up to see what he was holding, and her eyes widened. "Oh. It's just something I've been looking into. It's one potential route I can take."

Jealousy curled and wove its way through his insides. "What route is that?"

She went to the sink to wash her hands and wasn't looking at him. "Using a sperm donor to have the baby I've always wanted before I'm too old. But I haven't found anyone whose profile is a match for what I'm looking for."

"I… But…" He stammered like a fool and tried to calm the thundering behind his ribs. One way or another—and without delay—Sage was planning to have a baby, and that was definitely not part of his plan to slow things down.

She turned to face him and began speaking rapidly in a hushed voice. "I've been meaning to talk to you about something serious. I want to have a baby. A child of my own who I get to keep and raise and love every day. And I've been hoping…" She chewed her thumbnail and couldn't seem to look at him. "I'm in my mid-thirties, and I don't have time to mess around."

His skin went icy cold. *Is Loren right? Has Sage been after something from me this whole time?*

"Is this why you were so eager to hook up and started coming to the cabin so frequently?"

"Seriously?" She snapped her hands to her hips and shot him a thunderous glare. "Grayson DeLuca, I didn't do any of this alone. Who's the one who first asked me to come to the cabin? For sex," she hissed in a low tone.

He winced. "I did. You're right."

"I thought we were in this together."

"Wait." He swallowed the lump in his throat. "Are you expecting *me* to be your sperm donor?"

She gasped. "Oh, that's rich coming from you. You're acting like it would be some horrible thing, especially after what I did for you."

She hadn't exactly answered the question.

She snatched up the letter and waved it in the air. "I started this process before you ever came back to town. Before I had any idea that I would *ever* see you again." She briskly walked away from him.

He followed her out of the kitchen and had to lengthen his stride to catch up to her as she headed toward the stairs. "Sage, wait."

She came to a sudden stop and spun to face him. "Why does everyone find the thought of having a baby with me so repellent that they would even go to the lengths of getting a secret vasectomy?"

"Oh, sweetheart—"

"In any romantic relationship, isn't it normal to think about the future and plan what might come next, Mr. I Have a Plan?"

"Having another baby is something that's never been in my plans."

She straightened her spine and started up the stairs. "Message received."

This wasn't going at all like he'd planned. He hadn't expected to add a discussion about having another baby in his forties to the immediate topic of slowing down their relationship.

"My house in town is ready to move into," he said rapidly.

She paused at the top of the stairs. "Perfect timing to make your escape."

"Sage, it's not like that. It's not an escape."

She held up a hand to quiet him. "Remember last night when Loren said she needed space to think? Well, it's my turn to ask for the same. Loren is upset. You're upset. And so am I. We should take some time apart to…consider the future."

His first inclination was to argue against her suggestion, but it was exactly what he'd been telling himself needed to happen. "We're in agreement. Hitting the pause button is best." The words left a sour taste in his mouth.

"Great." With tears in her eyes, she left him standing at the bottom of the stairs.

Was Sage in love with him and truly hurt, or was he just a convenient guy who owed her and could help her get pregnant?

She's never said I love you.

Chapter Twenty-Five

The burn in Sage's throat matched the sting behind her eyes.

Do not cry. Hold it together.

She didn't want Grayson to know how much his withdrawal had hurt her so she went into her bedroom, closed the door and flopped face down into her pillow. No one needed to hear her frustrated growl. His alarmed reaction to her desire for a baby didn't bode well for her dream of them starting a family.

She rolled onto her back and rubbed her damp eyes. "He's got to be all in or it won't work."

She was not going to become a parent with a man who was anything less than thrilled about her getting pregnant. This felt like another nudge that was moving her closer to becoming a mom—on her own.

Her hands trembled and she clasped them to her flat abdomen, phantom sensations transporting her to another time when she'd experienced the joy of pregnancy. As Loren had grown inside her, she'd felt the first fluttery movement. Every kick and stretch and hiccup. Biology be damned... Loren was a part of her. And it wasn't only because she'd loved Grayson back then—and now.

She got up and went to the room Loren had been using and sat on the bed. A bottle of bright pink nail polish was on the nightstand beside her sketchbook, a novel, bangle bracelets and hair clips. Several items of clothing—none of them black—were scattered here and there. Such a teenage girl's room. Like it had been when it was hers before she'd moved into her current bedroom with the bigger closet.

For several precious weeks, she'd known what it was like to be a "mother" to Loren, and it had been wonderful. Rapidly changing teenage moods and all. But now…

Why did I open my big mouth and blurt out my desire for a baby at a time like this?

She had imagined he was feeling the same about them headed toward becoming a family, when sadly he was not. Her head understood why they needed to slow things down and really think about the future, but her heart didn't understand. Not really. Having Grayson so quickly agree to her suggestion that they take some time apart was like a dagger to her heart.

Would she ever find a man who would fight for her?

Footsteps approached, and she could tell by the quick rhythmic pace of them that it was Loren.

The teenager came to a halt a few steps in. "Oh, I didn't know you were in here."

"Hi, Ren." She stood. "Are you ready to talk to me, or would you like me to leave?"

"It's okay. You can stay." Loren sat on the cane-back chair in the corner and pulled off her black cowboy boots. The cat ran in and jumped onto her lap, snuggling her head under Loren's chin as if she knew she was leaving.

Sage wanted to do the same. "I'm so sorry we upset you last night. I never want to see you hurting."

"I know. Lizzy told me sometimes grown-up friends can't help but become more." She shook her head as if she couldn't imagine such a thing.

Sage wanted to smile for the first time since being caught kissing on the front porch last night. "What else did she say?"

"That you care about me."

"That's true. I care about you very much."

"Loren." Grayson's voice came from down the hallway. "Are you up here?"

"In my…" Loren frowned. "In here."

Sage knew what she'd been about to say, and she wished more than anything that this really was her bedroom.

Grayson rushed into the room and paused much like his daughter had done upon seeing her. "What are you two talking about?"

"Nothing," Loren said.

Sage had a feeling he wanted her to leave so he could talk to Loren about them moving to town, but she wasn't feeling that generous toward him at the moment and wanted to see how this would go down.

He shifted from foot to foot. "I have good news. Our house in town is ready. We can go as soon as our things are packed."

Loren jumped up from the chair, dislodging the cat, who hissed at Grayson and swatted his leg. He side-stepped and glared at the animal as she made a hasty retreat from the room.

"Why do we have to go tonight? We're supposed to watch the third movie in a vampire series."

"You can come over and watch it another time. I'm going to the cabin to get my stuff, and it shouldn't take me more than thirty minutes. Start packing, please."

Under her breath, Loren said a word she definitely wasn't allowed to say, but Sage couldn't blame her. Grayson paused in the doorway with his back to them like he'd turn around and scold her, but then he kept going.

"Want help packing your new clothes?" Sage asked.

"Sure." She said it so half-heartedly that her shoulders slumped. "What if my new stuff doesn't fit in my small suitcase?"

"I'll loan you a suitcase. In fact, why don't we put your hanging clothes in one of my garment bags so they don't get wrinkled."

"Good idea, especially since we don't have an iron or ironing board."

"You can borrow mine anytime. Ren, please know that you're always welcome here at the ranch."

Loren picked up a bracelet and twirled it around her finger. "Just me, or only if Dad is with me?"

"You are welcome with or without him. Always."

"Do you like my dad?"

Sage's throat tightened. She wanted to be as honest as possible without saying anything that might further upset the situation. "Of course I do. He's a wonderful guy. You're lucky to have him as a dad."

"I mean...do you *like* like him? As more than a friend."

Her body felt numb, and she sat on the side of the bed. "Yes, I do, but I realize it's not an ideal situation. How do you feel about me liking him?"

Loren shrugged and turned back to the closet. "Well... I don't really know."

"That's okay, honey. Take your time. We all will. Just know that you can call or text me or Daisy or Lizzy at any time. I'll wait for you to be ready."

The sun was setting, and Sage's spirits were as heavy as the glowing orb headed behind the horizon. She opened the outer sliding door of the horse stall and let Mischief out into the fenced-in exercise arena. The foal tossed his head and bounced around like he was on pogo sticks before running a lap. This was going to be one high-strung horse, but Loren loved him, and she couldn't bear to sell him.

"Where's Ren?" Daisy asked from behind her.

Sage sighed and braced a hand on the door frame. "They left this morning. Moved back to town."

"I didn't know they were leaving today."

"No one did. Loren was just as surprised as me when Grayson came back from town and announced their plans to immediately pack up and leave."

Daisy put an arm around her, and they watched the frisky foal enjoying his run. "Did he leave because of what happened last night?"

"Yes, I believe so. I know he feels guilty about being with me. I'm the woman his wife kicked out of their lives."

"I think he's also scared."

She rested her head against her twin's. "It's also because I suggested taking some time apart to think about the future, and he immediately agreed."

"Why did you tell him that?"

"The short answer is because he doesn't want to have another baby."

Daisy said a string of words that their mama would've scolded her for.

"My thoughts exactly."

"Want me to beat him up now or wait a while?"

"I'll get back to you on that." She really didn't want to have to decide between having a baby or having Grayson and Loren in her life.

Why in the hell do I have to choose?

Gray put the box of pizza on his new quartzite kitchen countertop. "Grab two paper plates, please?"

Loren closed the refrigerator and did as he asked but remained silent.

"It's been days since we moved into town. When are you going to start talking to me again?"

She shrugged.

Sage wasn't talking to him either. She hadn't called to say she'd had enough time alone to think about the future, and even though her distance hurt like hell, it was probably for the best. Moving on too soon was hurting all of them.

Several times over the last few days he'd turned to Britt for advice like he'd always done, but then a micro-second later came a wave of sadness that accompanied the reality that his loved one was gone.

Maybe I'm not ready to move on.

He dropped a couple of slices of pizza onto each plate, but his appetite was gone. It had been gone ever since Loren caught them kissing and freaked-out.

"Instead of taking it to your room like I know you're planning to do, sit at the table, please."

"But—"

"Table."

"Fine." She snatched up her bottle of lemonade and stomped into the dining room.

At least he'd gotten a couple of words out of her. He took a seat on the other side of Aunt Tilly's dining table. There were still boxes stacked in a corner, and even though he'd been here long enough to get them unpacked, he was too depressed and didn't care enough to do it.

"I need you to hear this, whether you talk to me or not. A new woman in our lives—no matter who it is—could never ever replace your mama. I'll forever love her just like you will."

"What's going on with you and Sage?"

He hadn't expected the direct question. "What do you mean? Nothing is going on." Just like his daughter had wanted.

"I mean..." She moved her hand around as if searching for the right thing to say. "You were good friends who laughed and stuff. And now you're not even talking. We don't see her or any of the Daltons. It's been days, and you're a big grouch."

He arched his eyebrows. "I'm not the only one who's cranky."

She spread out her arms as if to demonstrate the state of their house and the reason she was in a bad mood. "Why did you make us come here when the house isn't really finished like you made me think it was? You're sleeping on a mattress on the floor, your bathroom isn't ready and I can't bake cookies because we don't have an oven."

"The oven arrives tomorrow."

"Not the point, Dad." She shook her head and took a bite.

He knew exactly what she meant. Neither of them was happy, and he'd bet a million that Sage wasn't, either.

"You had a fight, didn't you?"

He couldn't go into all the details about why he couldn't be so close to Sage right now. He was still working it all out in his own head. Her longing to have a baby as fast as possible had thrown him for a loop. He'd known she wanted one, but he hadn't realized to what level she was willing to go.

"It's complicated."

She rolled her eyes. "Now who sounds like a teenage girl?"

He kind of felt like a teenager, floundering and second-guessing everything. "Sage asked for time alone to think."

"What did you do?"

"Why do you think I did something?"

Loren ducked her head. "It's because I got so upset about you kissing her, isn't it?"

"No, kiddo. It's not your fault. I'm sorry I put you through that. You were right about me moving on too fast."

"But you're not happy *not* moving on," Loren said. "Think about that."

Chapter Twenty-Six

Sage finished a phone call with another satisfied client and leaned back in the office chair. She should be thrilled about the new referral business they were sending them, but she was too confused about her personal life. She was hurting too much to get excited. It had only been a few days since Grayson and Loren moved back to town, and she'd almost called him a million times, but something always stopped her. It was a bit of fear, a dash of stubbornness and a mixture of disappointment and confusion.

Travis stopped in the doorway of the office. "Sage, I dropped your car off for the exhaust work, but they had to order parts, so it won't be ready for several days."

"That's fine. I can use one of the trucks if I need to go somewhere."

"Do you need me to do anything before I head over to my ranch for a while?"

"No. Thanks again for dropping off my car."

"You got it."

Her phone chimed with the sound she'd programmed for Loren's calls and texts, and her breath caught. It was the first time she'd heard from her since they'd left the ranch.

The message asked her to meet Loren at the fountain in the Old Town courtyard at sunset. It seemed an odd place for the teenager to want to meet, but she was missing her so much that she wasn't about to say no or question the location. She responded to the text right away.

I'll be there. See you soon.

Was she asking to meet there so her dad wouldn't know? That certainly wouldn't help the tension between her and Gray. She would ask Loren that question as soon as she saw her. After making herself look presentable, she took one of the ranch trucks and drove into town.

When she got to the fountain her nerves were rattling like rocks in a tin can. The quiet of the warm summer night would usually calm her, but tonight it wasn't working. She sat on the side of the fountain where she could look out over the park and Channing Creek down the hillside. She was early, and because it was a Sunday night and the shops were closed, there was hardly anyone else around.

A couple walked along the edge of the creek, just the way she wanted to do with Grayson, and a dad helped his little boy feed the ducks. Another thing she wanted to watch him do with a child. Their child.

She covered her face with her hands and willed the tears away. Right now, she was going to focus on seeing Loren. Trying to predict what would happen between herself and Gray was impossible. It all depended on the kind of future he wanted and if their visions aligned.

Grayson was loading the dishwasher when his phone chimed, and he pulled it out of his pocket to check the text message. Loren was out riding her bike, and even though they were in Channing and not Houston, he was still protective and worried. The message was from his daughter.

Meet me at the horse fountain ASAP.

He typed a response. Are you okay?

I'm fine. Just come, please.

"What is my teenager up to?" At least she was communicating with him again.

The courtyard and fountain were only a few blocks from the house, but he decided to drive just in case there was a problem with her bike and he needed to put it in the back of his SUV.

He parked in front of Glitz & Glam, where some of his money had been going lately, but every penny was worth it to get his daughter out of the dark clothes she'd worn for the last year or so. He wished he'd realized that the reason she'd switched to black was because she'd outgrown the clothes she'd bought with her mama. He hadn't been paying enough attention. He was doing everything he could to change that and do better by her.

Now that he was working from home, he planned to repair and build their relationship. She was his number one priority, just as Britt would expect. Doing right by Loren was so much more than fulfilling a promise. He loved her with all of his heart.

You love Sage, too, a voice said in his head before he could stop it.

As entered the courtyard, he looked around for his daughter, but it wasn't Loren that he saw. The tight band around his chest loosened a notch.

Sage's strawberry-blond hair glistened in the last of the evening sunlight. She was so beautiful inside and out, and he'd missed her so much. She hadn't seen him yet, so he took the opportunity to admire her. The gentle curve of her shoulders. The way she tilted her head in thought.

The way her nearness calmed his soul.

"Hi, Sage."

She jolted and put a hand to her heart. "Gray."

"Fancy meeting you here."

She looked around. "Where's Ren?"

"I was going to ask you the same thing. She sent a text asking me to meet her here."

"Same." Sage released a breath and smiled in a wobbly expression that revealed her raw emotions. "I think we've been set up by a teenager."

"I think you're right." He sat beside her, and they gazed out at the sun setting across Channing Creek. "Maybe she's smarter than either of us."

"That's entirely possible. I've picked up the phone to call you a ton of times but..." She shrugged.

"I understand what you mean. I'm floundering a bit myself. I'm pretty sure Loren got us together because she thinks it's all her fault that we're not talking."

"Oh, no." She shifted to face him. "I hope you told her it isn't."

"I did." Slowing down their relationship had started as a way to protect Loren, but Sage wanting to have a baby was one of the things they needed to discuss. He brushed a curl from her cheek. "Have you had enough time away from me? Because I have."

"More than enough. I miss both of you so much."

"We've missed you, too. I don't want an escape from you, sweetheart."

"That's good." She laced her fingers with his. "We're both trying to protect her. And ourselves. It's a tricky situation."

He appreciated her understanding more than she could know. "Look who's headed our way."

Dressed in a red boat-neck shirt and denim shorts, Loren was pushing her bike and studying them cautiously.

When she reached them, Sage stood and hugged her tightly. "Hi, honey. Are you okay?"

"Yeah. I'm fine."

"Want to tell us why you've brought me and your dad together?"

"You two should try dating," Loren said.

"Really?" Grayson and Sage said in synchronized surprise.

He hadn't expected this. "What brough on this change of attitude?"

"Dad, you're too grumpy to live with. You're like Shrek before he got out of the swamp and found Fiona."

"Are you calling me an ogre?"

"If the attitude fits…"

Sage chuckled. "If you ask my family, they'll likely say the same about my mood."

"I want to start going out to the ranch again," Loren said.

"Me, too." Grayson's tension eased another notch, but there was still so much to discuss and clear up.

"I'm not saying I want you kissing and making googly eyes at one another in front of me all the time, but I promise not to freak out like I did. That night after the opera, I'd just woken up from a bad dream and…" She shrugged. "It just hit me at a time I was really missing Mama."

He pulled her into a hug and then opened an arm for Sage to join them. Holding both of them at once gave him hope.

"You're crushing me." His daughter wiggled out of his bear hug. "Can we go out to the ranch tomorrow? Mischief has probably grown a lot since I've been gone."

Sage's smile was wide and glowing. "Tomorrow sounds perfect."

"Speaking of going out to the ranch, can Loren stay with you while I go out of town on business for a couple of days?" He rubbed his hand up and down the back of his neck. He hadn't yet told Loren that he had to go to Houston. He was worried about taking her with him because it would remind her of what they'd lost.

"Of course she can stay with us. It's the perfect opportunity for us to catch up on the list of movies we've been watching," Sage said to the teenager. "And if you want, you can tell me any concerns you have about me dating your dad."

"Okay. We'll see. Does Davy miss me?"

"Everyone misses you."

"Cool." Loren smiled and got onto her bike. "I'm going to ride home. Bye."

Once she'd ridden away, he turned to Sage. "Well, what now, sweetheart?"

"We have a lot to discuss and work out, but for right now let's just hold one another, enjoy the sunset and slowly ease back into figuring this thing out."

"I can do that." With his arms around her, she settled against his chest, and he breathed her in. "If Loren does ask you a bunch of questions, please remember not to say anything about the surrogacy."

"I won't say a word about it."

The upbeat melody of a country song could be heard as Grayson opened the farmhouse's kitchen door the following morning. Sage had Davy on her hip, and she was dancing around the kitchen island. The baby was giggling with pure delight, and she was smiling at the child with so much love that Grayson could almost feel it.

She should be a mother.

He pressed the heel of one hand to the thundering in his chest. Seeing her like this made him dangerously close to wanting what he'd thought he did not.

Sage looked up and saw him, but her smile didn't falter. "You caught us. Want to dance?"

He couldn't have resisted even if someone tied him up. He opened his arms and welcomed them both. Davy gave him a big wet kiss on his cheek, and Sage kissed the other. They took a few more turns around the kitchen. Too soon, the song ended, and they stayed that way for a few more moments as the DJ talked.

"Where's Loren?" she asked.

"She went out to the stable to see Mischief."

Davy arched his back and wiggled on her hip. "Dondon."

"That means he wants down. Standing still isn't near as exciting as dancing, is it, angel boy?" Sage put him on his feet, and he took two wobbly steps before dropping down to crawl over to the cat who was napping on a bed near the kitchen table.

She wrapped her arms around Grayson's neck and gave him a proper kiss. "I'm glad you came in to say hello before you head to Houston."

He let his hands roam up and down her back. "I needed a kiss to tide me over."

"I can grant that wish. I'm feeling very generous."

Her pretty mouth met his in a soft teasing kiss, and he allowed himself to enjoy the moment.

Davy giggled when the cat started licking the back of his neck, and Sage went to pick him up.

The back door swung open, and Loren rushed inside. "Mischief has gotten so big."

"Lala!"

"Hi, angel boy." She crossed the kitchen, lifted him from Sage's arms and kissed his cheeks. "I missed you so much."

Watching them together made Grayson's heart expand in his chest.

She would make a really great big sister, and Sage would make a great mom.

This was all hitting him hard and fast, and he didn't want to say anything to Sage about the possibility of them having a baby before he really considered it from every angle. They'd already discovered what could happen when they jumped into something without a well thought out plan.

Pressure built in his chest. He suddenly realized the full weight of what was causing such feelings of guilt. Because Britt hadn't been able to carry a child, the idea of having a baby with Sage seemed like a double betrayal.

But Britt is...gone.

Since returning to Channing, he'd felt like Sage was the one woman who was off-limits, but was his promise to stay away from her meant to be forever, or had it ended when he'd lost his wife? Their wedding vows had said *until death do us part.*

Did my promise end when she passed?

Maybe. But because Britt felt so strongly about her child not knowing they'd used a surrogate, the truth of Loren's birth needed to remain a secret. Not forever, but until she was more mature and could understand why he'd kept it from her.

The timing needed to be just right, or it could ruin the relationship he was building with his daughter.

He had a lot to think about on this business trip.

Grayson couldn't resist driving by their old house while he was in Houston. He parked on the street a few houses away and decided to take a walk through their old neighborhood one more time. Thunder rumbled in the distance, and it looked like it would rain at any second, but he didn't bother with an umbrella. If he was lucky, the weather would keep everyone indoors so they couldn't intrude on this moment.

Nothing had changed. Except him. He tipped back his head and stared up at the overcast sky. "Britt, you always liked rainy days, and they always make me think of you," he whispered.

A gust of wind blew the first misty drops of rain in his face.

"I hope that's a loving hello because I need to ask something of you, darling. You always told me that if you weren't around, I should do whatever it takes to make sure Loren is well cared for and happy. I need to believe that you would agree that Sage is doing that for our daughter. She helped bring her out of a darkness that I couldn't. So, I hope you understand and will forgive me for moving back to Channing and making Sage a part of our lives."

The rain began to fall in a soft, steady rhythm, cooling the summer air and bringing the scent of ozone. The drops hit the hot sidewalk, painting its surface darker one drop at a time until they all connected into a glistening sheen. The reflection staring back at him was a man he barely recognized—a man with hope.

"I'm going to trust in the love that we shared that you understand about me needing to move on and about Sage." He brushed his fingers through his wet hair. "One more thing. I don't think I can keep the promise to never tell Loren about her birth, but I can promise to wait until I know that she is ready to hear it."

Chapter Twenty-Seven

Sage stopped in the doorway of Loren's room. She was on her stomach on the bed, sketching a picture of the cat who was sleeping on her pillow. "Ren, will you come up to the attic with me?"

The teenager glanced up and gave her a suspicious look. "Why? Isn't it super scary up there?"

"Nope, not in the daytime. I want to show you something. I found an old art easel, but I don't want to haul it downstairs if you don't want to use it."

"Okay. Let's go see it." She followed Sage out of the bedroom. "I have an easel at the house in town, but it would be cool to have one here, too."

Sage thought so as well. At the opposite end of the hall from Loren's room, she opened the door to the attic, flipped on the light and they made their way up the straight staircase. "Daisy and I used to play up here on rainy winter days when it wasn't too hot."

"Like your secret hideaway?"

"Exactly. We even made tent forts with our mama's clean sheets, and she'd fuss at us."

"It must have been so cool to have a sister. I've always wished I had one." She stretched out her arms. "Wow. It's a lot bigger up here than I thought it would be. You can stand up straight and move around and everything."

There were stacks of boxes, old steamer trunks and random pieces of furniture. It should really be cleaned out at some point. She pulled out and opened the easel. "This is it. It belonged to my mama."

"That's cool. It's a good one, and I would like to use it."

"Perfect. I'm glad it will get some use rather than collecting cobwebs." Sage refolded the easel for easier carrying.

"Where can I set it up?"

"How about in my room by the big windows where you said the light was good?" She started down the stairs first.

"That would be great. You'll really let me paint in your room?"

"Sure. It's the perfect spot. Want to go into town and buy some new painting supplies?"

"Yes, please. I've almost used up all of my watercolors and a lot of my pastels. Is there a place in Channing to buy that stuff, or do we have to drive all the way to Fort Worth?"

"You're in luck. A new store opened recently, and I think they will have everything you need." Sage went straight into her bedroom and set up the easel.

"Can we go to the store soon?"

"Whenever you're ready."

"Cool," Loren said on her way out of the room. "I'm going to change my clothes."

Sage loved her eagerness, and she couldn't wait to go have some fun together.

Loren was glad to be spending time at the ranch once again. She had the easel set up in front of the windows in the sitting area of Sage's bedroom where the natural light was great this time of day. She had a fresh canvas, her paints laid out in the order she liked them and her new paintbrushes in a metal can.

The jingle of the cat's bell had her turning her head right as Lady jumped up onto the small folding TV tray and knocked the jar of paintbrushes off onto the floor.

"No! Naughty girl."

Lady scattered the brushes even further as she scampered from the bedroom. The old wooden floors weren't exactly level, and some of the brushes rolled under Sage's bed. Loren got down onto her hands and knees and peered under it. As she stretched her arm to reach for the brushes, she knocked over a shoebox, the lid came off, and papers and photos spilled out in a fan across the floor.

"Oh, shoot."

She used her arm to rake it all out from under the bed and started putting everything back into the box. Some of the photos were so old, they were black-and-white. Some were of the twins when they were little. A photo of her parents caught her eye. They were standing in front of a fireplace with another woman, and she quickly realized the third person in the picture was Sage.

And Sage was unmistakably pregnant, her hands resting protectively over her huge belly as she smiled at the camera.

"Sage had a baby?" she whispered to herself. What had happened to her baby? She'd never mentioned a child. Had the baby died?

She flipped over the photo, read the date printed with blue ink and gasped. It was dated a week before *her* birthday.

Her insides seemed to be swaying unsteadily, and she grasped the pink bedspread. She kept looking from the front of the photo to the back, as if it would suddenly change and everything would make sense again. But nothing changed. It was a week before her birth and her mama's stomach was completely flat, but Sage's wasn't.

"Oh my God. Is Sage my mother? Did she give me away?"

She jumped up from the floor, and her heart fluttered so hard she was lightheaded. She had the thought to run away like she used to do, but that was an old rebellion she'd outgrown. Leaving all the papers and pictures spread out on the floor, she clasped the photo with trembling hands and went downstairs in search of Sage.

She found her alone in the living room, rearranging things on the coffee table. "Hi, honey." Her brow furrowed. "What's wrong?"

She held out the photo. "Are you my real mother?"

Chapter Twenty-Eight

Sage heard the words, but they didn't make sense until she looked at the photograph. Her mouth opened and closed several times, but she didn't know what to say. She'd never meant for anyone other than herself to see that photo. That time in her life was precious, and she hadn't been able to get rid of it. Her blood thundered in her head, and she sat down hard on the couch.

Grayson was not going to be happy about this. Not happy at all. She'd just told him she wouldn't say a word about this exact thing.

But some secrets weren't meant to be kept forever.

"It's not what you think, Ren."

"Look at this date!" The unhappy teen had tears streaking her cheeks as she stabbed her finger at the back of the photo. "It's a week before my birthday and my mama wasn't pregnant, but *you* were. You didn't want me and gave me away?" Loren choked out.

"Oh, honey, no." She opened her arms to hug her, but Ren stepped back, bumping into the coffee table and making coffee slosh over the rim of her cup.

"A hug isn't going to make this better. I'm not a little kid."

"You're right. How about the truth?"

Loren studied her warily. "You're really going to tell me the whole truth?"

"Yes, I am." Sage internally winced. This was going to be another wrench in building a relationship with Grayson.

Years ago, she'd been in agreement about not telling anyone that she'd been a surrogate for money to save their ranch, but she couldn't have Loren thinking she was her real mom and that she hadn't wanted her. That thought made her physically ill, and she put a hand to her throat, willing herself not to get sick. She had wanted Loren even though she'd had no right at all. It had crushed her to give birth and hand the baby over to them.

"Sit down, and I'll tell you all about it."

Loren dropped onto the couch and stared at the photo still clasped in her hands.

"Your parents wanted a baby more than anything."

"Even my dad?"

"Absolutely. But your mama couldn't carry a baby, so I volunteered to be their surrogate." Sage held her breath while she waited for the teen's reaction.

"So that really is me in your stomach in the picture?"

"Yes, it sure is. When this picture was taken, you were kicking up a storm." Sage put her hands to her belly as if she could still feel the movements. "I'd eaten a big piece of chocolate cake, and all the sugar had you stirred up."

"Did you like being pregnant with me?"

"Oh, I loved it so much."

"Wait…" Loren wrinkled her nose. "*How* did you get pregnant? Did you and Dad—"

"No, no. It was all very clinical and done in a medical setting. You are biologically your mom and dad's child. I carried you for nine months, felt you kick and hiccup, and I sang to you. I gave birth to you. And fell in love with you."

Loren sagged back into the couch cushions, her body relaxing as if she'd been holding up the weight of the world. "You really loved me?"

"I always have."

"That's why you reacted the way you did that first day at the mill. Were you eager to help us move in because you wanted to see me?"

"Yes. I couldn't resist the chance to know you."

"This is so weird. It's like my life is a movie."

Sage understood that sentiment. "What other questions do you have?"

"I don't understand why they lied to me." She shook her head. "Why was this a secret?"

"I'm not completely sure of your parents' reasons. You'll have to ask your dad that question. But for me…" She took a breath and chose her words carefully. "At the time, I was young. I was in my early twenties and didn't want people to think that I'd accidentally gotten pregnant and was giving my baby up for adoption. People like to talk."

Loren tucked one foot beneath her. "I guess I can see why you did that. So, nobody knows?"

"Only Daisy. I'll tell you something I think is pretty cool. You, my dear, help save this ranch."

"Really? How?"

"Your parents gave me that last bit of money Daisy and I needed."

"You helped them, and they helped you?"

"That's right."

Loren stood and put the photo on the coffee table. "I think I need to go see Mischief and think about all this."

"I completely understand. It's a lot to take in."

"I promise I won't run away."

The knot of tension in Sage's belly began to ease. Once Grayson saw that Loren was okay with this big news, surely, he would be, too.

* * *

When Grayson drove up and parked beside her car, Sage went outside to meet him. She wanted to prepare him for what his daughter might say.

"Hi, sweetheart," he said with a smile, but his happy expression fell away. "Is something wrong?"

"No, not really. Everyone is fine, but there is something I need to tell you."

She moved into his arms for a hug, resting her head on his chest and soaking in his comfort, but she couldn't put it off any longer. She stepped back, took a deep breath and handed him the photo Loren had found.

He studied it and then smiled sadly. "I remember this day. But I don't understand why you're showing it to me now."

She wrung her hands. "Because Loren saw it."

His mouth fell open, and he jerked his gaze up to meet hers. "You had it out where she could see it?"

"No. Of course not. It was in a box under my bed."

"What the hell was she doing snooping under your bed?"

"It's not like that. Something rolled under there, and she was getting it out and found the photo by accident. She brought it to me with questions." She made a flipping motion with her hand. "There's a date on the back."

He turned it over and swore. "What did you say to her?"

"I had to tell her the truth."

He pressed his fingertips against his forehead and let out a long slow breath. "Sage, how could you do this? Telling her that her mother didn't give birth to her is the *one* thing I asked you not to do. I made a promise, and it wasn't your secret to tell."

"I'm really sorry, but I made the decision I thought was best at the time."

"You could've said the date on the photo was wrong." He shoved the snapshot into the breast pocket of his shirt.

"Gray, she's smarter than that. Loren was upset because she thought I was her biological mother. I couldn't have her believing for a minute that I would've given her up if she was my baby."

He squeezed his eyes closed. "You could've said that you had something shoved under your shirt and were just pretending to be pregnant."

"The photo clearly shows that Britt is *not* pregnant a week before the birth. She thought I didn't want her, and she needs to know that she was wanted. By three people—the parents who created her and the woman who carried her."

He plowed a hand through his hair and paced back and forth across the gravel driveway with jerky movements. "You've made me look like the bad guy."

"Gray, I'm sorry. That wasn't my intention. I would never paint you as the bad guy. If it helps, she doesn't seem all that upset. And not all secrets are meant to be kept forever."

"I wasn't going to keep it forever, but it was my secret to tell her when I decided the time was right. When she's more grown up. I should take Loren home." With long strides, he headed for the kitchen door.

"And then what?"

"And then…" He stopped and spun to face her. "And then I don't know." He studied her face as if he was trying to memorize it. "You and me together was never supposed to happen. We gave it a shot, but I can't do this with you."

She gasped, and the air burned her lungs.

"I'm sorry, Sage." He looked almost as devastated as she felt, but he turned and continued into the house. Without looking back.

Her heart was breaking, but it was her own fault. She

had a strong feeling that he was still mourning his wife. He hadn't been ready for a new relationship, and she'd pushed herself on him. Too much, too soon.

She never should've taken the pizza to their house that first day or invited them out to the ranch. Now…

Everything was falling apart.

Hazy spots floated in Grayson's line of vision, and he paused in the upstairs hallway with a hand braced against the wall. He had planned to come home from Houston and talk to Sage about having a child together, but now…

This would probably set back his relationship with Loren, and she might never trust him again. Every cell in his body ached.

When he felt steadier, he headed for his daughter's bedroom. Because honestly, the room here was more her bedroom than the one in their house in town. And that made this whole thing all the more sad.

"Loren, please get your things together. It's time to go home."

His teenager remained seated on the bed, crossed her arms and glared at him. "You can leave, but I'm not. I'm staying here, where people tell me the truth."

He winced and caught sight of Sage in the doorway. "We'll talk about this at home."

"Where you'll probably just lie to me. I recently asked you about the day I was born, and you could've told me the truth then." Her lips quivered.

He felt like his chest was caving in, and he needed some time to absorb this new reality. Sage had said Loren wasn't that upset, but it didn't feel that way to him. "I won't lie to you. We'll talk about everything, but not here."

Sage came into the room, hugged Loren and whispered

something into her ear. His daughter nodded and started tossing her things into her suitcase.

Why had she done it when Sage asked, and what had she whispered to his daughter?

Without looking at him, the woman he'd fallen in love with walked away, and it was his own fault.

In the car on the way into town, his daughter wouldn't even look at him. With her arms defiantly crossed and her body turned away, she stared out the side window.

"What did Sage say to you when she hugged you?"

"It's a *secret*," she said with extra emphasis on the last word. "I know you understand what those are."

He certainly did. So many secrets. Too many. He should've known better than to think this one could wait.

"I could see how mad you were at Sage for telling me about her being pregnant with me, but I don't understand why."

"There's more to keeping this from you than you know, and I made Sage promise never to tell you because I was honoring your mother's wishes."

"Why would Mama want the truth kept from me?"

"It broke her heart not to be able to have a baby, and I guess if you didn't know about us using a surrogate, then pretending it hadn't been that way was easier. I just know it was very important to her that you believed she gave birth to you."

"I would've loved Mama no matter what."

"I know, kiddo. Me, too."

The second he pulled into his driveway, Loren fired open her door and got out. "I'm not happy about any of this being kept from me." She slammed the door and stalked toward the front porch.

"I'm not, either." He dropped his head onto the steering wheel. He'd told Sage it was over between them, and the stark devastation he'd seen on her face was already beginning to haunt him. He should've moved to a whole new town somewhere far away from Houston and Channing.

Something crinkled in his shirt pocket, and his head snapped up. It was the tell-all photo. He pulled it out and studied the image.

What if Loren finding this photo was the universe trying to tell him something? Too bad the message wasn't clear.

Chapter Twenty-Nine

"That's it," Daisy said and slapped a magazine down on the kitchen table. "Enough moping and sadness and crying. Lizzy and Sage, pack it up, ladies. We're going on a girls' trip to the beach."

"But I—"

"Nope." Daisy cut Sage off before she could protest. "Travis, can you and the brothers handle things around here for a few days? We need to take your wife with us."

"Um…sure." Travis said it more like a question, but Daisy's pointed stare made him grin. "No problem. I'll ask the brothers to come stay here, and we'll have a guys' weekend. Poker, beer and—"

"Do you really want to finish that sentence?" Lizzy asked her husband with her hands on her hips.

He chuckled, then wrapped his arms around her and pulled her in close. "I was going to say *barbeque*."

"Good answer. No corrupting our son just yet."

Watching them share a chaste kiss made Sage even sadder. She had loved getting to that point in her relationship with Gray, but now… She just wanted to grab some junk food and watch movies in the dark.

"It's a really long drive to the beach," Sage said, trying to get out of it.

"Good thing we aren't driving," her twin said. "You know

how Roy Hall is always saying he wants to fly us somewhere in his plane? I asked him, and he's ready to go as soon as we are."

"Like in a private jet?" Travis asked.

"No, nothing all that fancy. It's a small six-person plane. He's taking us to Padre Island. He has a sister who lives there and is going to stay with her."

Travis, Lizzy and Daisy started talking and making plans, but Sage was too depressed to argue or join in the discussion.

"I'll go pack." She grabbed a bag of potato chips off the kitchen counter on her way to her bedroom. She really just wanted to be alone, but she pulled a suitcase from her closet and plopped it onto the bed. Normally she was meticulous about picking outfits and folding them just so, but today she just started tossing in shorts, shirts, swimsuits and sundresses, barely even noticing if they matched.

When she pulled out a T-shirt that belonged to Loren, it made her think of their shopping trips. She did some deep breathing to keep from crying. It didn't work.

She was mad at herself, and she was mad at Gray, too. Loren learning the truth hadn't been the traumatic event he was making it out to be. Especially since she seemed to have accepted the truth of her birth better than they could've hoped. It was Grayson who'd had the dramatic reaction.

"I should've known better than to pin my hopes on a man who's not ready to move on."

Sage zipped her suitcase, and as she was coming out of her room, she saw Finn Murphy moving stealthily toward Daisy's bedroom.

No telling what the jokester was up to. She tiptoed after him.

"What's up, Daisy Maisy," Finn said loud enough to make both of them jump.

Her sister dropped a bottle of shampoo, and it rolled across the floor to stop at his feet. "What is wrong with you, bonehead?"

"Do you want the whole list?"

"You're going to give me a heart attack."

From her spot out in the hallway, Sage could see her sister but not Finn.

"Sorry I startled you," he said.

Daisy tried to scowl but couldn't hold off her grin. "Why don't I believe you?"

"I'm not sure." He chuckled and walked close enough to the bed that Sage could see him.

"I'm going to smack Travis for teaching you to sneak up on me like that. Just because y'all think it's funny when he startles Lizzy, that doesn't mean you should do it to me, too."

Finn ignored her grumbling, flopped onto her bed and sprawled on his back. "Can I sleep in your bed?"

Daisy blinked rapidly and shook her head. "In my bed? When?"

"Tonight. Since I'm going to be staying here to help out Travis, do you mind if I sleep in your bed while you're gone?"

"Sure. I mean, no, I don't mind. It's fine," Daisy said. "But you better be clean when you crawl into my bed, Finnegan."

"I'm always clean when I get in bed. But once I'm there…" He said in a deep sexy voice and let his comment hang in the air.

Sage grinned and backed away from them. Those two were a mess. The best of friends who could talk in depth and share secrets but also bickered and picked at one another. And flirted. Why wouldn't either of them just give in to their attraction and—

She shook her head. *Maybe because they're a hell of a lot smarter than me.*

* * *

A few hours later, Sage dug her toes into the wet sand, noticing the chips in her red nail polish and not caring. Her heart felt heavy and her belly bound with barbed wire, but at the same time, it felt empty. A wave washed over her feet and then receded, taking with it sand and bits of broken shells. If only it could wash away the sharp, jagged pieces of her tattered emotions.

It was time to get over Grayson DeLuca, for a second time. After Loren's birth, he'd been hours away with no chance of seeing him, but now, how was she supposed to live in the same small town and always wonder when she might run into him?

She picked up a spiral shell that had once been home to a sea creature who'd probably left it for a bigger one. Now it was empty. Like her arms, her bed and her life.

She let out an exasperated sigh. She knew she was being overly dramatic. Her life was not empty. She had her sister and her niece's family. But no one of her own. Her heart felt as if it had been forced into a box that was much too small to hold all of her hopes and dreams. Like she'd have to pick and choose because she couldn't have it all.

It was up to her to make her wishes a reality or figure out a way to put them to rest and accept her future. If she went through with using a donor to get pregnant, she'd also have to accept that her child would have no father. No family history or stories to pass along. Never knowing if they shared features or stature or the gene that makes your pinkie fingers crooked.

The salty wind caught the brim of her big floppy sun hat, and she barely grabbed it before the sea claimed it. Why was trying to have a family so hard for her? The man she'd almost married had had a vasectomy to prevent having a baby with her. Gray had run away with his tail between his legs. And she was not eager to attempt a repeat with a third guy.

"Sage, are you hungry?" Daisy called down from the balcony of the beach house. "Lizzy made tacos and frozen daiquiris."

"Yes. I'll be right up."

She rinsed her feet and legs at the outdoor shower and went upstairs. Her sister put a cold fruity drink in her hand. She took a few sips, but her stomach protested. Stress did this to her. Especially stress that came with sadness.

"I think I need some sparkling water to settle my stomach before I can eat."

Daisy swapped out her drink and gave her a hug. "You'll get through this, and we're right here with you the whole way."

"What would I do without you?"

"Good thing you don't have to find out."

Lizzy turned on some music and dished out the food before giving Sage a big hug. "I have faith it's all going to work out."

"I hope you're right."

So many things were out of her control. Grayson hadn't been hers back then, and even though for a brief while she'd thought he was, he wasn't hers now. If he didn't want her as the mother of his baby, then he didn't want the real her. What she needed to do was find something that was within her power.

"I have got to stop this pity party," Sage said. "After we eat, let's play one of those card games that always makes us laugh."

After eating too much and laughing harder than she'd thought she could, Sage was exhausted and fell asleep almost immediately, but she woke in the middle of the night.

Daisy was sound asleep and taking up more than her half of the bed, which was no surprise. Her twin had always been a bed hog.

She was too restless to stare at the ceiling, so she slipped from the bed and went outside. The soft sand was still warm from the day's heat but became cool as she reached the dampness. Salt water lapped at her toes and wind tossed her hair. It was so peaceful, but at the same time the power of the ocean was consuming and she could feel the crash of the waves in her chest.

A fresh batch of tears trickled down her cheeks. One dripped off her chin and splashed into the ocean. One salty tear in a vast sea.

It certainly seemed like something that should earn a wish like you got with birthday candles or a shooting star. The question was, what wish to make?

To the universe, or whoever was listening, Sage made her wish. "I want a family of my own."

She was done waiting on a guy to make her dream of being a mom come true. Done waiting on a guy to be ready to man up and start a family with her.

"When we get home, I'm going to the sperm bank and picking a donor."

Sage was in her bedroom unpacking her suitcase from their short trip and doing her best to convince herself that everything was going to work out just as it should. Although she'd tried to get out of going to the beach, her twin had known just what she'd needed. Getting away from the place where everything reminded her of what had happened had helped her come to terms with the future and make decisions that were best for her.

If Grayson could so easily walk away, she wasn't going to

try to force a relationship he wasn't ready for or ultimately couldn't give his heart to. With so much tumultuous history between them, it was best to move on with her life as if he'd never returned to Channing. That was going to be a whole lot easier said than done. Her body felt heavy, and she dreaded the time it would take to heal her heart.

When her phone rang, Loren's pretty face appeared on the screen. It was a photo Sage had snapped of her while they'd been horseback riding. The strike of pain mixed with the joy was something she'd have to get used to. Just because she would not have a romantic future with Gray didn't mean she couldn't have a relationship with Loren, and she hoped he would understand that.

With her heart racing, she answered. "Hi, Ren. How are you?"

"I'm okay, but I need a new bra. Can you please help me?" The teen rushed the words as if her request was a matter of the greatest importance.

"Of course I can," she said but then hesitated. "Your dad is okay with me helping you?"

"Yep. When are you free?"

"I have a doctor's appointment this afternoon, but I'm free tomorrow."

"That would be great. I'll call you in the morning. Thanks, Mom."

The phone line went dead, and Sage's breath left her lungs in a rush.

Mom.

She stood frozen with the phone in her hand. Had it been a slip of the tongue, or did Loren realize that she'd called her Mom?

The sharp, sudden strike of hope and longing threatened to undo all the decisions she'd made.

Chapter Thirty

"Loren Grace DeLuca." Her dad's tone was a warning.

She turned just enough for a brief glance of him leaning against the kitchen counter. "Hi, Dad. Gotta go."

She dashed out the back door, and once she was out of sight, she stumbled to a stop, pressing her back against the side of the house. While she was on the phone with Sage, she'd known her dad was behind her, leaning against the counter beside the coffee pot, but pretended she hadn't. It was the only way she could think of to make him stop being a bull-headed dumbass.

She had to show him that he was making a mistake by pushing Sage from their lives, because she felt like she was partly to blame. When they'd first arrived in Channing, she'd been a brat, and then she'd made him feel guilty about kissing someone. Now she was thinking clearly enough to accept some of the responsibility for what had happened. Him getting upset with Sage for telling her the truth was wrong.

If she could accept another mother figure in her life, then he should, too.

Loren went to the garage and grabbed the pruning shears. There was still a ton of work to be done on this overgrown mess of a backyard, and since Daisy had taught her to enjoy gardening, it seemed like the perfect thing to do to stay out of her dad's way while he came to his senses. A row of old rose bushes ran along the back of the house, and she began clipping away the dead branches.

She'd thought using the word *Mom* for Sage would feel wrong and maybe even hurt, but it hadn't. It was different from saying *Mama*. Saying it hadn't been painful or felt icky at all. It had made a warm tingle run through her whole body.

But had she freaked out Sage?

She really hoped she hadn't. The woman who had given birth to her made her dad happy, and she made her want to start once again doing things she'd been denying herself since losing her mama. Loren also didn't want to give up having the Dalton family in her life. She'd grown to love all of them.

How could she make everyone realize that they could become a family? She had no doubt that her mama would want all of them to be happy.

Grayson watched his daughter through the window as she clipped away at the overgrown bushes. What was his precocious child up to?

Since ending things with Sage, Grayson had been miserable with a capital *M*, but he'd been trying to keep busy and be there for whatever Loren needed. He was trying to do the right thing for everyone, but his daughter's little phone-call stunt had him second-guessing his decision to end things. Suddenly she was okay with Sage and he was the one who was holding back and denying his feelings.

He went to the dining room table and started once again working on the architectural plans for the old grist mill, but his thoughts kept drifting back to Sage. Her cooking with Loren and dancing with Davy. In the bedroom, where she was sweet and sexy and tender. The way she'd brought Loren back to him. He owed her more than he could say for that.

I miss her so much.

And each time he thought of her, he changed the drawings a little more and a little more until the whole front half of the mill was a big open space—and looked a lot like a community center.

Just like Sage wanted.

He sat back in his chair, crossed his arms and studied the drawing. If he could so easily alter architectural plans, like he did all the time, why couldn't he extend changes into other parts of his life? Loren had found a way to move on and accept Sage. This is what he'd been waiting and hoping for, and he could no longer use his daughter as an excuse.

He stood and paced with his hands linked behind his head. He'd been searching for signs everywhere and telling himself what he thought Britt would say or do, but all the words and the fears and admonishments in his head were his. Not that of a ghost.

"It's time to stop dwelling so much on the past, and stop being a chicken about moving on with my life."

Sage had made an appointment with her doctor to check her hormone levels and make sure everything was in order so she would know the best time for the procedure that would hopefully lead to her becoming a mother.

She was sitting on crinkly white paper and shivering in a blue paper gown as she waited for her doctor to come in with a report. She'd made her choice of donors, and all there was to do was to get the timing right. Along with a lot of prayer that she hadn't waited too long.

The door opened, and she sat up straighter. "Hello, Dr. Aguilar. What's the word? How does all my lab work look?"

"Ms. Dalton, you won't be needing a sperm donor. You're already pregnant."

Her mouth fell open as her hands went to her belly. "Congratulations. You're going to be a mom."

Sage rushed into the house through the kitchen door, and baby Davy waved from his high chair. "Hi, angel boy."

Daisy looked up and frowned. "You look like you've seen a ghost."

She smiled bigger than she had since her argument with Grayson, and before she could get a word out, her sister squealed.

"You're pregnant."

"Yes."

She was pulled into a hug, but then her sister held her by her shoulders and studied her face. "If you're already pregnant, that means—"

"It's Grayson's baby. But I have no idea how to tell him."

Could she have the baby and let Gray believe she'd used a donor?

No.

She absolutely could not do that. There were already too many secrets, and secrets had a way of coming out at some point and almost always hurt people. She had to tell him she was once again having his baby. This time one who was biologically hers. This time one that she would keep.

This time one she prayed they could raise together, but first she had to figure out a way to tell him he was going to be a father.

Chapter Thirty-One

Grayson had been pacing around the house and was now staring out the kitchen window, watching a mama bluebird feed her nest of chicks. He was trying to get his thoughts straight when Loren came inside. "Do you realize what you called Sage when you were on the phone with her?"

She opened the refrigerator and stared at the contents. "Oh, you heard that?"

"You know I did."

She closed it without choosing anything. "I had to do something to get your attention. You're a total grouch since you pushed Sage out of our lives."

"So you've said several times." Grayson took a sip of coffee. "I'm sorry about that, kiddo."

Each of her fists snapped to her hips as if to punctuate her next two words. "It. Sucks."

He plunked his third cup of coffee into the sink, sloshing cold bitter liquid over the chipped rim. "Hey, you're pushing it, young lady. I get that we're both adjusting to a new way of life, but that doesn't mean you can be sassy."

She crossed her arms, reminding him so much of her beautiful, fierce, spunky mother. "Dad, you have got to get a clue."

"What clue is that?"

"I remember Mama going out of her way to take care of us. Would she want you to be happy or sad right now?"

"Happy."

"Does Sage make you happy?"

Unsure how to answer, he turned the question back around on her. "Does she make you happy?"

"I asked you first," Loren said.

"Yes, she does."

"Me, too."

Her smile was bright and the one he'd been trying to coax out of her before they'd moved here. It was like a warm blanket settling around his shoulders. "Your mama wouldn't want us to be sad or miserable. Not ever."

"My work here is done," she said with a smile, flipped her long hair over her shoulder and left the room.

When did she get so smart?

He'd learned that teenagers could change moods in no time flat, but his little drama queen had a good point. Britt would hate seeing them unhappy, and she also wouldn't want him to be lonely for the rest of his life. The only downside was the fact that she wouldn't have chosen Sage to be the one to fill the void. Tingles spread across his skin.

Or would she?

"My darling Britt, was it you who whispered in my ear and guided me back to Channing? Did you know what we needed before I did?" Maybe Sage was his guardian angel on Earth and Britt in heaven. That was a nice thought.

He walked through the downstairs rooms of his newly remodeled house. The place looked great, but it didn't feel like a home yet.

He'd come back to Channing with a surly, depressed child, but then they'd hung out with the Dalton family and his daughter had finally been happy once again. And he knew with one hundred percent certainty, Britt would want him to do whatever it took to give their daughter a happy life.

And right now, none of them were. Not him. Not Loren. And not his beautiful, sweet Sage. Would she forgive him for the way he'd so abruptly ended things?

His sudden urge to see Sage was overwhelming. He wanted the woman he loved to be part of their lives. Part of his family.

Grayson went to his bedroom for his cell phone and called her, but she didn't answer. Not the first, second or third time he tried.

It had been too much for him to ask Sage to keep a secret that *he'd* promised to keep. It had been unfair. Unreasonable. She hadn't made the same promise not to tell Loren the truth, and she'd been in an impossible situation when the photo had been found.

And he had not broken his promise because he hadn't been the one who told their daughter the whole story of who carried and gave birth to her. So, there was no reason for him to feel guilty that she now knew the truth.

Now that he was being completely honest with himself, he could admit that Sage had not been the only problem in his marriage. Even before she had become their surrogate, they'd had issues. He'd always loved his wife, that had never been in question, but they'd had their share of challenges. Their relationship had sometimes resembled oil and water. They could mix, but it had taken special effort to blend their time and lives.

Since her tragic sudden death, he'd been lying to himself about his marriage. He hadn't wanted to admit that he and Britt had both been at fault for not having a perfect marriage. But he was also smart enough to know that no marriage was perfect. You had to work at it, make occasional sacrifices and communicate.

And currently he was doing a really crappy job of communicating with Sage. She deserved so much better.

What an ass I've been.

He tried Sage's number again but still got no answer, so he went upstairs and knocked on Loren's door. "Can I come in?"

"Fine. You may enter."

He found her sitting in her window seat with her knees tucked up in front of her. "Will you please try calling Sage from your phone?"

She sat up straight and swung her feet to the floor. "Are you going to try to work things out?"

"I will if she'll talk to me. Will you help out your old dad?"

Loren grabbed her phone and made the call but frowned. "It's going straight to voicemail. You should call or text Daisy."

"Good idea." He started dialing her number as he went back out into the hallway, preparing himself for a tongue lashing from Sage's protective twin.

As expected, Daisy told him he was being an idiot, but she also told him Sage had another appointment with her gynecologist. The words "another appointment" along with the type of doctor she was seeing was making him nervous. She was really going ahead with her plan to get pregnant. Had he screwed up big time? Was he too late?

His gut twisted into a tight tangle of knots. If she got pregnant with someone else's baby, he'd...

What? Never forgive himself? Maybe. But as much as he loved Sage, he'd love any baby who was a part of her. Just like she loved Loren.

Grayson stood at the bottom of the stairs and called up to his daughter. "Loren, let's go find Sage."

She raced out of her room and down the stairs. "Cool.

Go put on something better than those ratty sweatpants and T-shirt."

He did as she'd asked as well as brushed his hair and teeth. They hurried to the car and drove across town—which was thankfully only five miles—to the doctor's office.

"I'll go inside with you," Loren said and flung open her car door. "You should let me do the talking."

He chuckled. "And why is that?"

"You'll see."

At the front desk, a plump middle-aged woman with silver hair twisted into a tight bun on the top of her head looked up with a smile. "Can I help you?"

"We're here for my mom's appointment. Sage Dalton."

The woman cocked her head. "Honey, Sage doesn't have a daughter."

"Well, technically, I'm her soon-to-be stepdaughter."

"Is that right?" the receptionist practically purred as she looked him up and down. "She's been holding out."

Grayson internally groaned and said a few curse words under his breath. Now the rumor that he and Sage were getting married would spread all over Channing before the day's end. What if she wouldn't take him back?

"Is she here?" Loren asked.

"I'm sorry. We had a cancelation, and I called her to come in early. She's already had everything done, and she's gone. But she said she was going to the coffee shop."

A spiky ball plunged into his gut. Had Sage just had the artificial insemination procedure only minutes before? He was too late. She hadn't been kidding about her urgency to get pregnant. She'd gone through with her plan to have a baby whether he wanted to be the father or not.

"Thank you." He turned for the door.

The *slap, slap* of Loren's flip-flops followed along behind him. They barely had their seat belts buckled before he was backing up and driving toward Old Town. At a red light, he glanced at his daughter. "Next time, it's my turn to do the talking."

"Sorry, Dad." She gave him her best puppy-dog expression. "I thought they would only give information to family members. I forgot that this town is so small that everyone has known everyone for forever."

"It's okay. We found out what we needed to. Let's get to the coffee shop." He parked in front of Crafty Coffee. "I don't see her car."

"Let's just go in and check," she said and opened her door.

They quickly walked around the small place with no sign of Sage.

"Are y'all lookin' for someone?" the twentysomething barista said as he handed an order to an elderly couple.

"Yes." Loren braced her hands on the countertop. "We're looking for Sage Dalton. Have you seen her?"

"You just missed her. She ordered a decaf, which is weird for her, and then took off."

Decaf?

She never drank decaffeinated coffee. Was she drinking it because… He shook his head. Finding her fast was more important than stressing over what he couldn't control. "Did she happen to say where she was going?"

"Let me think…" The young man hooked his thumbs in his black apron and gazed into space.

Grayson was about to explode with impatience and anxiety. He had to find the woman he loved.

"Nope, I don't believe she said where she was going."

He growled under his breath and spun for the doorway.

"Thanks," Loren said to the young man. "Time to go to the ranch, Dad."

* * *

While keeping an eye out for her little silver sports car, they drove out to Dalton Ranch. His mood did not improve to see her usual parking spot empty. Where was she?

As they neared the back door of the farmhouse, Daisy saw them through the window and waved them in.

"Where's Sage?" he said as soon as he had the door open.

"Hello to you, too, Mr. DeLuca." She hugged Loren but glared at him.

"Sorry, Daisy. I really need to see her, to talk to her. Do you know where she's gone?"

"First, tell me why." Her eyes narrowed on him.

"Don't worry," Loren said before he could. "It's good. He loves her, and he's finally come to his senses."

"Well, okay, then. I like sensible men." She grinned. "She's in the stable."

"But her car isn't here."

"It's in the shop."

"Loren, you stay here, please. I'll go find her."

Daisy held up a measuring cup. "She can help me cook."

He ran all the way to the stable, but when he burst through the open door, the only one he saw was Travis. "Is Sage in here?"

"She was, but she left just a little while ago."

He'd missed her by a few minutes—again. He took a deep breath because he was on the verge of screaming. "Where did she go now?"

"I guess back up to the house."

He leaned his back against the wall and plowed his hands through his hair. "I just came from there, and Daisy said she was out here."

"Are you trying to get yourself out of the doghouse?"

"Something like that." He pushed away from the wall as

an idea popped into his head. "I bet I know where she is. See you later, Travis."

She was probably at the cabin. Why hadn't he thought to go there first? His nerves kicked up as he neared the place where they'd talked and laughed and fallen in love. The door was partially cracked open, and he heard the sound of crying.

When he saw her with her face in her hands, he rushed forward and dropped to a knee in front of her. "Sweetheart, what's wrong?"

She uncovered her face, eyes going wide as if she was startled to see him. "Gray. What are you doing here? How did you know I was here?"

"It was harder than you'd think to find you. You weren't answering your phone, and I should've known to come here first, but I've been running all over town looking for you."

"My phone is in my bedroom charging." She wiped her tears. "Why are you here? Wait." She pressed her fingertips to his mouth before he could answer. "I have to tell you something first. I'm pregnant."

His whole body went numb, and his mind screamed for it not to be true. "How can you already know you're pregnant? You've only just had it done today."

Her head tilted inquisitively. "Had what done?"

"The…" He moved his hand around searching for the words. "Donor stuff," he growled and then winced. The last thing he wanted was for her to get more upset. This situation they found themselves in was all his fault.

He gathered both of her hands into his. "Sweetheart, I'm in love with you. I'm the one who wants to be the father of your baby. But I'm also the one who's been a huge dumbass and waited too long."

Sage's lips were pressed together but not in an angry line. It was an obvious attempt not to smile. At least she was no longer crying, but did she think that her having someone else's baby was funny? He could feel his face morphing into a frown. Did she understand what he was saying?

"Sweetheart, if you can forgive me for the way I've behaved, I want to have a family with you. I love you with all of my heart, and I'll love the baby because he or she will be a part of you. The biology doesn't matter. You've taught me that."

She clasped his cheeks and kissed him hard. "I love you, too. And I'm so glad to hear you want to have a family with me because you, my darling, are this child's father. I'm having your baby."

He was stunned. "How?"

She chuckled and her hands went automatically to her lower abdomen. "The old-fashioned way."

"The baby is mine? Truly?"

"Yes. Truly." She gazed down at her fingers, interlaced over the spot where a miracle was happening. "We made this baby together, right here in this cabin."

He was so filled with love and happiness and renewed hope for their future. He pulled her up to stand and held her close, and they swayed together in a slow dance. "Why were you crying when I came in?"

"I was trying to figure out a way to tell you, and I started overthinking what you might say or do, and you know how my imagination can take off into wild places. I knew you would do the right thing by your child, but I wasn't sure if you would want anything to do with me."

"My sweet, sweet Sage, I love you and want you in my life every single day. I will love any baby who is a part of you, but I'll admit, I'm so incredibly happy that you're having *my* baby. Again."

She buried her fingers in his hair. "This time you can sleep next to me and feel the baby kick. You can talk to our child growing in my stomach."

"And find out what it's like to make love to you while you're pregnant." He kissed the spot behind her ear that made her giggle.

"Oh, I like the sound of that, too. Where's Loren?"

"She's with Daisy. They're cooking."

"So, we have some time to ourselves?"

"We do." He nuzzled her neck. "Do you know how amazing you are?"

"I think you should show me."

"With pleasure, but first I have something to say. I know we still have plenty of things to learn about one another and there will be stuff we don't agree on, but if we try, I know we can find a way to make it work."

"I completely agree. We will have to keep our communication open and share our worries and joys and all the stuff in between."

"That sounds like a good plan, because I have a question." He dropped to one knee and kissed her stomach. "Sage Dalton, will you marry me?"

Her smile went from happy to glowing. "Are you free weekend after next?"

"Name the place and time, and I'll be there. So, is that a yes?"

"It's a yes, my love."

He stood and cradled her face. "Now let me show you how amazing you are, my beautiful fiancée."

"I like the sound of that," she whispered against his lips.

They continued kissing and pulled at one another's clothes while stumbling into the bedroom, where she toppled them onto the bed.

* * *

The cake batter had been mixed and was baking, filling the farmhouse kitchen with a delicious scent that made Loren think of the holidays. She was usually excited about baking, but she was distracted and pacing around the farmhouse kitchen. Waiting to find out what happened when her dad found Sage was making her stomach hurt, and she was going to be so mad if he screwed this up.

Daisy took the cake out of the oven, and Loren moved closer to have a look. "What kind of cake did you say this is?"

"Butter pecan. It's Sage's favorite."

"Are you baking it to make her feel better?"

"Yes. And hopefully to celebrate."

"I hope so, too."

Daisy held out a big wooden spoon. "Could you please stir those chopped pecans into this cream cheese frosting?"

"Sure." Loren took a seat on one of the two stools they'd pulled up to the island. If they didn't get back together, she might have to give up her time on this ranch with this family. That wasn't a good thought.

"You have to move the spoon around to mix in the nuts," Daisy said with a chuckle.

She looked down into the bowl in front of her and laughed. "I'm a little distracted waiting to find out what the rest of my life looks like."

"Completely understandable." Daisy hugged her. "I have a really good feeling that everything is going to work out just fine. Try not to worry."

When her dad and Sage finally came in through the kitchen door, they were holding hands and smiling, and Loren's anxiety eased. She rushed over to them. "Please tell me y'all are dating again."

Her dad held out his arm to pull her in on his free side. "Are you okay with it being more than just dating?"

"What kind of more?" She gasped. "Like married?"

Her dad chuckled and put an arm around Sage. "Yes. We want to get married as soon as possible."

She had a brief moment of panic, but when Loren looked around at all the smiling faces, she knew this was a good thing. Everything was going to be okay, and no one would forget her mama just because they kept living life.

Daisy rushed over to join in the hugging. "I was hoping this would be a celebratory cake and not one we ate whole in front of the TV with wine."

"Daisy, I hope you're ready to be my maid of honor?" The twins hugged and squealed.

Sage held out a hand to Loren. "Will you be my bridesmaid?"

"Of course. What color dress should I wear?"

"Any color other than black," her dad said.

"I'm thinking pink." Her life was entering a whole new phase, and starting over small-town style was going to be pretty cool.

Chapter Thirty-Two

Not that long ago it had just been Sage and her twin living on the ranch, but now their family was growing, and it was such a beautiful thing. She sat at her dining room table with all of the people she loved the most—her sister, Lizzy, Travis, Davy and now Grayson and Loren. And one on the way.

Travis spooned a bite of mashed potatoes into Davy's mouth. "We can set up the backyard like we did for mine and Lizzy's wedding. The arch that y'all covered with flowers is still in the barn."

"Great idea." Lizzy passed the plate of fried chicken. "If we all work together, we can pull off a wedding in two weeks. No problem."

"It can be simple," Sage said. She just wanted to be married to the man she loved and officially be a stepmom to the child she'd given birth to.

"It can't be too simple," Loren said. "I want to help Lizzy and Daisy plan the wedding. Can we go shopping for your wedding dress tomorrow?"

"That sounds perfect," Sage said with a smile so big her cheeks ached. She was looking forward to lots of shopping trips and outings in the years to come.

After dinner, they took Loren upstairs to Sage's room so they could tell her she was going to be a big sister. They wanted it to feel special that they were pulling her aside so she wouldn't get lost in the mix of a group announcement.

"Why did you bring me up here?"

"We have something big to tell you," Grayson said.

The teenager looked wary. "Is there another life-altering secret?"

Grayson and Sage smiled at one another, and he sat on the foot of the bed beside his daughter. "It's something we just found out, and we don't want to keep it secret from you for one moment longer. There have been enough secrets."

"And it is life altering," Sage said. "You're going to be a big sister."

Loren jumped to her feet. "You're having a baby?"

"I sure am."

Loren looked very thoughtful and then a grin spread across her face. "The baby and I will have the same dad and, in a way, the same mom because you carried both of us in your stomach."

Sage opened her arms, and Loren moved into the hug. "I love that way of thinking. And I love you so much, honey."

"I love you, too."

Sage thought her heart couldn't get any fuller, but hearing Loren saying those words was like a miracle.

"Since the secret is out, can I tell everyone, please?" Loren asked as she clasped each of their hands.

Sage looked at Grayson, and his mouth curved into the smile that made her breathing come in a nice steady rhythm. A smile that said they were letting go of the past and moving forward with their lives.

"Yes," they said together.

"You can tell them," Grayson said and kissed the top of his daughter's head.

"Cool. Let's go have cake and celebrate." Loren went out the door first, and her feet clattered down the stairs.

Sage laced her fingers with his. "I think she is adjusting to life in Channing."

"We both are, and it's all thanks to you, sweetheart."

The whole family was gathered in the living room, eager to hear what had Loren so excited.

Lizzy took a seat on the couch and snuggled against her husband. "We're already planning a wedding. What more good news can there be?"

"Loren is going to share something important," Sage said. "It's been a secret for too long, and the time has come to have everything out in the open."

Daisy's green eyes widened, and she shot her twin a questioning stare. Sage gave her their private signal for yes. The big secret they'd been keeping for years was about to be revealed.

Well…her half of it. Daisy's part of how they'd saved the ranch was hers to reveal only if and when she chose to.

Travis and Lizzy leaned forward on the couch with eager expressions, and Davy banged on his toy drum.

The smiling teenager moved to the center of the living room. "My mama, Britt, couldn't carry a baby in her tummy, so someone else had to do it for her."

"Like a surrogate?" Lizzy asked.

"Yep." Loren bounced on her toes with her hands clasped. "And it was Sage!"

Lizzy's mouth open like she was about to sing one of her operatic notes, Travis grinned, and Sage tipped up her face to steal a quick kiss from Grayson.

"I had a really awesome mama, but I also have a woman

who carried me and gave birth to me. So, I think Sage is also kind of like my…mom. Don't you think so?"

Everyone was in full agreement.

"And now," Loren said with dramatic flair. "She is going to make me a big sister."

"We're having a baby," Grayson said and wrapped his arms around Sage, smiling at her with so much love.

"I'm so happy for all of you." Daisy wiped a tear that leaked from the corner of her eye.

After all the congratulations, Loren came to stand beside Sage and Grayson. "Did I do okay?"

"You did perfect," she said to the child she adored. "This has been a most excellent day. One I'll remember for the rest of my life."

"I completely agree." Grayson cradled Sage's still flat stomach with one large hand. "I love all three of my girls."

"Dad, how do you know it's going to be a girl?"

"I just have a feeling."

The love in his smile made happy tears gather in Sage's eyes. The life growing inside her was just the beginning of a beautiful dream come true.

Epilogue

"Mom, where are you?"

Every time Loren called her Mom, Sage smiled and her heart filled more than she could've imagined. "I'm in the kitchen."

Her daughter breezed into the room wearing a turquoise shirt, jeans and pink boots. "I found someone who will look at the artwork. I think I'm getting closer to discovering the artist who did the drawings and paintings we found in Aunt Tilly's secret drawer."

"Oh, that's great news. I bet it will lead to something exciting." Sage was also trying to find more information about Tilly's baby who'd been adopted so many years ago. She pushed herself up from the chair and cradled her rounded belly. She took two steps but then paused when her stomach tightened enough that she hissed.

"What's wrong?"

"That was either a really strong Braxton-Hicks contraction or—" Before she could finish the sentence her water broke and splashed onto the hardwood floor between her bare feet.

Loren pressed her hands to her cheeks. "Oh, snap. It's time, isn't it?"

"I believe it is. Get your father, please. Hurry."

"Dad," she yelled on her way out the back door. "It's time. My baby sister is coming right now."

Sage chuckled, tossed a couple of hand towels onto the floor and then waddled to the bathroom to change her clothes. Excitement mixed with nerves, a little fear and a lot of love. She was so ready to meet her baby girl.

Hours later in the hospital delivery room, Sage breathed through another contraction. They were one right on top of the other, and she knew what that meant. It was almost time to push.

"Was this how it was when you had me?" Loren asked as she wiped Sage's forehead with a cool, wet cloth.

"I don't remember it hurting this much." She gritted her teeth and groaned.

Grayson massaged her foot, using the acupressure points he'd researched. "You did great then, and you're doing just as well now, sweetheart. You're amazing."

"Ready to push?" the doctor asked.

"Ready or not, let's do this." She smiled at Gray on her right and Loren on her left.

"You got this, Mom. We're right here with you."

"I love you," he whispered and kissed her cheek.

Another contraction started, she inhaled deeply and began to push with all of her strength. Time moved in a circular way, and she wasn't sure if it had been ten minutes or ten hours.

"The baby is crowning. Don't push again until I tell you."

"Okay." Sage panted to keep from bearing down and squeezed her husband's hand. Any minute now she would meet her newborn. It couldn't happen soon enough.

"Push, Sage."

She did as the doctor told her, and after only a couple of minutes, hand in hand for a second time, she and Gray welcomed a tiny infant into the world.

"Congratulations. You have a beautiful baby girl."

Happy tears streamed from her eyes as her child was placed on her chest.

"Welcome to the family, little sister."

Grayson wiped away a tear and cradled his daughter's tiny head. "She so beautiful. You did so good, sweetheart."

She was exhausted, overflowing with love, and the sound of her newborn's cry was the sweetest sound Sage had ever heard.

* * * * *

HARLEQUIN
Reader Service

Enjoyed your book?

Try the perfect subscription for Romance readers and get more great books like this delivered right to your door.

See why over 10+ million readers have tried Harlequin Reader Service.

Start with a Free Welcome Collection with free books and a gift—valued over $20.

Choose any series in print or ebook. See website for details and order today:

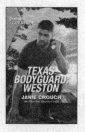

TryReaderService.com/subscriptions

RSBPA24R